WILD TENDY

THE ICECATS SERIES

TONI ALEO

Editing by: Lisa Hollett of Silently Correcting Your Grammar

Proofing by: Jenny Rarden

Cover Design: Lori Jackson Design

Photo by: FuriousFotog

Created with Vellum

To everyone who has ever doubted me, this book is for you.
In this book, my characters overcome inner doubt—and the doubt of others.
They prevail, they fight for their happiness, and they do it without apology.
I hope that for you, as I hope it for myself.

FOREWORD

This book deals with a medical situation which has many variations. Please bear in mind that no one experience is identical and that I've made every effort to represent a unique issue accurately. Also, if you give me the ultimate reward of a review, please try to keep it as spoiler-free as possible. I want everyone to experience the plot as it develops. I hope you enjoy *Wild Tendy*. I happen to love it very much.

Why don't you join my newsletter for updates on new releases, sales, deleted scenes, and more? Sign up with confidence. NO SPAM EVER! JOIN NOW!

CHAPTER ONE

ico

I LOVE WOMEN.

I know what you're thinking—you're not surprised. I'm a twenty-seven-year-old, really good-looking—if I may say so myself—franchise and league-starring goalie. Ask anyone who is around the league, and they'll say I am the best. My save percentage is the best hands down. Just look on my mantel, and there you'll find the photo of me with the Vezina Trophy from when I won it this summer. It was a first for me, and I'm not even embarrassed that I cried a little. I worked hard for that fucking trophy. I wanted the Cup, but we were robbed.

Fucking Nashville Assassins.

Fucking Aidan Brooks. Such a douche nozzle.

But none of that matters now. A new season has started, which means a new start. We have the arsenal needed to win the Cup, and we will. No matter what, I'll get us that Cup. It's number one on my goal list at home. A new season also means a new set of puck bunnies wanting all my attention. I, for one, will never deny them that. I'll block every puck I'm physically able to, even some I don't think I can, but I'll never block an advance from a lovely woman. Nope, I love them way too much.

I love the smell of them. The feel of them. A great ass and set of tits will bring me to my knees. A beautiful straight, white smile will make me harder than a frozen pipe. I love how good they make me feel. I love how they scream and squirm. The little noises that bring me to the edge. But most of all, I love their hair. I don't know what it is about a woman's hair, but it drives me wild. Especially when it's fanned out across my thighs and my cock is so far down her throat, there is no way I can think of anything else.

Not the sounds outside. Or the way the clock keeps flashing. Or so I thought… But, really, why hasn't she set that clock? Why doesn't she have an iHome or something? Who still has plain old digital clocks? It's odd, but I wonder where she got it. It's sort of retro. Neat, even.

"You need to set that clock?"

A pair of striking blue eyes looks up at me. They remind me of a certain someone who got away, which is why I swiped right for this sweet piece of ass. Around my cock, she asks, "What?"

I lean back on my hand to hold my weight as I point at the clock beside her bed. "It needs to be set."

She removes my cock from her mouth. She licks her lips before setting me with a look. "If you're worried about my clock, I must not be doing a good job."

I shrug. "It's a distraction."

She draws her brows in, and those blue eyes deepen in color. A flush runs along her cheeks, down her throat. She really is beautiful. Real long and deep-blond hair, and I love the swelling of her lips. She reaches over me, her breast pressing into my taut cock, and yanks the plug for the clock out of the wall. She throws it over her shoulder, the crash making me jump a bit. The clock must have been cheap, because it shatters all over the floor. The light is gone, but now there are pieces everywhere. "Didn't like that clock anyway, but I love how huge this dick is."

I know I should be more thrilled about her comment on how big I am, but instead, I'm worried about the pieces on the ground. I'm not a fan of mess, which is why I usually bring girls back to my place. After a few stalker issues, I had to relocate, and since then, I've found myself at hotels. This is the first time I've been to a woman's house, and I don't think I'm a fan.

Don't be weird. Just get off. That's what you're here for.

I blink a few times and repeat that to myself as she drops her mouth back down over my cock. Ah, it feels good. I enjoy her mouth, and I'm soon proud of myself for letting go about the mess. Thank you, new therapist. I feel my eyes roll up in my head, and soon, I let my head fall back. I sense my load building. My stomach tightens as her nails dig into my thighs. My balls pull up, and this is exactly what I want. I want this release. I need this release. I start to explode, and at first, I don't notice that she has come off my cock. But when I do, I shoot my eyes open just in time to watch myself come all over her neck and breasts.

Don't be weird. Ignore it. It's fine. Some would say it's hot... I'm not some, though.

Ick.

I self-talk, something I've been working really hard on. My therapist urges me to do this more often than I should, but it's hard. Especially when my come is all over her. It makes my skin crawl.

When I'm done, she grins up at me. "Man, you know how to come."

"Well, I'm a man," I say offhandedly, and then I hold my breath because I think I know what she is about to do. I watch with laser focus as she grabs the side of her comforter and wipes her chest. I almost come out of my skin. She must have noticed, because she raises a brow at me in question.

"I'll wash it later."

My throat starts to close. "Are you going to use a wet rag for your chest?"

"Why?"

"Because you're covered in come."

"So? Sex can be messy."

I hold up a finger as she crawls up into my lap, stopping her. "Key word, *can*. I'm not a fan."

"Are you a germ freak?"

"Eh, not really. It's more the texture and the thought of it just sitting there. Getting drier and—"

"It came from you. What if I swallowed it?"

I shrug. "As long as you brush your teeth, I'm good."

"Seriously?"

I nod. "Seriously." *Don't be weird. Ignore it. It's fine.* "Also, can we throw this comforter in the wash now?"

* * *

"She kicked me out."

My best friend, Chandler Moon, bounces his newborn son in his arms as he waits for the bottle to warm in the bottle warmer. He kisses Carter's head before he curves his lips. I'm sure my latest sex debacle is amusing. Chandler doesn't know that life anymore; he's all about his domesticated one. He's happily in love. A family man. Something he's always wanted and something I can't seem to fathom right now. One woman? For life? I tried that, and she figuratively kicked me in the balls because she was in love with another man.

I move through their place, picking up diapers and mess. Chandler and his girlfriend, Amelia, are not dirty people. The clutter of baby shit isn't normal. I've known Chandler for years and he always picks up after himself, and Amelia is OCD about cleanliness. Now that they've multiplied by two, it's a little more challenging. I understand that. They're really overwhelmed with the demands of twins. I am too, and they're not even mine.

"You really don't have to clean," Chandler says as he picks up the bottle, but I wave him off. "And why do you get so grossed out by body fluids? It doesn't bother me."

I look to Amelia, who is sitting on the couch with their daughter, Hannah. She grins. "I mean, I like when he comes on my chest."

I hold out my palm to her. “Do you wipe it on the bed?”

She makes a face. “No, but I also have a towel handy when I know things are about to get nasty.”

“See?”

Chandler laughs. “So, have a towel handy.”

“I didn’t know she was going to do that. I thought she was gonna swallow!”

He shakes his head as he directs the bottle into his son’s mouth. “I know you thrive on formulas and routine, but you know sex isn’t like that when you’re sleeping with different women every night.”

I roll my eyes. “Keep your judgy, ‘I love one woman’ shit to yourself.”

He snorts. “Just saying. Did you have this problem with Shelli?”

I give him a dry look. “She always swallowed.”

Amelia gags. “Wonderful to know about my cousin.”

“She always brushed her teeth afterward too.”

Amelia throws a hand up. “Well, thank God. I taught her well,” she jokes, and Chandler laughs.

“You never brush your teeth.”

She cries out in embarrassment before throwing a rubber duck at him. “Chandler!”

He dodges the duck with ease. “Hey, I’m holding our son! And Nico knows we have sex and that you swallow. Hello, we had twins.”

She raises one eyebrow. “You know that’s not how twins are made, right?”

“I’m not an idiot,” he calls to her, and then his eyes meet mine. With a playful grin, he adds, “I’m an idiot.”

I laugh loudly, which unfortunately startles little Carter. He lets out a wail that sends a chill down my spine. I back up slightly, hoping the noise will die down. Babies freak me out a bit. I’m getting better being around the twins, but still, they’re so unpredictable in my opinion. “Shit, I’m sorry.”

Chandler waves me off. “No big,” he says quickly as he shushes the baby to calm him down.

“If you’re particular about sex, Nico, you should really let them know before you go at it," Amelia says to me, and I look over at her. She's still as beautiful as the day I met her. I wanted to holler at her, but then I saw the look on Chandler's face and knew I had no chance. He was completely and utterly in love with her. It's been a pleasure to watch their story unfold. Or just begin. The twins really add to their fairy tale. "Or even put it on your Tinder."

Chandler snorts and I smirk. "Yes, in the additional info: 'Please don't wipe my come on the bedsheets, and brush your teeth if you swallow it. It's icky, and I don't like it.'"

With an unamused look, I say, "I'm a man. I don't use the word *icky*."

Chandler flips me the bird. "Fine, it's fucking gross."

"Better," I agree, though I'll never put that on there. Maybe I will be a bit more honest, though. I'm always so worried people will think I'm weird. It freaks me out so badly that I'm not even completely honest with Chandler about my issues. He just thinks I'm OCD and a germ freak.

Amelia grins. "I don't think it's a bad idea. How many times have you had this problem since you and Shelli called things off?"

"I didn't call it off. Shelli called it off for that fuckbag, Brooks," I remind her.

I'm not saying I was head over heels in love with Shelli Adler, but I may have been tripped up on her. She's a goddess, and hell if she didn't fuck like a dream. She didn't care for me the way I did for her. Her excuse that I didn't even really know her was bullshit. Yeah, I didn't know her family shit, but I knew how she liked to sleep, her favorite foods, and what made her squirm. It may have taken a lot of therapy, but I know for a fact that it wasn't me. It was her. I fell for a girl who was in love with another man.

A fuckbag, in my opinion.

Amelia rolls her eyes. "Hey, that fuckbag completes her."

I'd wanted to complete her. She didn't give me that chance, though.

"But that doesn't mean you wouldn't have. I loved you two together, but she has loved Aiden since she was a kid."

"Ugh, Amelia, please. I don't need you stroking my ego," I groan. "I'm over her."

I am; I'm just bitter about that fuckbag. He not only took my girl from me, but he took my Cup. I don't like Aiden Brooks. At all.

"I'd rather she didn't stroke anything of yours," Chandler says then, which sends us all into a fit of laughter. "But in all honesty, bro, she isn't wrong about the whole sleeping around thing. Especially if you're going to keep up with the Tinder," he says as he rocks back and forth while Carter eats.

"Huh?" I ask, confused.

"The whole letting people know beforehand what you like and dislike so that you don't get kicked out of women's houses."

"Oh," I say as I start to wipe down the counters. I didn't expect him to change gears so quickly, but then, Chandler doesn't speak of Shelli with me. He knows I'm still upset about it. "Yeah, maybe I shouldn't use Tinder anymore."

"Now that's a great plan," he says, pointing at me.

Even Amelia nods. "I never liked you on Tinder. You meet crazy people, and with the twins now, I can't have you bringing nutcases around."

"Yeah, I mean, I wasn't thinking about the twins, but you're right."

She rolls her eyes. "Of course not. Nico Merryweather, think of anyone but himself? Never."

I glare, and Chandler shakes his head. "Hey, he's not that bad." He then looks at me. "She's emotional."

"I know Amelia loves me," I call over at her, and her look says otherwise, but I know the truth. "While I'm thinking of the twins now, it also has to do with the fact that I'm not meeting good people."

"Mainly because you're on a hookup app," Amelia says dryly. "Go to a bar."

Both Chandler and I shake our heads. "Nico doesn't do bars. When he does, he drinks entirely too much."

I nod. "And then I make even more bad choices."

"Fine, join a church group."

I give her a look. "Do I look like the kind of guy who's getting into heaven?"

She doesn't laugh or even smirk. She just nods. "Yeah, you're self-absorbed, but you're a good guy. You'll be a nice addition to heaven."

I wave her off. "Don't you have friends you can hook me up with?"

"I do, but none of them could handle you," she says simply. "You need the kind of woman who is strong and can deal with you and your extra-ness."

"Extra-ness?"

She gives me a look. "Nico, you are over the top. You're loud, and you say what is on your mind with no holds barred. Half the time, I'm not sure you even think about what you're about to say. You're extravagant. You spend money as quickly as you move your glove to stop pucks."

I shrug. "Women love that."

"Gold-digging women, yes, but not decent women. You need a good woman. Someone who will love you and your quirks. Not get their feelings hurt when you say something you don't think through because they wiped your come on the bed."

I bite the inside of my cheek as I throw the towel I was using to clean up with. "I don't think there is another Shelli out there."

She gives me a small smile. "Nope, but there is someone who is made for Nico Merryweather. You just have to find her, and she isn't on Tinder. She'll be the one you never saw coming."

Chandler goes to her, kissing the top of her head before sitting beside her. He looks at her, this overwhelming expression of love on his face. "All I wanted was a cup of coffee, and I got the world."

She leans into him as she beams, and my heart actually feels it. It's not often that emotion takes over for me, but right now, it's happening. I really enjoyed watching Chandler fall for Amelia. It's almost like she was made just for him. I look around at the home they've built. When they got pregnant, Chandler had an addition added to their beach house to make room for the kids. The house doesn't look like a bachelor pad anymore. It's a home for his family.

I think I want this. It would be so much easier. I could find someone who gets me, like Amelia said. I could have the house and someone who would love me for my craziness. Shit, do I want a wife? I watch as Chandler kisses his son's head and then his daughter's. When Sadie, Chandler's dog, climbs up with them, I feel like I might die from the cuteness. But then Chandler's eyes meet Amelia's, and this little smirk covers his lips. He looks as if he's on the highest cloud in the sky. I've known him for a really long time, and only Amelia does that for him.

One woman.

One woman makes him that happy…

Interesting.

CHAPTER TWO

viva

I BLOW at a piece of hair that has fallen out of my ponytail as I take the fresh bread out of the oven. I place the pan on a cooling rack before rushing to put in the next tray of bread. I'm dragging ass this morning. I woke up late since I was up late with Callie, being a good big sister by helping her with her project on Queen Elizabeth. One thing for sure, I wish I had the queen's life. Instead, I'm the queen of a sub shop.

I'm so winning at life.

I rub my eyes as I set the timer, another yawn taking over as I start cutting up veggies after washing my hands. Usually Callie helps in the mornings, but with how late we stayed up and her having gymnastics today, I felt she needed the sleep. She works her ass off at school, here at the shop, and at the gym. She can sleep in while I suffer. That's what a good big sister does. Or a stupid one.

Ed Sheeran's "I Don't Care" blasts through the shop as I sing at the top of my lungs. It's the only time I can listen to music from the current decade. When the shop opens, 90s is all that plays since we're a 90s-themed sub shop. The shop is full of crazy bright colors. The booths are all retro greens and yellows. The walls are decorated with memorable images from the 90s. *Rugrats, Fresh Prince of Bel-Air,* New Kids on the Block, *Friends...* Anything that happened in the 90s adorns the shop. My mom used to be a tour manager before she opened the shop, so the walls are plastered with pictures of her and many 90s stars. It's pretty badass, and while I love the 90s, sometimes I want to listen to some Five Seconds of Summer or Dan & Shay. Yes, the best music was made in the 90s, but there are some bangers now. Problem is, I refuse to change anything about this shop. It's vintage, it's my mom, and I won't mess that up.

Alec Benjamin starts singing his jam, "Let Me Down Slowly," and I bob my head to the beat. This is Callie's favorite song, and usually she sings it from her soul as she's busy doing whatever needs doing in the shop. Our subs are the best here in South Carolina. Each sub is themed after something from the 90s. Our "How You Doin'" salami sub is our best seller. But then, our "Carlton" tuna is right up there. Really, everything sells well.

Everyone in town comes to the shop, and we stay busy as hell, which is tough since it's only Callie and me who work here. Thankfully our customers are pretty patient. They get distracted by the ambiance of the place, which gives us time to get subs out. Plus, our subs are damn good. Our secret vinaigrette is what brings all the people in. I was taught how to make it when I was seven. Back when things were the best. Now...now, things are a bit suspect.

When I hear the shower running, I glance at the clock. Oh good, Callie woke up to her alarm. I really wanted to get all this done, and if I'd gone upstairs to wake her up, I might have gone back to bed. I don't have time for that, though. It's a Thursday, our biggest sub day because it's Throwback Thursday. All subs are buy one, get one fifty percent off. It's gonna be one of those days that I fall face first into my bed by eight. A yawn leaves my body at just the thought. Which reminds me to start the espresso machine.

After I click it on, I get back to work as I wait for Callie to come down. I turn on the stove to make her a breakfast sub, something she has been urging me to sell, but the lunch and dinner rushes already kill me dead. I don't think I could do a morning rush too. Especially with her not being here. She offered to homeschool so she could help me, but I refused before she could even finish her sentence. I was homeschooled through high school, and I missed out on everything. I don't want that for her. I want more for her. I have to give her more.

I finish her sub and put it on the warmer so it's toasty when she comes down, which won't be for another thirty minutes. The shower is still running. But to my surprise, as I'm thinly slicing the tomatoes, I hear her walking down the stairs. I glance back as she rushes to me in only her towel, her hair wet and panic on her face.

"Aviva!"

My heart jumps in speed as I quickly wipe my hands. "What? What's wrong?"

"Is this a lump?" Her voice is full of horror, and my heart stops in my chest. I meet her halfway across the kitchen as she drops her towel so her left breast is out. She developed early and had a full B cup at thirteen. She puts my fingers on the spot she was holding, and I dig my fingers into her breast. I lift her arm with my other hand and feel around, biting my lip as I try to calm down.

When I'm satisfied, I shake my head. "No. You're about to start, right?"

"Yeah," she says, gathering her towel, tears welling up in her eyes.

"It's just that. You're fine."

Her shoulders drop in relief, and I admire my beautiful sister. She's thin, thanks to the many hours she puts in at the gym next door. We share the same dark hair that curls naturally along our shoulders. Her deep green eyes are a bit darker than mine, but they have the same catlike shape to them. Her lips are a dark pink and very thick. While my bottom lip is thicker than the top, her lips are even and perfection. Her face is round, almost like a cherub. And just like a cherub, she's a complete angel. My sweet, beautiful sister.

"Aviva, I can't keep doing this."

I turn back to the tomatoes as I nod. "Callie, the doctor said eighteen."

"That's not fair! I have two ticking time bombs on my chest."

"I know, Cal. I know."

She is frustrated, as am I. Her breasts give her an anxiety that hurts my soul for her. "With our history, I think I should be able to do it now. We have the money for the implants. Why can't we do it?"

"Probably 'cause a sixteen-year-old doesn't need implants," I say, and she gives me a frantic look.

"Then I'll wait for those until I'm eighteen. But please, I need these things off me."

I meet her gaze. We've talked about this before, and she's always wanted to wait so she could just have one surgery. "Are you sure?"

"Yes, I hate them, and they freak me out."

"I know, but with gym—"

"I'll be down for a week at most."

I bite the inside of my cheek.

Callie continues, "You did it, and you're awesome."

Physically sure, but mentally, it's up in the air. I nod. "I'll make another appointment."

She wraps her arms around me, and I lean my head into hers. "Thank you."

"Of course. Now, go get ready so you aren't late."

She nods before she turns and heads upstairs. Out of my control, tears well up in my eyes, and I collapse into the counter as a sob shakes me to my core. I draw in a deep breath, trying to calm down. But for the love of God, she terrifies me. Like she said, those breasts are two ticking time bombs on her chest, and they freak me out too. I know she thinks it's a good idea to just get rid of them, but it worries me that she's scared and wants this out. I did that; I was terrified and went that route. It was painful and fucked with me mentally, but I didn't have a choice. Callie needed me. I really don't want that for her, but what other option is there?

Cancer takes who it wants.

* * *

While I wanted to fall face first in my bed once I closed the shop, Callie had texted me that her coach wanted to see me. It was a rough day. We were busy as all hell, and meanwhile, my mind has been consumed with thoughts of Callie's breasts. Not really a great thing to think about, but they haunt me. Since I don't have any, I have to worry about hers. I made the appointment with the doctor, but it isn't for another week. I have to figure out a way to keep Callie from freaking out until we can go. Hopefully she'll be too busy to think about it. Though, it didn't matter how busy I was… I always thought of mine.

The walk across the parking lot to GymMasters is short. My mind is flooded with things I need to do in the morning, but I try to push that aside when I enter the gym. It's a huge, state-of-the-art facility that brings in a lot of business. Callie has been coming here since she was two. She loves it, it's a wonderful outlet for her, and we're thankful for everyone here. When things got rough, they helped and still allowed Callie to come and work with the team, even though we don't have the money to pay for her to compete. She hasn't competed in four years. I know she misses it, but I just can't swing it.

Debt is a nasty thing.

I walk down the side, past the recreational section, to the back where the team girls practice. I spot Callie on bars and smile as she does some little twist thingy. The girl is a beast, and it kills me that I can't afford to let her compete. But she's very forgiving. She knows I try. Even though I feel like I suck, she doesn't allow me to tell her that. She's a damn good kid.

"Aviva."

At the sound of my name, I turn to see Callie's coach, Amelia, coming toward me with one baby on her chest and one on her back. To say Amelia Justice is beautiful is an understatement. How she looks that good after having twins is beyond me. She has the prettiest blue eyes too. She's stunning. She just had the twins a month ago, and I have no clue how she is back in this gym. Yet here she is. The owner is very family-oriented and allows Amelia to bring the babies with her. I smile as I get to the main floor.

"Look at these babies. They're adorable! Hannah and Carter, right?"

Amelia beams. "Yup. Thank you! Chandler had a game tonight, so they had to come with me. Makes spotting the girls a bit hard when all they want is to be held."

"I bet. How are you, though?"

"I'm good. Thanks for asking, and thanks for coming in. I know you're busy."

"Well, I gotta make sure Callie isn't in trouble."

Amelia laughs. "Far from it." She looks over to where Callie is doing some kind of release to the low bar, and she beams. "She's amazing."

I grin. "I like her."

She meets my gaze. "Listen, I talked to Dominica, and she agrees. Callie needs to compete."

My shoulders droop. "Amelia, I don't have the money—"

"We feel she has the potential for a scholarship for college. She's damn good and so smart. She's a perfect candidate."

"I know, but I can't afford it. I'm still paying so many medical bills and trying to keep the shop afloat—"

"I know," she says, cutting me off once more. "Which is why we want to pay for it. Almost like a scholarship from us."

"To get a scholarship? How does that make sense?"

She smiles. "It makes us look good. It brings in business 'cause everyone wants their kids to be college-bound gymnasts. Most kids won't make it, but Callie could."

I swallow hard as I watch her do a double layout dismount, landing it with perfection. "I don't know. I hate handouts."

"It isn't a handout, I promise. We want her to succeed."

My pride won't let me. "Let me try to swing it. Can you get me the monthly dues?"

She pulls in her brows. "Yes. Let me ask Dominica to get it to you."

"Thank you."

Just then, Callie comes to me as she takes off her grips. "You say no?"

I give her a dark look. "Actually, I said yes."

She squeals before wrapping her arms around me and kissing me hard on the cheek. "I thought you wouldn't do it. You don't like handouts."

"No, I don't. But I'm gonna try to swing it."

She cocks her head as she backs away. "Can we afford it?"

I nod. "I'll figure it out."

She looks between Amelia and me. "Okay."

I can tell by her voice she isn't convinced, and to be honest, I'm not surprised. I'm not even convinced I can make this work, but I really don't want the gym doing anything more than they already have for Callie. After she puts away her gear and gets dressed, we head back to the shop. When we lost our house on the beach, I had no choice but to upgrade the apartment over the shop so it was livable for us. I'm still paying that off, along with everything else.

I wrap my arm around Callie's shoulders and kiss her forehead. "I'm proud of you."

"Thanks," she gushes, leaning into me. "I'm excited. I really want to compete again. I could get a scholarship to pay for school. That would be awesome, and you wouldn't have to worry about me."

I scoff. "I'll always worry about you, Cal."

"You're the best, Veev."

I kiss her once more. "Gotta be the best for the best."

She grins at me as I open the door of the shop. She walks in before me, hitting the code for the alarm before I lock it back up. She resets the alarm as I pick up some trash I missed earlier. I turn from the trash can to find Callie looking at me in horror from behind the counter.

I raise my eyebrows. "What?"

I walk toward her to see the cash drawer open and the safe in the same state. My heart falls into my stomach as I rush to check the obvious, and I pray it isn't true. But it is. All my money is gone.

I close my eyes to keep the tears in. The alarm hadn't gone off, so the person who came in knew the code. "Callie, please tell me you didn't give Dad the code again."

She doesn't answer me at first. Not until I open my eyes do I see the tears streaming down her face. "He said he needed it so he wouldn't wake us up when he came home at night."

"Callie, he doesn't live here!"

Her tears fall faster. "But Aviva, we can't expect him to stay in shelters. We're his family!"

"Yes, we can. Because if we don't, he fucking steals from us!"

She snaps her mouth shut and lets her head fall.

I slam the drawer shut and kick the door to the safe closed, a big mistake as pain radiates up my leg. "Fuck!"

She jumps at my outburst as I crouch down, shaking my head. I cover my face to keep in my tears. I was going to go to the bank tomorrow to deposit everything. He took it all. A week's worth of profit. Fuck me.

"So, I guess I won't be competing."

It takes everything inside of me not to scream at her, but it isn't her fault. My dad could talk an Eskimo into buying ice. He's a huge manipulator, and she's young. I stand up, wrap my arms around her, and kiss her forehead. "I'll figure it out. But do not give him the code again. Do you understand me?"

"Yes," she says, and I wipe her tears. "How are you gonna figure it out?"

"Don't worry about that. I got this."

Which is a complete lie, but I can't let her know that.

CHAPTER THREE

viva

I PINCH the bridge of my nose as I squeeze my eyes shut.

"I am aware I let the account lapse. That's why I'm calling, to pay the bill and then to get a new code assigned. I also need to put in cameras."

The lady on the other line is probably sick of my shit. This isn't the first time I've missed a payment, and it probably won't be the last. Not when I have a poor excuse for a father stealing from Callie and me.

"Yes. Absolutely. My card number is—"

I quickly rattle off the number of one of my many credit cards. Once I have an appointment, I hang up, letting out a long huff. I waited until Callie went to school to deal with all this. I didn't handle it well last night and was a bit of an asshole when I realized a week's worth of profit was gone. I needed time to calm down. To get a game plan. I can't let Callie see that. Things haven't been easy for us, so when I can take the burden, I will.

The shop doesn't open for another hour, so I dial the number I've been dreading dialing since I found my money missing. My father's raspy voice fills the line, and I know he spent most of the money on alcohol the night before.

"Hey there, sugar."

I cringe at his nickname for me. I know I should be more forgiving. He lost the love of his life, but I lost my best friend. I'm not out drinking and doing drugs. I'm raising my sister and running the shop in her honor. "Why, Dad?"

"What?" he asks. He almost sounds genuine, but I know it's all a fucking ruse.

"How can you steal from me?" I ask, emotion clogging my throat. "I have bills to pay for the shop. I gotta pay for Callie's gymnastics and Mom's medical bills. How dare you? I needed that money."

"I don't know what you're talking about. You were robbed? Call the police."

"And if I do, you'll go to jail. Shit, I probably should call," I jeer. Problem is, I have no camera proof, and he had the code. His name is also on the lease for the building, but that will change today. Even if I have to sleep with the landlord to make it happen, I will. Lord knows I need to get off, and he isn't that ugly. "I'm not naïve, Dad. You asked Callie for the code, and now, all my money is gone. You're so fucking greedy. You took it all. Couldn't even leave me a little."

"I am appalled, Aviva. How dare you accuse me of this?"

"I know it was you." Damn it, I'm gonna cry. "And know this—this is the last straw. You come around me, or even Callie, I'll call the police."

"For what? Seeing my daughters? Be real, Aviva. You have nothing on me, which is why you haven't called the cops. No cameras or witnesses."

"How do you know that?"

"'Cause I know you can't afford it," he says bluntly, and my blood boils as traitorous tears fall down my face. He's admitting to it without admitting. What a bastard. This man is not my father. My father was kind. He was a great guy. He loved us. He loved himself, and he would never do this to us. This man…I don't know. One thing is for sure, though.

"I hate you," I sneer as I blink through my tears.

The line goes dead, and I let my head fall to the counter with a thud. It hurts, but not as bad as the sob that racks my body. I feel it everywhere. I don't understand how a man, a father, could do this to his children. Especially after everything I've done. I've kept Callie and myself alive through everything. I tried to help him. Tried to get him help, but he didn't want it. Oxycodone and alcohol were and are more important than us.

I want to blame it all on the cancer, but the cancer didn't make my dad take my mom's pills. He did that on his own. To cope with what was happening. What the hell did I get to help me cope? Nothing. I was the strong one. Hell, I still am. And damn if it isn't hard as fuck. I have no choice, though. I've got to keep Callie stable. She is going to do great things, and I can't let the burdens that keep weighing on me affect her.

I swallow hard as I sit up, wiping my face free of tears. He doesn't get my tears. He already took enough. And hell, I can't change him. He is on his own; he is no longer my father. That may be a bit harder for Callie since they used to be so close. While I was close to my mom, Callie was close to Dad. They were two peas in a pod, so I know this won't go over well. But we'll be okay. We've always been okay.

When my phone rings, I see it's my landlord returning my call. "Dusty, how's it going?"

"Good, Aviva. How are you?"

"Living my best life. Listen, my dad broke in last night and stole all my money—"

"You're still paying me, though?"

"Yeah, I have that. Focus, Dusty. I need to get him off the lease so if this happens again, I can call the cops on him for trespassing. Please help me."

"I'll need his signature to do that."

I roll my eyes. "You didn't need it to put me on the lease, and you sure as hell didn't need it for me to pay you monthly. Would you like to go after him from now on?"

I'm met with silence, and I find myself crossing my fingers. It's silly, but my mom always used to do it. "Let me call my dad," he says finally.

"Ugh! No. Dusty Senior hates me."

"He doesn't hate you. He just doesn't like how hostile you get."

"I wouldn't get hostile if he hadn't raised my rent when he knew damn well I had just lost my mom!" I'm not going to make it. My blood pressure is through the roof, and I'm pretty sure I'm about to stroke out. "Please, Dusty. I need to make this happen."

"Let me call him. I'll call you back."

The line goes dead before I can ask him otherwise. I drop my phone to the counter and let out a shout.

Could my day get any worse?

When my laptop sounds with an email, I see that it's from Dominica. The subject is, *The payment schedule you requested.*

Of course it can.

Fantastic.

I open the email to find prices I wasn't expecting. Leotards, warm-ups, and meet fees, *oh my*! I'm not gonna make it. I feel the stroke coming. At the end of the email, she tells me they don't mind helping me out. I just can't seem to allow her to. I'll figure it out. Maybe I can sell some stuff. Or maybe I'll win the lottery. Gotta buy a lottery ticket for that, though. I can buy one when I go out for the mayonnaise.

Oh my God, I forgot to get the mayo!

I glance at the clock, and I only have thirty minutes to get to the store and back before we open. Man, life is really coming for me today. I slam my laptop shut, but then because I'm worried, I reopen it to make sure I didn't crack it. When I find I didn't, I shut it again, a little more gently, and rush out with my keys, throwing my phone into my purse. I get into my Kia and head toward the store. My mind is going a million miles a minute. I have so much to do today along with running the shop. I'm gonna have to pull money out of Callie's savings account, and that alone has me almost in tears. That money was for college and her boob job. I'll put it back; I always do.

I'm heading south toward the store when my phone rings. I reach over to my purse, digging into it as I try to watch the road. It keeps ringing, taunting me, and I worry it's Dusty. When I finally find it, I see it is Dusty. Frantically, I answer it as I bring it to my ear.

"Hello?"

And then I look up. Just in time to see myself driving right into a bright-red car's ass. There is no way I won't hit it. I brace for impact as I slam on my brakes. It doesn't matter, because I hit the car. Hard. I hear the crack of my car and the car in front of me. Pain radiates through my head, and instantly, I deem this day complete shit. How else can it get any worse?

But the disaster isn't over, for Dusty says, "Listen, Dad wants to sit down with you and discuss it. But I don't think there's a way around needing your dad's signature."

I wish life would use lube when it fucks me.

CHAPTER FOUR

ico

"How's the new therapist?"

Coming through my Bluetooth, my mom's voice is full of tension. She didn't like that I switched therapists, but the last one moved to start a family with her husband. I had no choice but to wish them well. My mom always calls after practice, and usually I love talking to her. But today, I'm beat. I want to go home and pass out. Practice was tough after our loss last night. Our power play was shit, and Coach was not happy. So he tortured us today. The last thing I want to talk about is my therapist.

"I like her. She's right out of school, but everyone thinks she's amazing. She came highly recommended. She actually interned with some of the best therapists in New York. She moved here for her family."

"Is she pretty?"

"Why?"

"Future wife?"

I laugh. "Mom, I cannot get involved with my therapist. I need her to help me, not distract me."

She isn't my type either. Too supermodel thin. I like my women a little thicker than Ms. Amaya Jenkins. Plus, she looks like she's nineteen. A baby.

"Fine. I just think it's time to settle down."

"What? I'm too young to settle down," I say in an almost joking manner. I mean, I was just thinking about settling down after watching Chandler and Amelia together with the twins, but that was yesterday. It wouldn't be bad, especially if it were with the person who was made for me. Problem is, I don't know if that person is out there. As my mom says, I'm pretty special.

"When you find someone to be with, I won't have to be so overprotective."

I snort. "You'll still be overprotective, and you'll have her do your dirty work."

"Exactly."

Her laughter warms my heart. "I'm too young, Mom."

"I had you at twenty."

"Mom, that was a poor life choice. Should have waited," I tease, and she laughs.

My sperm donor ran out on her when I started having health issues. Back then, there wasn't much support for my situation, but my mom loved me enough for two parents. I had a damn good life, a full life, and it's all because of her. When the doctors said I needed something to focus all my energy on, she's the one who put the glove on my hand. It was my grandpa's old glove, and I was fascinated by it. He played hockey his whole life. He didn't make it into the NHL, but he worked his ass off for what he had. He'd go from playing for the local team to working in the factory back home. I miss him. I miss my mom, but there is no way in hell she can be here.

She has a tendency to smother me.

"Ha. I bet your grandfather and grandmother would agree," she laughs, and I smile. "So, are you any closer to interviews?"

My chest seizes up at the thought of it. Interviews and I don't go together. At all. "I don't know. Her goal is to have me ready by January first."

"January first? Ashley was saying she would have you ready for the beginning of the season."

"I know." I am annoyed with how upset she is getting. I know interviews are a part of my job, but I honestly can't handle them. Thankfully, the organization supports me and understands. The media, and the fans, don't, but I gotta do what's best for me. "But Amaya is saying with the change of therapist, she wants to ease me in slowly."

"That's unsatisfactory. We had a goal. You know how I am about goals."

I do, which is why I am also so obsessed with goals. It's probably why I haven't put "Find a Wife" on my goal list. Then I'd really have to commit to that. "I know, but I don't think I'm ready."

She takes in a deep breath, and I can hear the disapproval. "I don't know why Ashley had to go start a family." I laugh, but she doesn't. "Listen, send me Amaya's number."

"Why?" I say, coming to a stop at a red light. I scrunch up my face at her request.

"I want to speak to her."

I roll my eyes as I tap my fingers on the steering wheel. "Mom, you can't keep being my advocate. I'm almost thirty—"

"I don't care, Nicolas." Damn, she used my full name. "You can be ninety and I'll be on my death bed, and I will advocate for you." She's impossible. "Don't make me come there."

"Jesus, fine. I'll send it to you once I'm ho—"

But before I can finish my sentence, I'm thrown forward, and my chest hits the steering wheel. The loud crunch of my car getting smashed behind me makes me breathless. Or maybe it's from slamming into the steering wheel.

"What in the world was that?"

I look behind me to see a car almost in my back seat. "Fuck, I just got rear-ended. Let me call you back."

"Are you okay?"

"I'm fine," I say, hanging up and throwing open my door. I get out and look at the other car to find the driver with her head on the steering wheel. I rush to her, praying she's okay. When I reach her, she's lifting her head. Tears rush down her face, along with blood from a cut on her forehead. I pull open her door, and she looks up at me.

"I am so sorry."

"Are you okay?" I ask, ignoring her apology. She has to be okay.

"My head hurts," she says, wiping her forehead. "Oh, because I'm bleeding. Awesome. Could this day get any fucking worse?"

I crouch down to her eye level, panic rushing through me. I couldn't care less about my sports car; I don't like blood, and it's running fast down the side of her face. I pull off my shirt, and her eyes widen.

"Usually when you get rear-ended, you get pissed, not naked."

I smirk as I press the shirt to her head. She takes it with a smile as I ask, "Do you feel dizzy?"

"No, just a little pain. I'm okay, though," she says, and then she starts to get out. I stand up, helping her out as she looks at the damage. She's tall. While I'm way taller, she's taller than most girls I meet. She's almost to my shoulders and thick in all the right places. Her eyes are a stunning dark green and flooded with tears. Her lashes are really long, giving her catlike eyes a dramatic look. I don't usually look people in the eye, but hers demand my attention. Her dark brown hair is up in a messy bun, and I think that's a pen or two in her hair. She's wearing a tight white tee with some kind of logo on it and a pair of tight black leggings somehow containing her ass. She seems completely annoyed, and when she holds out her hand, I look toward it as she says, "I'm assuming you have insurance with that flashy car."

"I do. Do you?"

"Yeah," she says with a sigh. "Man, I can't believe I did this."

"It's no big deal," I say offhandedly. "As long as we're both okay. It was an accident."

"I was trying to find my phone, which I know is awful, but I had to answer it. Damn it, I'm so sorry."

"It's fine. Don't worry about it," I say once more, looking her over. She's really pretty.

She swallows hard as the cops and ambulance arrive. "Well, I'm glad you're not being a dick about this because that would be the cherry on my shit sundae of a day."

She looks distraught, and I believe today hasn't been her best. An officer comes up to us to make sure everyone is good, and she's led away to have her head tended to while I give my statement. I notice people have gathered, watching as the tow trucks come and begin to load up our cars. A tingling starts in the back of my throat as I answer the questions from the officer. The questions are endless. I know he's just doing his job, but I need to move from this spot.

"Can I go check on her?"

"Who?"

"The lady who hit me."

"Oh, Ms. Pearce? I have more questions, Mr. Merryweather."

Pearce. Hm. I wonder what her first name is? "And I've got you, but I need to breathe for a second." I don't even give him time to stop me or even disagree before I head to where she is stepping out of the ambulance. There is a bandage on her head, and she has a no-nonsense look on her face.

"I hear you. I will go to the ER if I have any of that. I'm fine, really. I just need to get back to my shop." The look on her face says otherwise. She has no intention of doing anything they say. When she sees me, she lets her shoulders fall. "Both our cars are un-drivable, which is fantastic. Again, I'm so sorry."

I shrug. "It's fine. Are you okay?"

"I'm fine. Thanks," she says, tapping on her phone. "I know this probably put a wrench in your plans for the day."

"Nope, I was just heading home. Probably go lie on the beach for a bit."

She scoffs. "Must be nice. I gotta get home and open my shop."

"Shop?"

"Yeah, I own Willz Sub Shop—"

"By GymMasters."

She nods. "Yeah. My sister, Callie, goes there."

"My boy's girl works there as a coach."

"Oh? Who?" she asks, dropping her phone to her side.

"Amelia Justice."

She smiles. "That's my sister's coach."

"Wow, small world."

"Small town," she says simply. "Listen, I gotta go. They have all my info, you know where I work, and yeah, so sorry again. Come on in for a sub on the—"

"What's your name?"

She presses her lips together, her green depths meeting mine. Her lashes taunt me. I want so badly to pull her hair down to see how long it is. "Aviva. Aviva Pearce."

I nod and hold out my hand. "I'm Nico Merryweather." She takes my hand and shakes it. I feel the heat of a thousand suns radiate up my arm, but Aviva doesn't appear to feel it. She looks annoyed and ready to go. "You should let me take you to lunch. Maybe turn that day around."

She seems taken aback. "I possibly total your car, and you want to take me to lunch?"

My lip quirks at the side as I look away. "I'm not worried about the car."

She scoffs. "It's a nice car that I'm sure will up my premium, which again, is just how great my day is going." She laughs, shaking her head. "Thanks for making me feel good about myself on this shitty day, but I don't have time. I gotta open the shop and do sub shit. Again, sorry. Nice to meet you. Hopefully we don't meet under these circumstances again."

"I don't care what circumstances as long as I see you again," I say, stopping her mid-step.

She curves her lips, but she's got a suspicious gleam in her eyes. "Are you messing with me?"

"Messing with you?"

"Yeah, because let's be honest, I look like roadkill run over twice and picked through by vultures. I'm living on dry shampoo and a prayer, and you are far from that. You probably wake up on gold sheets with someone wiping your ass. Like, hello Greek god, go find a Greek queen."

I can't help but grin. "All I see is a Greek queen who may need something to smile about."

She narrows her eyes, and it wasn't the reaction I was expecting. Usually when I say that to a woman, she's ready to get naked. Nope, not this girl. Fire fills those green eyes. "What is wrong with you?"

"Huh?"

"I legit just met you because I rammed my car into yours, and you're hitting on me? Is this a tit for tat?"

"Huh?"

"Like, I hit you physically, so you hit on me figuratively?"

I look around myself, confused. "Yes?"

"Why? It's not funny. My day has been complete shit, and I don't need you fucking with me. So yeah, fuck-you-very-much."

All I can do is blink. What just happened here? I hold out my hands in complete confusion as I watch her walk away. I'm about to run after her when the officer comes back, and he's asking me more questions. I'm pretty sure Aviva just blew me off, and wow, that doesn't happen to me. The only time it did was by the girl I thought was my match. I know Aviva's day has been shit, but I meant what I said. I want to give her something to smile about.

And I think I just added an item to my goal list. To get Aviva to believe me.

CHAPTER FIVE

ico

I WOULD HAVE CALLED Chandler to come and get me, but then I remembered he'd had to stay late to film his stuff for the sports network. Since I don't do that stuff, I was able to leave. Maybe if I had stayed for the filming, I wouldn't be sitting between the twins in Amelia's new minivan, with my legs across the console in the front seat while I hold the bottles for Carter and Hannah. But I also wouldn't have met Aviva.

"Thanks for coming to get me."

Amelia waves me off, and even though she's driving, her eyes are like hawks on the kids. "I was out and about anyway. I can't believe Callie's sister hit you. She's usually so safe when she's driving."

I want to laugh because I know Amelia has already decided Aviva is never driving her kids. I, too, have been removed from that list. I'm pretty sure the only reason I'm feeding them is because she didn't want to wait around for them to eat. She's a busy lady, and since her nights are dedicated to the gym, she'll settle for me feeding them.

"It was an accident. She didn't seem to be having a good day."

Amelia laughs. "Aviva never has a good day. I'm pretty sure the universe is out to get her, which I really don't understand. She's absolutely lovely. Great big sister and super business-savvy."

"And really hot." My comment makes her groan.

"Nico, no. You're too much for her."

"How so? I'm hot. She's hot."

I annoy Amelia, and I find it funny. "She has absolutely no time for you—at all. Like, not even kinda. She is always busy, always trying to make ends meet. And I can tell you right now, she doesn't do handouts. So if, for some crazy reason, she gives you the time of day, don't buy her shit."

I slack a bit, and Carter chases the nipple of the bottle. I hold it better for him. "I'm a little confused. What girl doesn't like gifts?"

"Aviva Pearce."

"She has a really hot name."

Amelia rolls her eyes. "It's unusual, for sure. But really, Nico, I don't think this is something you should pursue. With the season starting and Shelli breaking your heart—"

"Whoa. Shelli didn't break my heart," I say sternly.

"Nico."

"Amelia," I say back. "Don't get me wrong. I liked her a lot—"

"I heard you say repeatedly you could love her more than Aiden does."

I meet her gaze in the mirror. "I could have if she had given me the chance."

"You obsessed over her for months."

"It wasn't obsession. I wanted to know everything so when I got the second chance, I wouldn't fuck it up," I say simply as Hannah finishes off her bottle. "Chance never came. I moved on."

She shakes her head. "Aviva isn't the kind of girl you sleep with and move on. She doesn't have the time for a fling...or hell, maybe she does. I don't know. I just know she is special. I know Callie, her sister, is talented and so damn kind. That's all Aviva's doing, and I don't want anything hurting that family. They've been through a lot."

"Like what?" I find myself asking.

Amelia's shoulders fall a bit as she turns onto the road where the car rental office is. "It's in no way my story to tell, but just know someone like Aviva should be worshiped—not played with. So, get your intentions in check before you bother her."

I blink. "Why do you always think the worst of me?"

She doesn't even laugh. "I don't try to, and I honestly don't think you're a bad guy, Nico. You and Chandler are best friends, and Chandler is perfection in my eyes, so I know you aren't evil. I think you make decisions and do things to hide what is really going on inside you. I don't know what that is, or even if Chandler does, but I feel your outlandish ways won't be perceived well when it comes to Aviva. She has too much going on, and she has too much to lose."

"So, you're saying I'm too weird for her?" I ask, my own insecurity about the word making it hard to breathe.

She shrugs. "I don't think you're weird, Nico. I feel you're self-absorbed and only care about yourself. Someone like Aviva can't stroke your ego like Shelli did. She doesn't even have time to stroke her own."

I nod slowly. I've heard this self-absorbed shit a time or two. I don't feel I'm that way. Do I like to get off? Fuck yeah. Do I love women who fawn over me? Every day of the week. Do I like hearing good things said about me? Yes, especially when I have a tendency to put myself down. I like feeling good, and I won't apologize for that or even think I'm self-absorbed. I'm not. Amelia doesn't know me. She knows the Nico I allow her to know.

"I don't know, Nico. It's odd because I say that, but then I see how you are with the twins. Or Chandler and his parents. You're a good dude—I know this—but I feel like you'd hurt Aviva."

I scrunch up my face as I remove the bottle from Carter's mouth as Amelia comes to a stop. I wipe the kids' mouths and then hand her the bottles. "I'll make sure to bring you something to eat tonight as a thanks."

I won't look at her as I pull my legs back from the console, and I know she notices.

"I upset you."

I scoff. "Nope. Too self-absorbed to be upset," I say as I get out. "Bye, babies. Be good."

"Nico, I'm sorry. I'm emotional—"

I shut the door on her and head inside to get my rental car. I love Amelia. I do. I also know she's going through a lot of hormones right now and has absolutely no filter. I can appreciate that since mine has been missing from birth. Amelia is wrong; I wouldn't hurt anyone. And I may not know Aviva from Adam, but I know I wouldn't hurt her. She may have told me to fuck off in three different ways today, but my intentions were never to get in her pants and leave. I wanted to take her to lunch to make her feel better. I wanted to make her smile since her day was so awful. I hadn't even thought of getting in her pants at all. Would I like to? Yes, because leggings were invented to be peeled off someone with thighs like hers. But it was more than that for me. I saw a girl having a hard day, and I wanted to make it better.

Yeah, Amelia is wrong. I know she is.

On my goal sheet that is currently only in my head right now, right under make Aviva believe me, is prove Amelia wrong.

And I will.

* * *

THE PARKING LOT of Willz Sub Shop is packed. It could be the overflow from the gymnastics parking lot, but it seems the shop is busy as all get-out. I park my rented Ford truck between GymMasters and the shop before getting out. Amelia has tried apologizing a billion times since earlier, but what she doesn't know is I thrive on being doubted. She thinks I'm self-absorbed? Fine. I'll prove I'm not by bringing her dinner every night, and I'll get to see Aviva. Two goals, one puck. Let's go. I want to bang on my chest, not for the manly exhibition but more to try to beat the anxiety out of me. Not sure. But before I can explore that, the door to Willz flies open, and a pint-sized girl yells back inside.

"You're ridiculous! We could get this done in five, and now it's gonna take you twenty!"

"Your job is not this place, Calliope! Your job is school! Get to work!"

Well, I know for a fact that the voice yelling back is Aviva.

The girl slams the door shut and sits at the table by the entrance, opening her book as she lets out a huff. She looks up at me, and wow, she's the spitting image of her sister. Only difference is she's miniature. "Take a picture, bruh. It'll last longer. Though, I am only sixteen and it could be considered child porn or something like that, and I'll turn your ass in."

I can't help it. I laugh. "You must be Aviva's little sister."

She raises her brows. "Who are you?"

"The guy she hit today."

She nods. "Ah, yeah. Hot guy with the red sports car."

I grin. "She said I was hot?"

"She did, and I hope that embarrasses her." She lets out another huff before opening her notebook. "She's impossible. We have a rush, and I can help. But no, I gotta work on stupid angles."

I peek inside the shop, and yeah, it's packed. I want to help Aviva, even though she looks like she can do this with her hands tied behind her back. "I think she's got this."

"Of course she does. Aviva has everything," she mumbles as she presses her fingers to her temple. "Meanwhile, I have no clue how to do this."

I look down at the book, and then I find myself sitting down. "I love this stuff. Angles are my jam."

She gives me a weird look. "Angles are your jam?"

"Yeah. Did you know in a triangle, the largest angle is opposite the longest side, and the smallest angle is opposite the shortest side?"

She blinks. "I think my teacher may have said that."

"And then in an isosceles triangle, where two sides are equal, the angles opposite the equal sides are equal. In an equilateral triangle, where all sides are equal, the angles are all 60 degrees. That shit is so cool. It's like when I'm blocking a puck. The angle I turn—or throw out my leg or glove—makes it so the puck can be caught because of that angle. It's actually really interesting," I say quickly, turning her book so I can see it. "And then here, a 180-degree angle. You do that in a leap, right?" She looks from me to the book. Then she nods. "And you know how that feels and looks?"

"Yes!"

I can see the pieces clicking and the excitement building. She's figuring this out. I wish everyone had the teacher I had. She made sure to put real life into my studies so I could understand. Reason number two million why my mom is the best.

"So, when you get this problem and it equals this," I say as I draw out the problem and then the answer. "You know what the answer looks like 'cause you're in this position. Right?"

The biggest, brightest grin covers her little face. "Yes. Thank you."

"Anytime. I love math. I was able to connect to it. Really understand it. It was fun for me."

"Well, I hate it, but maybe I can convince you to stick around and help me out. I have free subs."

I laugh as I nod. "How about a date with your sister? Do you have that?"

The hysterical laugh that comes out of this little person is a bit troubling. I don't think I've ever seen someone laugh so hard. "Aviva? Aviva doesn't date. Free subs. I have subs, not a date."

"She doesn't date? Everyone dates."

Callie lets out a long breath. "Not my sister."

"Maybe I can change that?"

Her eyes light up, making her look like a little doll. "Please let me watch."

"The date?" I ask, confused, and she laughs.

"No, you asking, 'cause I'm sure it's gonna be awesome."

The girl is not giving me any confidence here. "I don't like the sound of that."

"I'm telling you, man. Take the free sub," she urges, and I smile. "But can you help me with these three problems to make sure I do it right before you go for the sub and the epic turndown my sister is gonna provide you with?"

I flash her a grin. "Wow, you doubt me so easily. I'm known to be a smooth talker."

"And Aviva is known to make grown men cry. Ask our landlord."

We share a look that tells me I'm walking into a lion's den and I should run the other way. Problem is, I need a sub for my best friend's girl who doubts me, and I need Aviva to smile. Hopefully she'll go on a date with me.

All that involves me going into Willz.

I want to go in.

I will go in, and maybe, just maybe, the lioness won't bite my head off.

CHAPTER SIX

viva

WHEN THE BELL over the door rings, my eyes cut to the entrance to see how much I need to speed up. Big party, fuel to the fire. One person, I can keep my speed. Two people, a little faster. But none of that matters when he walks in. Nico Merryweather. Super-hot dude with a real nice ride. Who also asked me out for no damn reason at all. I've been going over and over it in my head to try to figure out his motive, but I can't come up with anything. It's obvious he's got money. And he also can have any girl he looks at, but he wanted to take me to lunch? After I hit him? Makes no sense whatsoever. But now he's here.

What. In. The. #7?

Highway to Ham.

A little sub shop humor.

I cut the sub for Mr. Tuna—that's not his name, but he legit gets a tuna with bacon every day. What can I say? I know how to add mayo to a can of tuna, and people eat it up. I am still a little worried about buying mayo from the gas station next to where I hit Nico, but I'll know soon enough what Mr. Tuna thinks. All that doesn't matter, though, because it's hard to pay attention with Nico taking up the whole doorway. I mean, the whole damn thing. He has to bend over to enter my shop, and seeing him…it rattles me. Thankfully, I don't cut myself as I quickly check Mr. Tuna out. As I start on the next customer, I notice Nico doesn't get in line. Instead, he lowers his gigantic self to the table by the door, and he distracts me.

I'm somehow able to make the #2, It's Gonna Be Beef, but I can't stop glancing back at him. When I first saw him earlier, I thought he was handsome, but I didn't realize he is completely gorgeous. He's got a boyish look to his face. Thick cheeks, but a sharp line to his jaw. His eyes are a dark brown, and the color somehow seems to make his eyes look bigger. Or maybe it's his lashes. He has this wild blondish-brown hair that isn't long but is not short either. Surfer-style, almost. His nose is wide, and Grilled Cheese Jesus, he has the whitest teeth I've ever seen. That smirk he's wearing is dangerous, and of course, I almost cut myself when he flashes it my way.

He must have noticed that I noticed him.

Damn it.

When the door opens once more, Callie appears, and I almost cry out in relief. She comes around the counter quickly, throwing her books down as I ask, "You're done?"

"Yup," she says as she starts to check people out. "Your admirer is a math genius."

That does make me cut my finger. "Son of a beef sandwich," I groan as I turn to the sink to wash my hand. Behind me, Callie puts on a pair of gloves and gets to work as I clean my wound. Of course, it's hard to put on a damn Band-Aid when I'm shaking everywhere. First, I didn't suspect Nico would be a math genius. Second, I didn't anticipate the whole admirer thing. Surely Callie is messing with me. After wrapping my finger with tape and a fresh pair of gloves, I jump back in line. Soon we get through our dinner rush.

When the bell rings over the door with the exit of the last customer, I glance over at Callie. "Don't mess with me like that when I'm making subs."

Callie just grins, and her gaze moves past me. I follow it to find Nico looking down at me. I come to his shoulder, but still, he towers over me. Even with a cooler of sub fixings between us, I feel him all over. He takes up the whole room. When he licks his lips, every single fiber of my being is set on fire. Man. Two minutes. That's all I would need with him. Shit, probably one minute, given my hiatus.

"You changed your hair."

Oh, that deep voice. It's raspy and oh so sexy. I blink, and I notice he's looking at my head. I move my bangs out of my eyes. "I brushed it."

"You didn't have bangs earlier."

I refuse to be impressed he noticed. "They were pinned back, and I didn't want customers asking me what happened, so I covered the cut."

"By the way, thanks for not being an asshole to my sister," Callie says then, and I set her with a look. But Nico, Greek god-looking dude, he flashes her the sweetest grin.

"Don't you have something to do? Cut something, Callie."

Callie's eyes are teasing as she grabs the bin of almost empty tomatoes. I look back to Nico, resting my foot on my calf as I lean into the counter. "What brings you in? Didn't get the info you need earlier?"

"I got the info, but I wanted more."

I furrow my brow. "More?"

"Yeah, a sub for me and my friend. She picked me up from the wreck, so I owe her."

Her must be his girlfriend. Lucky bitch. Not that I have time for that. Nowhere in this shittastic life of mine is there time for a dude. Dudes need attention. They're like cute little puppies. Gotta feed them, pet them, and love on them. I hardly have time to love myself. Someone else? Please. But man, what it would be like to be loved on by this fantastic beast of a man. "Two subs coming up, on the house."

"No way. I'll pay."

I wave him off as I grab two pieces of French bread. "What can I get you?"

"What's your favorite?"

I look back at our menu. My mom and Callie painted it when we opened the place. I refuse to change it. If I have special subs, I usually put them on the board. "The I Need a Hero is the best sub here. It has this amazing sauce that is fantastic."

"Can I get two of those and then a Carlton?"

I look at him in confusion. "I thought you were getting one for you and your girl?"

"My girl?"

"Yeah, the one who picked you up."

"My best friend's wife-to-be. Amelia."

I swallow around the lump of embarrassment in my throat. "Oh, my bad." Then I blink and ignore the heat that creeps up my neck. "Still two Heroes?"

He nods. "Yeah, one for me and you."

I hold the two pieces of French bread in my hand as I stare at him. He leans into the glass guard that protects my fixings. His eyes are dark, like two sweet pieces of chocolate, and the way the side of his mouth turns up is downright wrong. "While I do need subs, I'd really like to sit down and get to know you."

"Get to know me?"

"Only you."

He's messing with me. I cock my head. "What's your game here?"

"Game?"

"Yes, this is the second time you've asked me out in one day, and mind you, I still look like vulture food—"

"I think you're magnificent."

I put down the bread and start to wipe off my arms.

He brings in his brows. "What are you doing?"

"Wiping off the spray from the game you're spitting. I mean, holy hell, dude. You don't even know me."

"I don't have to know you to think you're beautiful." His voice drops an octave. Within seconds, heat runs up into my belly and ignites. "There is no game here. I just want to get to know you."

I blink. "Okay, skipper—"

"Skipper?"

I shrug. "Everything else isn't appropriate to say in front of my sister."

I hold up my hand as Callie snickers. "That hasn't stopped you before."

"Shut it," I call to her as I cut my eyes back to Nico's. "I'm pretty sure you're the one who hit your head today—"

"I didn't hit my head, and even if I had, I'd still want to get to know you."

Wow, his bluntness is a little surprising. And those eyes are unstoppable. They're locked with mine, daring me to look away. "There is nothing to know."

"I don't agree."

Our gazes lock, and I swear I feel him all over me. I really need to get laid—but not by him. He'd break me in two. Figuratively and physically. "I'll get your *one* Hero and Carlton," I say then, dragging my gaze from his. I get to work on his subs, and I can feel his gaze on me. I won't give in to it, though. I can't. When I'm done, I hand them over to him and meet his gaze, even knowing it's a bad idea. "Come again."

His laughter fills my shop. It's raw but sorta dorky. Something I didn't expect from such a big man. "You're gonna make me work for it, huh?"

"Work for what?" I ask with a grin. His laughter makes me smile.

"Your time."

I look up then. "I don't have time. In all reality, I'm saving you time. My life is this shop and that snot-nosed brat behind me. You'd be wasting your time trying to get mine."

"Or I'd be spending it the way I want to." He somehow touches my hand as he grabs the subs. The simple touch has me catching on fire all over. "I'll see you soon, Aviva."

I'm breathless as he looks past me and says to Callie, "I'll come check on you at the end of the week to make sure things are going good with math."

"Thanks, Nico."

His gaze meets mine once more, and then he walks out. I watch as he crosses past the windows toward GymMasters. My heart is pounding in my chest, and I don't know what's happening, but man, he's got my blood pumping in a good way.

"I think you should give him a chance."

I shake my head. "No. I don't have the time."

Truth is, I know a man like him would get bored with someone like me. He's dripping with money. He could have anyone. He probably just feels bad for what happened today. No one like that would want someone like me. Especially when he finds out there is nothing under this shirt but two scars and a whole lot of heartache.

Someone like him? Walking perfection? Ha, yeah. He wouldn't want me.

CHAPTER SEVEN

viva

"I DO NOT UNDERSTAND why you are making this a big deal."

Yes, I am being a bitch. No, I do not care. My landlords make me crazy. Dustin Sr. stands in front of me at the counter, while Dusty is stuffing his gob with a #10, Don't You Wish Your Chicken Was Hot Like Me. It's our take on Nashville Hot Chicken. It's also Dusty's favorite, so I made sure to have it ready for him when I knew he was coming in.

"I need this done. He stole over $20,000 from me." My voice is strained, mostly because I'm trying not to cry. "I had the locks changed, upgraded my security, and bought a new safe. I really need him off the lease so that if he trespasses, I can call the cops."

Dustin is an older man who is supposed to be giving his business to Dusty. Dustin is not impressed by me. Dusty, though… I sneeze, and he gets a boner. With his bushy brows coming together, Dustin leans on the counter. "The problem is legal, Aviva. I went into an agreement with your parents. Both of them. I was nice enough to add you on to the lease when your mom passed."

"You were, thank you. But the thing is, it's my business. You know it is. You haven't had a payment from either of them in over five years. It's all from me. Would you like to contact my dad?" Dustin looks away, shaking his head. Everyone who knows my family knows my dad is a druggie. "I need this done. To protect myself and Callie. Please, Dustin."

I glance at Dusty, but he's stuffing his face, ranch dripping down his jaw. Dustin looks off toward the windows, and I have a feeling I'm not going to like his answer. "I'll do it, but your rent will go up a hundred to protect me in case your dad tries to sue me."

This. Money. Hungry. Fuck. Hippo.

Instead of saying that, I take a deep breath. I have no choice but to make this work. I hold out my hand, and he takes it. "Deal."

"I'll have the new documents drawn up and sent to your lawyer. Raventorn, right?"

"Yes, Jaylin Raventorn."

"Right. I'll get that done today."

They walk out without even a goodbye—or paying for the sub. Bastards. But at least that's over. At least my dad will be off the lease. Man, it would be great if I didn't have to deal with this. I hate that my eyes are full of tears as I dial my lawyer's number. I went to school with Jaylin, and we've been close friends ever since.

"How'd it go?" she asks as soon as she answers.

"He's raising my rent by a hundred dollars, but he's gonna do it."

I can hear her rolling her eyes, if that makes any sense. "He's such a fuck."

"I know. Listen, I won't be able to pay you for this until next month."

"Aviva, when have I ever asked you for money? We're friends. You'll get it to me when you can," she says softly. I know she means it to be kind, but I feel like a piece of shit.

"Thank you."

"Anytime. Can I get you to come have a drink with me this weekend? Please? One drink or six."

I laugh along with her, even though I hesitate. I know I can't say no. Plus, it's been forever since I've seen her. "Not at a club. I'll do the pub."

"Sounds good. Nine on Saturday?"

"Nine? Jesus, Jay, I'm old and tired."

She laughs. "I'll get you the paperwork then."

Before I can tell her I wasn't joking, she hangs up. I do the same and lean on the counter. I can't even remember the last time I went out. I open my laptop and navigate to my budget. I stare at it for almost an hour before I start to move some things. I hate taking from Callie's savings, but I have no choice. I've crunched and crunched the numbers, but there is no other way than to take from her. I'll pay it back; I always do. When the shop's phone rings, I'm thankful for the distraction.

"Willz Sub Shop."

"Hello. Is this Aviva Pearce?"

I honestly want to lie. The lady sounds like a debt collector. "It is."

"Hi, my name is Joann Williams, and I work for the IceCats."

"The what?"

She chuckles softly. "The IceCats? The NHL hockey team."

"Oh. Duh, sorry."

I want to say I'm a fan, but I'm not. I have no freaking clue what is going on with that sport. I can never find that stupid ball thingy. They start fighting for no damn reason. There are too many rules, and it confuses me. I know people think the guys on the team are gorgeous, but I haven't met one with a full set of teeth yet. The only good thing is that penalty box. I wish I would only get put in a box for doing something wrong. All the things I want to do would result in jail.

"It's fine. I hear you're very busy." How in the hell does she know that? "Anyway, the reason why I'm calling is one of our players has raved and raved about your subs. He insists we have them for game days. If you're interested, I would love to sit down and talk to you. How much we'd pay, what we would need from you, and so on."

I just blink. "I'm sorry. I'm not following."

She giggles. She's a giggler, apparently. "Which part?"

"You will pay me to make subs for your team on game days?"

"Yes," she says excitedly. "I would love to meet with you as soon as possible. Our season is already in full swing, and he wants them as soon as possible. We're all about keeping our boys happy so they'll win for us."

She's giggling while I'm standing here dumbfounded. "Um. Okay? When would you like to meet?"

"You're off 4th, right? I can come by tomorrow before you open or during a lull in traffic."

"Nine thirty? That would give us about an hour. As long as you're good with me working while I listen, then I can kill two birds with one stone."

"I love a hardworking woman. That sounds wonderful. I'll see you in the morning."

"Thank you." Before she can hang up, I ask, "Who is the player?"

"Oh, sorry. I should have said. It's Nico Merryweather. Our goalie. Huge fan of your food."

It's as if she knocked the air out of me.

I can't seem to process what I've just learned.

"Okay, so I'll see you in the morning."

"Yes. Th-thank you," I stammer out.

"Thank you."

The line goes dead, and I just stand there with the phone to my ear. I slammed my car into Nico Merryweather, the golden boy hockey goalie, whom everyone in town is in love with. He asked me out. And he helped my sister with her homework. And now he loves my subs?

What. In. The. Living. Hell. Is. Happening?

When the door opens again, I look up with my jaw hanging open. Callie looks at me, and she brings her brows together. "Oh no. Did Dustin say no?"

I shake my head. "Actually, he said yes. It's not that."

She does a little jig. "Thank God. Then what's wrong? You look like you've seen a ghost."

I just gawk at her. "Nico, the guy I hit? He's a hockey player. Like the goalie everyone loves from the IceCats."

She blinks. "No. Way."

"Yes."

"You know, I thought he might be something hockey-ish, 'cause he talked about it when he was helping me the other day."

"You didn't put two and two together?"

"I have no clue what hockey is," she says simply.

"Touché," I say with a nod. "But he asked for the team to have my subs on game days."

Her eyes light up. "Veev, that could be huge money!"

My eyes widen with hers. "I didn't even think of that."

"Wow, this is awesome! Such a blessing," she gushes as she walks over to me. "Like seriously. Be excited."

"I'm finding it hard to breathe," I say softly, and she laughs.

"And just think, if you guys got married, you'd be rich! He's, like, super loaded. Can you take me to Barcelona when you're loaded?"

I roll my eyes. This girl. "For one, you don't marry a man for money—"

"Um, after everything you've been through, you should."

I shake my head. "No way. I work for what I want. And for two, he isn't interested in me."

She gives me that teenager's look of boredom. "Yes, he is. He asked me to get him a date with you. And he is getting you a huge job, which is helping your business, just like he helped me with my homework. He likes you."

I laugh nervously. "He just feels bad for what happened."

"Or he thinks you're smoking and wants to hit it."

I widen my eyes. "Calliope!"

"What? You're the one who sent me to public school."

"Still!" I scold. "And he doesn't want to hit it."

She doesn't seem convinced. "Veev, you need to let him hit it."

"Calliope!" I cry out, my eyes about to fall out of my head.

"What? Public school!"

"What does that even mean? Are you having sex?" I ask, horrified, and the little asshole laughs.

"No, I don't have time for that. And while I know you don't either, I think you should make time. You probably would smile more if you were having sex."

What. In. The. Hell?

It's moments like this I hate cancer for taking my mom. "I am fine, and also, another life lesson—sex doesn't fix everything."

"That's not what I'm told or what TV shows say. You're sad? Sex. Mad? Sex. Happy? Sex. I mean, I think sex goes with any emotion. Kinda like chocolate and ice cream. Or better yet, swiss and ham with mayo. Mmm, I'm hungry."

She sends me the toothiest grin before she starts making a sub. All I can do is let my head drop onto the counter. "Where did I fail?"

"I think it was letting me watch *Pretty Woman*."

"But it's a classic."

"*Friends* too. *Friends* opened a whole can of sex worms."

I point at her. "I will not apologize for *Friends*. Everyone needs to watch the whole thing at least a hundred times."

"Oh, I don't disagree. I'm just saying. I learned a lot from my uncle Joey."

I groan even louder. "Please stay in the gym and keep your nose in books."

She's still laughing as she heads through the kitchen to go put her stuff away. "Will do. And you go get laid."

Curse you, Joey Tribbiani!

I lift my head from the counter and shut my computer. I know I shouldn't put all my eggs in the IceCats basket, but man, I hope doing that will put me ahead. That would be awesome. It would help so much. If I could get out from under my mom's medical bills and get my dad to stop stealing from me, Callie and I would be great. One day at a time. We'll get there. I just hope it's before she graduates so I can spoil her a bit. Pay for her gymnastics. Take her on a trip. Hell, hire someone to work in this place so I can go. It's all so overwhelming. I just want to give her a good life. *I* want a good life.

I don't hate my life, not in the least, but I sure wish I could stop getting kicked when I'm down. Maybe a few good things could happen. This IceCat thing could be a turning point for me. I'd never get this opportunity on my own, and as much as I could think of it as a handout, I won't. Nico loved my sub. He suggested it to his team, and that's why they called. He didn't do it because he felt bad for me…right?

Something in my chest starts to seize at the thought he did it out of pity. Did he hit on me out of pity? Did he know I was at rock bottom? I bite the inside of my lip before I look back down at my phone. I could call Amelia and get his number. That would make me crazy, though. But I have to know. I pick up my phone and look for Amelia's number. But before I can hit her name, the door opens. Probably an act of God to keep me from looking insane. Though, when I look up to greet the customer, it's the man who is filling all my thoughts.

With a brightness in his eyes and an easygoing grin, he says, "Hey, Aviva."

Be cool. Be cool. Don't be a psycho.

I hear Callie behind me as she says happily, "Hey, Nico!"

He grins at her. "Hey, Callie. How was math today?"

"Totally awesome. You helped so much."

"Great. Let me know if you need more help."

"I will. A Hero, right?"

"Yes, ma'am. Can you make me two so I can have one for tonight?"

"Of course."

Well, I'm glad they're so chummy, but damn it, I need to know. "Did you tell Joann Williams to call me and get me to make subs for your team because you felt sorry for me?"

He actually stops mid-stride, and the look on his face says I went full crazy chick on him. I even feel Callie staring at me like I'm nuts as she makes his subs. Nico's eyes cut to Callie and then back to me. "Um. No? I told her I wanted your subs for lunch before games because they're good and I'm hungry. I don't like pasta salad. There is something about olives. They freak me out. Then the little red things they say are tomatoes but don't look like tomatoes and get caught in your teeth, I don't like them either. I love your subs, though. I know what I'm eating."

"Oh," I say after his word vomit.

"I don't like pasta salad either," Callie says, and I want to scream.

"Did you ask me out because you felt sorry for me because I looked like trash?"

He squints at me, and my beautiful sister says, "What is wrong with you?"

"Shut it," I snap as I meet his gaze. "I don't like being messed with."

He just blinks. "Nothing about you looks like trash."

"That's untrue, and I don't need you kissing my ass. I just want to know the truth."

From beside me, I hear, "Hey, wanna tuck in your crazy?"

I'm about to knock her out with a loaf of French bread. The low tenor of Nico's voice steals my attention. "Is it so hard to believe that I would ask you out because I want to?"

I snort. "Dude, look at you. You are famous. Everything on you is name brand. That watch is worth more than my shop. Those shades you have hanging on your shirt are more than I make in a week. I would be scared to touch your shoes. I mean, I'm worried there is mayo on the floor and it'll get them dirty. You are dripping money, and meanwhile, I'm rocking some Target yoga pants that I found on clearance."

His eyes darken a bit. "So, you're judging me?"

I'm a little taken aback. "Excuse me?"

"You're judging me." He comes to the counter, and I swear, if it weren't between us, he would go toe-to-toe with me. His eyes capture mine, and I feel a slow creep of heat crawl up my neck. "I have money, so obviously I can't be interested in a girl who apparently is wearing Target clearance. That's unfair. The thing is, I don't care what you wear or what you don't wear. I don't see any of that. All I see are these stunning emerald eyes that I want to know. Thick lips that I want to make smile. And other inappropriate things that I can't say in front of your sister."

I can't believe him. "I don't like games, and I sure as hell don't like handouts."

He holds out his hands. "Neither of those things is being done here." He then leans forward toward me, and I arch my back since I don't know what he is doing. Holy Grilled Cheese Jesus, he smells like heaven. His eyes, they're like little nuggets of chocolate, and everything inside me tingles. His voice is so low as he says, "A little advice. Not everyone is out to ruin your day. Some of us just want to make it a little better."

He stands back up, handing Callie a twenty before taking the subs. "Thanks, Callie. You ladies have a nice night."

"Bye, Nico. Sorry my sister is crazy," Callie calls to him.

He looks over his shoulder, those darn eyes dangerous as all hell and only on me as he calls back, "It's okay. I like a challenge."

The door shuts behind him, and I'm flabbergasted.

Beside me, Callie starts giggling. I glare down at her. "What?"

"He so wants to hit it."

I have no clue what I am going to do with her.

Or better yet, with Nico Merryweather.

CHAPTER EIGHT

ico

I PICK AT MY NAILS, my heart in my throat. I know Dr. Jenkins is staring at me.

"Nico?"

I bite the inside of my cheek as I shrug. "I don't miss her."

I look up as she nods gently. Today, her hair is down, and she's wearing a very expensive-looking pantsuit. I know she is trying to look older, but with that baby face, she'll need more than just a new suit. "Okay, but do you understand why it didn't work?"

I shoot her a deadpan look. "She was in love with someone else."

"How does that make you feel?"

"Like shit. Like I wasn't good enough for her."

"Elaborate, please."

I lean on my knees, looking down at her green heels. Not the color choice I'd make for shoes, but to each their own. Let your freak flag fly, as my mom always said. I swallow hard. I hate talking about Shelli. About me. But apparently this is supposed to help. "I felt I was getting comfortable. I was only sleeping with her. I was only calling her after games, and we were always texting. I felt like I wanted to open up to her."

"Have you ever opened up with anyone?"

"No."

"No one?"

"Not even Chandler, my best friend."

She looks surprised. "You haven't told Chandler your diagnosis?"

I look away. "No."

"Management knows?"

I chew the inside of my cheek. "Somewhat. My last therapist was very discreet."

"Why is that?"

"Because I'm terrified," I say softly, meeting her gaze. "Right now, I'm a full-on hockey god. Nothing can touch me. People think I'm perfect and—"

"Why does it matter what people think?"

Her question has me pressing my lips together. I swallow hard as the emotion clogs my throat. "I grew up the weird kid. No one wanted to play with me because I couldn't keep myself in check. Every little thing bothered me, I felt every single emotion, and I couldn't shut up. No one liked me. People love me now. I don't want to mess that up."

"Have you thought maybe they love you, the hockey player, and not you, Nico Merryweather?"

I pause. "Yeah, and I like that." She smiles, and I curve my lips a bit. "I don't want to put myself out there to be ridiculed or made fun of."

"It's a different world now, Nico."

"But still an unkind one," I answer back, and she nods, compassion on her face. Silence fills the space between us as I look around the conference room. It's empty. Nothing that tells you anything about Dr. Jenkins. It's plain, and for some reason, that bothers me. I want color in here.

"Can we try something?"

"What?" I ask as I look back at her. I'm a little nervous about what she's gonna want me to do.

"I want you to confide in someone."

"Confide?"

"About who you are. The real Nico."

I blink at her. "Why in the hell would I do that?"

She just smiles. "I think it would help."

"I don't."

She's stern as she asks, "Is there someone you'd like to tell?"

Why in the hell am I thinking of Aviva? That girl won't even give me the time of day. I doubt she'd care if I told her. She'd probably laugh in my face, think I'm lying. That it's some ploy to get her to go out with me. Hey, it's not a half-bad idea, in all honesty. I shake my head. "I don't know."

"Well, you have a week. I won't ask on Friday or Monday. But I will ask Wednesday, and I want you to have done it. I think this is something you really need to do to help yourself."

I don't agree at all. "I can't tell my mom?"

She gives me a look. One of those no-nonsense looks. Kind of reminds me of Aviva. "Your mom is aware…and also has called me four times."

I smile shyly. "She's a mama bear."

"To the fullest. I'm terrified of her," she laughs, and I smile. "But that being said, I want to help. So, help me help you."

Her words and request feel like a ton of bricks as I leave the conference room the IceCats let her use for our sessions. They want everything to be on-site, and I like it that way. I park my car, go to practice, go to therapy, go to lunch, and then go to meetings. It's nice this way, and I like it. As I head through the halls of the IceCats' compound, I realize I don't know how I am supposed to do what Dr. Jenkins has asked. I don't even know how to start that conversation. How do I bring up who I am, when I have been hiding it for so long?

I don't want people to think differently of me.

Around the corner from the video room comes Chandler with our teammate, Kirby Litman. They both nod at me. "How's it hanging, bro?"

"A wee bit to the left."

"Mine's to the right," Chandler says.

"Mine's at my knees." Kirby laughs, and like the teenage-acting men we are, we snort with laughter. "You ready for some lunch?"

I nod. "Starved. How was tapes?"

"Boring as fuck," Kirby says as we head to the lunchroom. "How was therapy?"

I shrug. Kirby bringing it up reminds me of Amaya's request. I could tell them, but the thought makes me gag. Kirby is a showboat, loud as fuck, and loves to tease people. I don't want him teasing me about this. He's a good friend, but I can't. I won't. I could tell Chandler, but then he's all sensitive and shit. He'll probably feel sorry for me. My mind keeps circling back to Aviva. I don't know, though. I don't think she'd care.

"Therapeutic?"

They both chuckle. "Is that doctor still so fucking hot?"

"She isn't ugly," I comment with a smirk just as we enter the lunchroom. Out of nowhere, Jo, our player relations rep, stops in front of me. "You were right. Those subs are bomb dot com."

I grin. "Aren't they?"

"Now Ms. Pearce, she's a tough cookie."

My grin grows. "She gave you a hard time?"

"No, but she was stern, and she wouldn't be lowballed. I tried because that's my job, to save us money so we can pay you guys, but she wasn't having it."

Sounds about right. "Did you get her?"

"Yup, she's gonna do it."

Awesome.

When I pull into Willz's parking lot, I see Callie outside at the patio table. The lot isn't empty, so I'm unsure why she's outside, but it is a beautiful day. I get out of my rental, heading toward her as she looks up. "Oh, thank God," she gushes, and while I'm starving for a sub, I don't mind sitting with her and helping her. Twenty minutes turns into an hour and then two. She's smart as a whip, but math trips her up.

"I wish it was easy like gymnastics is for me. I hate math."

I nod as I stretch my back. After being bent over on this crap seating, my spine is crying. "That's why it's hard, because you hate it. Enjoy it a bit, and I think you'll find it easier."

She doesn't look convinced. "I'll try that, but you're a godsend. I am actually going to make it to practice on time when I'd thought I wouldn't."

I glance at my watch to see she has about twenty minutes to spare.

"You're honestly the best, Nico. Thank you."

"Can you tell your sister that?"

She laughs as she stands and stuffs everything into her backpack. "She doesn't listen. But keep at her. I think she likes you."

I smirk up at her. "Yeah?"

She nods, and that excites me. I really thought she might hate me. I open the door for her and follow her into the shop. Just as the door shuts, Aviva yells out, "Is that you, Callie, or a customer?"

"Both," Callie calls back, and then she waves at me. "See ya."

"Bye. Have a great practice."

She sends me a sweet grin, and my heart warms. She's a good girl. As Callie walks into the back, Aviva comes out. When she notices me, she doesn't look too happy to see me. But my inside source says otherwise. I just have to remember that. "Hey, Aviva."

She nods as she puts on a pair of gloves. "Hey, Nico. How are you?"

"Good. You?"

She holds up her hands. "Living my best life."

I smile since I'm pretty sure she's being sarcastic. When she starts to make two subs, I perk a brow. "Already assuming I'm getting two? You're not wrong."

She laughs. "Oh, did you want two?"

"Please."

She starts to make three. "I only need two," I confirm.

"I'm actually making one for myself."

My heart kicks up. "To eat with me?"

She looks up at me through her lashes. "Nope."

I grin. "Where are you going to eat?"

"At the counter."

"I guess I will, too."

A little smirk pulls at her lips. "I guess that would be okay."

Man, she's beautiful. Her hair is up in a messy bun again, with her bangs covering her forehead. She's got her Willz tee on and a pair of black shorts. No makeup and no frills—and I think she's stunning. When the subs are done, she bags one and hands me the other. She sits up on the counter, and I lean on it as we both dig in.

"I have about twenty minutes before my dinner rush will start."

"I want more, but I'll take what I can get." When her eyes meet mine, I wink at her, and a blush creeps up her neck.

"No one has ever winked at me."

"Do you like it?"

She shrugs. "It's not awful."

I chuckle and do it again to tease her. This time, she laughs, and the sound is like hearing the puck knock off the post. It's magic. I have to keep her talking, though. I can't get distracted.

Around my bite, I ask, "Do you get sick of eating subs?"

She laughs. "God, yes. I'd love to go out for lobster and steak, but I don't have the time."

"You should make time. I'd love to take you."

She rolls her eyes. "You don't have time either, Mr. Hockey Goalie Guy."

I shrug. "I'd make time for you."

She grins. "I walked right into that line."

"Like a blind man into a wall," I tease, and we laugh. "So, Jo said it went well today."

"Yeah." She nods. "I'm only going to do it for a month at first to see if I like it and they like it."

"They'll love you, and I hope you love it too."

"I hope so," she confirms softy. "It will be great for the shop."

"Great. I just want the food."

Her eyes meet mine again, sending jolts of lust straight to my cock. "Thanks for that, by the way. The recommendation."

"Hey, I love this sub."

She covers her mouth as she eats and says, "It was my mom's pride and joy. One that I've made mine."

I look around the shop. The 90s is in full force in this place; even the music is 90s. "She was a 90s fan?"

She nods. "Yeah, she worked as a tour manager and managed some awesome 90s bands."

"Cool. Is she off touring or something? I've never seen her. Just you and Callie."

She presses her lips together before shaking her head. "We lost her about nine years ago to breast cancer."

I pause. "I'm so sorry. I didn't realize—"

She waves me off. "It's fine. How would you know?"

A weighted silence falls over us as we eat. "My mom lives in Quebec. I don't have a dad. He ran out on us."

She points at me with a fake grin. "Hey, we have deadbeat dads in common."

I hold up my hand for a high five, and thankfully, she hits it with her own palm. Her hand is soft, and I want to hold it. To keep from doing that, I say, "Go us." She nods in agreement, a small smile on her face before she takes another bite. I watch her for a second and then ask, "So, it's just you and Callie?"

She smiles. "Yup. She's honestly what keeps me going."

"She's pretty freaking awesome."

Warmth fills her eyes. "I saw you helping her again. I appreciate it."

"I love math, and she's a good kid."

"She is," she says, finishing off her sub. "I was sixteen when she was born, so I'm more a mom than I am a sister."

"That's nice. I don't have siblings."

She nods. "How did you get into hockey?"

The truth is right there. Dr. Jenkins's request is right there, but I ignore it all. "My grandpa played."

Aviva cocks her head with a smile. "I hear you're pretty damn good."

"I am," I say with a wide grin. "Ever been to a game?"

She shakes her head as she laughs. "I don't want to say I don't like it, but I really have no clue what is going on."

I laugh. "I'll have to take you to a game."

She gives me a skeptical look. "How? You'd be playing!"

"A rec game, so I can teach you."

She actually looks excited. "Oh, that would be cool, I guess."

"Callie should come, too, since I'm sure you don't want to leave her," I say, and her eyes fill with such light.

"You'd want to include Callie?"

I nod. "Yeah, why wouldn't I?"

"Most guys who want to hang with me don't want Callie around."

"What dicks. She's a cool girl."

She shrugs. "Well, I know that."

"And so do I," I say, and then the bell over the door rings. The sound is like my dick being ripped off. I don't want this to end yet. I want to keep talking.

"Duty calls," she says sadly, and it fuels my fire even more. She doesn't want this to end either.

"Yeah," I say as I hear the door open once more. "I guess I'll see you tomorrow."

She laughs. "Another sub?"

"Duh."

Her lashes kiss her cheeks as she gets up and gathers our trash.

"And I'll want to see you again."

Her cheeks fill with color as she bites her lip. "This was nice."

"Told ya." She wrinkles her nose at me, and I can't stop the grin from taking over my face. "We should do it again."

"Maybe."

With that, she saunters away with that fine ass. Everything inside me is red-hot, and there is no maybe about it. We're doing this again. I'll make damn sure of it.

I wave to her as I leave, and there is no contempt in her tone as she says, "See ya."

I actually can hear kindness in her voice, and it fuels my fire. As soon as the door shuts behind me, from around the side of the building comes Callie. I pull my brows together. "I thought you went to practice."

"I had to eat and get a few things together before I head over. I saw you two talking. Things look good!"

I laugh. "Yeah, it was."

"So, don't tell her I told you this, but I heard she's going to Bill's Tavern this Saturday with her friend. You know, if you're around and happen to go, bring a friend to distract Jaylin. They'll be there at nine."

Man, I love my inside source.

CHAPTER NINE

viva

"SEE? I can't even find the puck!"

Callie gets off the couch and walks to the TV, looking back at me as she points to the puck. In the goalie's glove. Is it called a glove? I need to ask Nico the next time he comes in. I hope it's tomorrow; I want to ask how everything went with lunch.

With a dry look, Callie says, "It's right there."

"Thank you," I deadpan as I apply my lip gloss. The IceCats game never would have been on before, but it's easy to say Callie and I have some inspiration to watch. Starts and ends with Number 0. I hate that the camera doesn't stay on him. I guess it's good that it doesn't, 'cause when it is, he's moving like a damn octopus, guarding the hell out of that net. I don't know how he does the splits like that, but my vagina hurts just looking at him.

As I watch the game, I curl my hair so that it's full along my shoulders. I haven't gotten ready in a long time. I can't even remember the last time I wore real clothes or makeup. Or even went out. Oh, wait.

No. I had that date six months ago, which was really just a hookup with an old friend. I got dressed up for him. That was a good night. A night where he told me he couldn't see me anymore because he was getting married.

Good times.

I ignore that, though; I need to have a nice night. I haven't seen Jaylin in a while, and I want to enjoy myself. I *have* to enjoy myself, before I lose it. With my eyes on the TV, I pin back a piece of hair as Nico lifts his helmet. He shakes out his wet hair, running his fingers through the strands, and soon, I'm wet everywhere.

Good. Lord. Almighty.

"Breathe, Veev."

I glare over at my annoying sister as I finish up my hair. I act like I'm not watching the game, but I am. I still have no clue what is happening, but Nico hasn't let one goal into the net. I like watching him fling his limbs to stop the puck. It's intriguing, but I hide that. Callie is obviously digging Nico. She thinks he's amazing, and I don't want her to get her hopes up. He's interested in me now...but not for long. He'll find someone who is worth his time. Not some scarred-up sub shop owner. One night, though... That's all I would want. I bet he'd give it to me, too. Get his fill, get mine. That's not a half-damn-bad idea. I might need to think on that a little longer. I doubt he does relationships.

Once I'm ready, I head out in a pair of heels that make my calves look amazing. My thighs and ass are crying in the tight skirt I stuffed them into, but if I know Jaylin, she's gonna look like a billion bucks. The haltered crop top I'm wearing is covered with a blazer since I don't want Callie to know I dress like this. Especially since I won't let her dress this way. She doesn't need to exude sex, but I sure as hell do.

When I reach for my keys, Callie looks back at me. "Aren't you gonna wait for the game to be over?"

I want to, but I don't want her to know I want to. She'll think I like Nico. Then she'll want me to date him, get married, have babies, and be rich. Since I don't want to tell her the truth or open a can of Nico worms, I shake my head. "No, the sooner I get out, the sooner I can come home."

She rolls her eyes. "Or you can stay out and have fun."

I wave her off. "No, I've got things to do in the morning." *My excuse for everything.* "Plus, I have to prep for the subs on Monday. You saw how long it took to prep for today."

Boy, was it some work. I made over a hundred subs and side trays with all the fixings. It was awesome, but the pay was even better.

"I'll help you. Just stay out. Have fun. Go home with someone."

My jaw actually drops as my phone dings, letting me know my Uber is here. "With who, Callie? Any Joe Schmo I meet?"

She shrugs, looking a whole lot of guilty before she says, "Whoever catches your eye. Just have fun. Let loose."

I put on my crossover bag and shake my head at her. "You're gonna give me an ulcer at the thought of sending you to college."

She snorts. "Don't worry. I'll make good choices and some bad."

"The bad are what worry me," I call to her before saying goodbye and heading out the door. Once I'm downstairs, I lock everything up and head out to the car. I can't help but look up at the apartment window, the TV light filling the room my sister sits in. I shake my head. That girl is crazy. I have no desire to go home with some Joe Schmo. But Nico Merryweather...that's a whole different story.

Not that it would ever happen.

THE PUB IS PACKED when I arrive. I soon realize it's because the game was on. Apparently I'm so in the dark about the IceCats that I didn't even know people actually gathered to watch them. Thankfully, once the game is over, the pub starts to clear out, but there is still a buzz going on. Pretty sure it's from how hot Jaylin is. Her skin is the color of milk chocolate, while her ebony hair falls straight along her shoulders. She has the perfect caramel eyes that are framed by dramatic lashes. Her lips are so thick I envy them. She's in a tight yellow skirt and a black crop top containing her huge boobs, and it's easy to say

I'm jealous of my friend. She's utterly fantastic, and all the guys are checking her out. Hell, *I'm* checking her out.

"Did you go up a size?" I ask, tipping my head toward her boobs.

"Yes, I told you that. Porn star titties is what I am going for."

We snort with laughter as I shake my head. "I'm so jealous."

"Get them done. It's so easy."

"I can't," I say on an exhale. "I'm saving back up for Callie's, and then maybe I'll do mine."

While we were close in high school and all through college, it wasn't time that morphed our friendship into a sisterhood. It was the pain we went through. After I lost my mom from breast cancer, not six weeks later, Jaylin was diagnosed with stage 2 breast cancer. And then I found out I had the gene for the same cancer my mom had. Jaylin and I went through the double mastectomy surgery together. We lay in bed together, watched movies, and mended with Callie at our feet. Cancer may tear apart some things, but it does bring other things together. Jaylin and I are closer because of it.

"You've been saying that for years," she scolds me, and I nod.

"I promise I will," I say. I wait for her to mention that I've said that a time or two, but thankfully, she doesn't. Instead, we both take sips of our wine. When she looks over at me, I smile. "Anyone new?"

She shrugs. "You know how it is. Guys suck. Or at least the dudes I've been meeting."

"Get off Tinder," I say dryly.

She laughs. "I don't have time to go looking for a guy—"

"Then get a dating profile. Stop with the hookups."

She shoots me a look. "You need a hookup for sure."

"Please," I say, waving her off. "Why don't you have your mom set you up?"

She snorts. "'Cause I am in no way, shape, or form ready for a Christian man. I need a bad boy. Someone who will make my mom pray for me more than she already does."

That sends us both into a fit of laughter. "I don't know why you drive her crazy."

"Because it's fun. She wants to put me in this perfect little box.

Successful lawyer, seven kids, good, godly man, and a huge house. Instead, I'm sleeping around, and I skip church more than I should." Her face is bright with happiness as she laughs from the soul. While I wish she'd calm down, I get it. She could have died from the cancer, and because of it, she's living life to the fullest.

It makes me envy her more.

She's living, and I'm hiding. It's pathetic and the real reason why I wiggle out of seeing her. She makes me feel a certain kind of way. Like I'm missing out on life, when all I'm trying to do is make sure Callie is taken care of. She's my main priority; I'll get to me later. Unless I die a horrid death, and then it will be for nothing. That's a truly depressing thought.

"You're a mess," I tease, and she flashes me a grin. "I envy you, though," I admit, and soon, her smile falls.

"Callie is doing great, Veev. You don't have to—"

"I know," I say simply, stopping her. "You've said this a few times."

"She's almost seventeen. She's not a baby. She doesn't need you up her ass."

I laugh ruefully. "Did she ever?"

We share a small smile. Callie has always been self-sufficient. She hardly ever cried when she was a baby, and she was always just larger-than-life. I don't know if it's because there is such a huge age gap between us or what, but like Jaylin said, Callie isn't a baby. She's almost an adult. "I just want to keep my promise."

Jaylin smiles before covering my hand with hers. "Aviva, you've kept that promise tenfold. Your mom is looking down on us, and she is beaming from ear to ear. You are the reason Callie is so perfect. You're the reason the sub shop is thriving. You've done it all. Now take some time for yourself."

I lace our fingers together and cover our hands with my other. Jaylin is my best friend, the one person who knows me inside out. The one who has seen me break down and has helped me back up. I can tell her anything. And I don't know why, but I want to tell her about Nico.

"There is this guy."

Her eyes light up as she scoots to the edge of the barstool.

I hold up my hand to keep her from squealing. "Relax. I doubt anything will happen!"

"No, something will. You have never spoken about a guy!"

I shrug, looking away as my face fills with a grin.

"And I've never seen you smile like that. Tell me everything!"

It must be the alcohol, because I feel goofy. "It's the guy I hit with my car."

Her lashes almost pop off from how wide her eyes go. "No way. The hot red-sports-car guy?"

I laugh, nodding before taking a swig. "At first, he tripped me out by asking me out. I thought he was just being nice—"

"No. He thinks you're hot!"

I roll my eyes. "I guess, because he's been coming around the shop. He's been helping Callie with her homework, and he got me a job with the IceCats, making subs for game days."

She blinks twice, and I'm pretty certain her lashes will come off this time. "Wait."

"What?"

"The guy you hit was Nico Merryweather."

"Yeah."

"Nico Merryweather, as in the star goalie of the IceCats?"

I bite into my lip. "Yes?"

She blinks once. Then twice. And finally, she starts laughing hysterically. I'm beyond confused as I watch her laugh. "Want to let me in on what is so funny?"

She looks up at me from where she is bent over laughing and shakes her head. "You've gone from not even being interested in anyone but Mike, who was never good enough for you, to now getting the attention from Carolina's most eligible bachelor? Girl, when you do things, you do them big."

I shake my head. "It's not like that at all. He's just intrigued by me because I'm not bending over and taking it up the ass from him at the drop of a puck."

She points to me. "Nice hockey analogy."

I giggle, though I am pretty pleased with myself. "I actually came up with it on my own."

"Impressive."

"Right?" I shake my head, waving her off. "But seriously, he's damn hot, and I wouldn't mind. But he'll get bored."

"Why do you say that?"

"You know why. He's who he is, and I'm who I am. Plus, he's probably a titty man. I don't have those," I say with a shrug, but something catches her eye halfway through my sentence. Within seconds, she's staring off to the side, and I roll my eyes as I take a sip of my wine.

Before I can turn to see what she is staring at, her eyes meet mine. "Well, sis, I don't think he gives two fucks if you have them. Not with the way he is looking at you."

I'm confused, and I turn in my seat just in time to see Nico coming toward me. He looks like a runway model in a crisp, expensive suit. His hair is wet and brushed back, and his face bears that smirk that makes it hard for me to form coherent thoughts. His brown eyes hold mine, and my whole body breaks out in gooseflesh. I swallow hard and notice that he is looking nowhere but at me. I brush my hair off my shoulders as he leans on the bar, that damn smirk devilishly handsome.

"Were you talking about me?"

It's like there is a frog in my throat. "Excuse me?"

His smirk gets bigger. "Since I haven't met your lovely friend, she sure did pick me out of a crowd and tell you I was here."

I recover somehow. "She's a fan and was telling me you were here."

His eyes darken. "Or you were telling her all about me and how much you wish I were here?"

"Your head is getting bigger by the second."

He chuckles as his eyes move down my body. "You look incredible." I lick my lips, and he inhales sharply. "Don't do that."

"Do what?" I ask, confused.

"Lick those lips," he says roughly. I swear, I think I'm going to fall out of my chair.

I look deep into his eyes. "Why not?"

His gaze doesn't leave mine. "Makes it real hard not to kiss them."

Suddenly, Jaylin is at my shoulder. "Please do. She really needs to be kissed."

"Jaylin!" I scold, glancing back at her in shock, but she just shrugs.

"I don't even care how embarrassed that makes you," she says with no fucks to give, and I refuse to look at Nico. I know my face is beet red; I feel it everywhere. "Hi, I'm Jaylin Raventorn."

They shake hands, though I notice Nico doesn't look her in the eye. That's weird. Everyone looks at Jaylin. She's stunning and, to be honest, totally his type.

She has boobs. Boobs I wouldn't mind punching since she thinks it's funny to throw me to the wolves, but boobs nonetheless.

"Nico Merryweather. It's nice to meet you."

"You too," she says, but I'm still fuming mad. I can't believe she said that. Then again, she had been drinking for an hour before I got here.

"Hey, Aviva."

I don't want to look at him, but I also don't want to be rude. I glance up at him, and he's holding a beer. Where did that come from? "Yeah?"

"Seriously, you are stunning. As always."

More heat fills my face, and that damn heart of mine skips a beat. It must be drunk. "Thanks."

"And don't worry. I won't kiss you." Why does that upset me? I mean, I knew the truth. But still. When he leans forward, his eyes dark and demanding, he whispers, "Yet."

CHAPTER TEN

viva

"THIS IS MY BUDDY, KIRBY LITMAN."

Kirby isn't even looking at me. He's zeroed in on Jaylin. Of course, she notices and leans toward him, her breast on full display. She taps my shoulder, and I hook a thumb at her. "These are my boobs…I mean, my best friend, Jaylin."

She gives me a dry look, but I shrug while Nico chuckles. She and Kirby shake hands before Nico bends to ask me, "How do you know her?"

"We were next-door neighbors growing up."

"Nice. All my close friends like that are back in Canada."

I lean on my hand. "That's where you're from?"

"A little town outside of Quebec City. My mom and grandparents are still there. Though, I bet my mom wishes I'd let her live here."

"Why don't you?"

He shakes his head. "You know how you are with Callie? Times that by a hundred, and that's my mom. So overbearing."

I try not to be offended, but of course I am. "You think I'm overbearing?"

He shakes his head quickly, holding up a hand. "Not at all. You're protective and make sure things are good for her. My mom does that and then some. She calls my trainers and doctors…and I'm twenty-seven."

I grin. "I think I'd love your mom."

He scoffs. "Don't play. My mom would love you. She likes strong women who work for what they want. Know how they want things."

I feel a little light-headed, but in a good way. "You think that about me?"

He nods. "Fuck yeah. I've never met anyone like you." He takes a long pull of his beer. "The last girl I was with came from money. She never knew what hard times were. Don't get me wrong, she was strong as all shit and badass. She was smart and awesome, but she wasn't self-made, in my opinion. You are." He laughs. "I could be being an asshole about her. She chose some other guy over me."

I can't help but think she isn't that smart, but to each their own. I notice Nico watching Jaylin, and when he looks back to me, he grins. Before I can ask about the girl from the past, he says, "Based on how she's dressed, I would say she doesn't look like your type of friend, but I've never had the privilege of seeing you like this."

I hold out my hands. "Get your fill because tomorrow it's back to shorts and tees."

"Will the shorts be short?" Nico asks with a devilish gleam in his eyes.

"I'll pull them up when you come in." Whelp, it's possible I've had too much wine.

"Such a tease," he says, waggling his brows at me, and I laugh.

"That's the wine talking."

"Well, please keep drinking," he jokes before ordering another beer and a glass of wine for me. "How's your night going? I know you don't like coming out. Since I've asked, and you've turned me down."

I giggle as I glance over at Jaylin to see her getting to know Kirby. Nothing is holding her back. She's having a blast, and I want that. I meet Nico's gaze again, and it's nice to see him somewhere else. Callie isn't here...I'm not running my livelihood. I'm just a girl in a bar, in a skirt that is making it real hard to breathe.

Or maybe it's all Nico.

"It's okay. I don't know how to be out. I'm used to being home and running shit."

"Well, for someone who doesn't know how, you're doing a damn fine job," he says, glancing around. He looks nervous, which is funny to me. He's gorgeous, and all the girls in here are checking him out. While he does stand out in his elegant suit, it's also that he is just so big. Shoulders thicker than boulders and a body that is a dream. I bet he looks real good naked. Wow, I do need to slow down on the wine. "Have I told you how hot you are?"

I try not to grin as my face heats up. "It's the dress—"

"Nope, it's you." I hide behind my wineglass, and he laughs. "I'd say dress like this all the time, but then when I come in for a sub, I'll be fighting off all the guys. That would be bad for business, and then you'd hate me for running off your profits. So, I'm gonna need you to wear a bodysuit at work, a loose one, maybe one of those baggy onesies, and then this when you're with me."

I snort with laughter. "With you?"

He shrugs. "Yup. Don't know if you are aware, but this moment? It's ours."

My heart is pounding in my chest, and I'm sure the wetness in my palm isn't from my wine. "How so?"

"Things are about to change for us," he says, and those eyes are so dangerous. They travel along my body as he takes a long pull of his beer.

"Change?"

"Yeah. This is the moment we decide if we want more."

Lord, he makes me breathless. "Or we could just be hanging out."

He nods. "That's exactly what we're doing. Getting to know each other so that you can decide if you want to pursue me. Which I'm all for since I really want to pursue you."

I can't fight my grin. "Is that right?"

"You know it's right. You knew from the moment you ran your car into mine."

"I was concussed."

He flashes me a devastating grin. "Or completely overwhelmed by my sexiness."

I can't help it. I snort with laughter, like, from my soul. I am laughing as I shake my head. "You're crazy."

"I try," he says, leaning on his elbow as he finishes off his beer.

He signals for another one, and when the bartender brings it over, he says, "I'll add it to your tab, Nico."

"Thanks," he says as he takes a swig, yet his eyes stay on me.

My eyes travel along Nico's face, and I sense he's doing the same to me. Maybe this is our moment. That sounds so silly, though. "Do you come here often?"

He curves his lips. "Only when I know there is a gorgeous girl here."

"Who are you here to see?"

His eyes don't leave mine. "You know it's you."

"I don't." I'm not fooling around. Why would he be here for me? Also, how would he know I was here?

"Don't play like that, Aviva. You're extremely confident and smart. That's why I'm attracted to you."

Oh, the desire in my gut is going crazy. I'm a bit breathless as I say, "How would you know I was here?"

He waggles his brows at me. "I had a source."

I tip my head as I try to read him. He has a source… That brat! "Callie?"

"I won't confirm or deny that."

I smack him playfully. "Don't use my sister to get close to me."

He grins. "Hey, I'm not. If she was the one, she gave up the info without me asking."

She would do that. I roll my eyes. "She's a thorn in my side. As are you," I accuse, and he grins.

"How am I a thorn in your side?"

"You're always there. Flirting and being cute. I am busy. I have things to do."

"Can I be one of those things?"

"Nico!" I exclaim, smacking him once more. But this time, I lean in closer. It was unintentional, but now that I'm here, I don't want to leave. His eyes have lighter flecks of gold in them. His lashes are long and lush. Lord, he is beautiful.

"You know you like it. You know you like me."

Oh, my face hurts from grinning. "Do I now?"

"You do," he says, and then he winks again. I don't know why more men don't wink like that. It really sets my panties on fire. He swallows hard as he orders another beer. When he takes a long pull, I eye him. "Thirsty?"

He looks around as he shrugs. "I don't like bars."

That surprises me. "Really? I thought this would be your scene."

He shakes his head as he leans toward me. His body is so big, and he smells absolutely sinful. "No, I like being home."

He holds up his finger for another beer, and I raise a brow. Being the daughter of an alcoholic, I know the signs. Plus, I'm pretty sure I read an article that said athletes struggle with vices. Drinking, drugs, both, and that is not something I want to be a part of. Not when I have Callie, and not when my dad is enough to handle. "Wow. Another one?"

He sighs heavily. "I really don't like bars, and usually, this one is not this packed. Or so Kirby said. I guess they were running a special or something. I don't know." He must have noticed that I don't like that excuse, for he stands up taller as he looks down at me. "Drinking numbs the need to run out of this place."

I perk my brow. "Why do you want to run?"

"There are too many people. I feel like I'm suffocating, but drinking makes that feeling go away."

"Claustrophobic?"

He shrugs, and I can tell he's holding back. "I guess. I don't know. I'm good on a bus with the team or on a plane. But when it's people I don't know, in a place like this, all these people…it makes me feel a certain way."

"Oh."

"Yeah, and since there is no way I'm missing this opportunity to be with you, I'm gonna drink to numb myself so I can stay."

The narcissistic part of my brain wants to tell me that it's a line, but I feel it isn't. I feel he's being truthful, and I know I don't know him that well, but I've never seen him look like this. He looks nervous, freaked out, and my heart goes out to him. I put my hand on his wrist, stopping him from lifting his drink. "If I'm getting to know you, I want to know real you, not drunk you."

My hand is tingling with desire as his eyes meet mine. He pushes the beer away and takes a deep breath. "So, I'm about to fast-forward our moment."

I perk my brow. "How?"

"By asking you to leave with me."

"Leave with you?" I ask, my heart jumping into my throat. "Where to?"

"The car, a restaurant where we can hide in the back, a park, the beach, anywhere." He runs his hands down his face, and when he looks back at me, I can see the panic in his expression. "I swear I'm not just trying to get in your pants. I just want to get to know you, and I can't here. I'm too worried about what's going on around us—"

I don't know what the hell has gotten into me, but I cup his jaw. His words stop immediately as his eyes bore into mine. I run my thumb along his bottom lip as I inhale deeply. I honestly don't know what the hell I'm doing, but I need him to feel better. If leaving is what will do that, then we need to leave.

And yes, I know I said we.

Holy Grilled Cheese Jesus.

"Let's go."

He exhales in relief as he stands up, throwing a few twenties on the bar. "For hers and mine," he calls to the bartender as I turn to Jaylin.

"We're leaving," I say because I don't know what else to say. The excitement on my best friend's face makes me feel like an idiot, but I don't care.

I want to fucking live.

"Okay. Call me tomorrow?"

"I will."

"And have fun."

I feel giddy. "I will?"

"You will," she says with a nod.

As I stand, I glance back at her. "Can you drive by the—"

"I'll text you if anything is wrong."

I swallow hard just as Nico's fingers thread through mine. I look up at him, and I'm out of breath. How in the world did this happen? I've never even noticed a guy before, but this guy… I see and I want. Badly.

"Do you want to run by the shop? We can do a drive-by to check on things."

My heart is pounding like a drum. One of those big steel drums they use in the symphony. "Yes, please."

"No problem," he says, and it really doesn't seem like a problem. It's almost like he wants to. Like he cares about Callie, but I guess I know he does. Before he can turn away, I grab his tie and pull him toward me. I don't know what I am even thinking, but I rise up on my toes and press my mouth to his. The hand that is holding mine wraps around my waist, pulling me closer to him as he grasps my face. I fall into the kiss as my insides clench, and every single inch of me is set on fire. He tastes like beer and everything naughty. His lips are soft, inviting, and when his tongue meets mine, I'm in utter heaven.

I swear, it's like an out-of-body experience.

When I pull away due to the intense catcalls from my so-called best friend, I look up at him through my lashes. His lips are curved, his eyes playful as he whispers, "Hey, no fair."

"What?" I ask breathlessly.

"I was supposed to kiss you first."

I swallow hard. "I couldn't resist."

He smirks. "I know. It's hard to resist me."

Oh, I'm in big trouble with this one.

CHAPTER ELEVEN

ico

"I KNOW it's silly that I wanted to check on her."

I shut the truck door behind her and shake my head. "No, it's totally cool."

"I should be fine with all the cameras and the new security system, but she makes me nervous."

"You don't leave her much."

I feel like there is more to the story, but Aviva just nods her head. I could tell how important it was that we checked on Callie. Thankfully, everything was fine, and it seemed Callie was already in bed. The apartment was dark. I almost thought Aviva would want to stay, but she was the one to ask where we were going. With everything closing and the weather a bit chilly, I suggested my house. I thought she'd say no, but here we are.

"I really don't," she laughs as she walks beside me up the sidewalk. "This is a really beautiful home."

"Thanks." I dig my keys out of my pocket. "I actually bought it from Amelia's grandparents. She used to live here, but when she and Chandler got together, she moved in with him. The place was for rent for a while, but then I had a few stalkers, so they let me buy it."

I could have left out most of that, especially the stalkers.

"Stalkers?"

I nod. "Yup. Bad choices lead to bad women."

"It's easy for that to happen nowadays. Especially with your profession."

"Yeah," I agree, and then I laugh. "But I really seem to attract the crazy."

She grins. "I'm not crazy."

I wink. "The jury is still out."

She laughs as I open the door for her, and she steps in. I lock the door behind us, and then I walk through the house, turning on lights.

"Wow, this is a nice place."

"Wasn't what you were expecting?"

She shakes her head. "Nope. Expected it to be a bachelor pad."

I chuckle as I kick off my shoes and set my keys in the bowl by the door where I always put them. As I unbutton my jacket, I notice she is looking around. She looks damn good in my house. I like her here. "Do you want something to drink? I have beer and cider. We can go out on the deck or the beach if you want."

"A cider would be great, and the deck looks awesome."

"Coming right up."

I watch as she kicks off her heels and throws her jacket on the couch. Her back is fucking sexy, and I want to run my tongue along all the muscles that make it up. I usually don't notice things like that on women, but her back is fucking magnificent. All that slinging of sub dough does a body good.

"So, where did you meet these stalkers?"

I laugh as I grimace. "Tinder."

She laughs. "I tell Jaylin to stay off there. She gets in trouble with those guys."

"That's the damn truth," I agree as I walk into the kitchen, putting away some stuff I left out before I went to the arena for the game. "It's a cesspool, for sure."

She nods as she looks at the different photos on the wall. A lot of them are of me growing up and then some of my family. "So, the girl you were speaking of before... How long did you date?"

"We didn't date," I say as I open the fridge. "We were just fucking, and when I wanted more, she told me she was in love with someone else."

She looks over at me. "Well, that's unfortunate."

"Eh, it is what it is," I say, pulling out some ciders. I stuff a piece of cheese in my mouth before shutting the fridge with my hip. "She's happy with him. Getting married and all that jazz."

"Did you love her?"

I shrug as I get the bottle opener. "I thought I did a bit, but my therapist says it was more infatuation."

"Oh," she says softly as she leans into the bar and checks out a goalie helmet I have lying there. When she reaches out to touch the helmet, my breath hitches.

"Sorry, can you not touch that?"

She pauses midway and jerks her hand back. "I'm so sorry."

"No, it's me. I'm weird about my equipment."

I lean into the other side of the bar and hand her the cider as she says, "It was rude of me to assume I could touch it. I'm really sorry."

"Don't be," I say, waving her off. I know I need to explain more about the helmet. But instead, I find myself extremely embarrassed. I watch as she takes a long pull of her drink, and I don't miss the side-eye. She probably thinks I'm a crazy person.

The silence is killing me, but then she says, "I was in love with the last guy I was with."

Why does that bother me? "How long were you two together?"

"It was complicated." She shakes her head. "We grew up together and dated in high school. When we went to college, it was very much a hookup when it was convenient for him. I started to realize that I was falling in love with him and he wasn't with me. I tried to cut it off, but I was lonely."

"Lonely? Aviva, you can have any guy you want."

"Hush, you," she teases, smacking my hand. She's handsy when she's drinking. I fucking love it. "I don't know. I had a soft spot for him. But the last time we hooked up, he told me he couldn't do this anymore because he was getting married. I was devastated. But then I realized he was only with me because he felt sorry for me."

"Sorry for you?" I ask, confused.

She must have decided she'd said too much because she shakes her head. "Oh, is this your mom and grandparents?"

Ah, fun. Secrets. "Yup. That's the fam."

"Your mom is stunning."

I come to stand beside her. "Thanks. When my dad left, I think he took a lot of her confidence."

"Well, that's shit."

"Agreed," I say, tapping my bottle to hers.

We both take a sip before she points to another picture. "What trophy is that?"

"Vezina. I was voted best goalie last season."

"Wow, that's cool."

"Yeah, not to toot my own horn—"

"Because you're so humble and all," she teases, and I grin.

"This is true, but I'm pretty badass."

"I know. I was watching tonight." Her face flushes a bit with color, and it sets me on edge. She's fucking gorgeous. "Don't read into that."

I move her hair off her shoulders, and the stars in her eyes are beautiful. "Why? I like that you watched me."

She rolls her eyes. "Just gonna make your head bigger."

I waggle my brows at her. "You being here is making my head bigger."

She perks her brow at me. "Which head?"

Her grin lights up her face, and I find myself unable to hold in my laughter. She laughs with me as I open the door to the back deck. She walks out in front of me, and I watch that sweet ass sway. I want to touch it so bad, but I don't want her to think I only want her for sex. While I wouldn't mind taking her right into my bedroom, she deserves more than that. If she's gonna give me her time, I'm gonna value it. As I shut the door behind me, I look over at her while her hair blows in the ocean breeze.

"Yup. I'd never leave this spot if I lived here."

I walk over to stand beside her. "It's pretty awesome."

"It's exquisite," she gushes. I love the look on her face. The blissful, carefree one. I haven't seen it on her before, and seeing it now leaves me fighting for my next breath. Unable to resist, I lean toward her, kissing her jaw. I linger longer than I should, but then my need for her is rewarded when she turns her face so that her lips meet mine. I place my bottle on the railing and gather her up in my arms, wanting to consume her completely. She feels so damn good in my arms. Her lips are tender, soft, and she tastes like the cider I just gave her. I run my hands up her spine, the muscles in her back teasing my fingertips just the way I wanted. She cups my face with one of her hands as her other hangs between us, the coolness of her bottle against my chest.

I deepen the kiss, needing to taste every single bit of her mouth. I feel myself getting harder with each sweep of our tongues. She kisses like a fucking dream, and I really don't know how she does anything but kissing. She needs to be kissing someone every second of the day. Me, preferably. I press my nose into hers, drawing the kisses out as I slide my hands down her back to her ass. It's thick and utterly flawless. She gasps for breath as we part, and I find myself taken with the way her lashes kiss her cheeks.

When she looks up at me, her lips are swollen, and it takes everything out of me not to capture that mouth once more. Ah, fuck it. I want—no, I need to. I drop my mouth to hers once more, and she meets me eagerly, her lips as wanton as mine. She wraps her arms around my neck, her bottle hanging against my back as we kiss and tease each other. Her teeth are dangerous and have me harder than a pipe as she rakes them across my lips. Heat is radiating off her, and soon, I can't control myself. I run my hands over her butt, and when I lift her off the ground, she wraps her legs around my waist. Thank God she wants me just as much as I want her.

Against her lips, I whisper, "I think we should take this inside. My neighbor is a peeper." She smiles against my lips, hard, and I notice her dimples for the first time. "You have dimples."

She covers her face quickly. "I hate them."

"What! Why? They're amazing!"

She shakes her head. "They're funny-looking."

I pull her hand down and kiss her lips. "They're stunning."

She bites her lip as she gazes down at me. The heat between us is molten-hot and unstoppable. In a low and raspy voice, she whispers, "I think we should take this inside."

She doesn't have to tell me twice. I capture her mouth once more and hold her so close to me. She squeezes her thighs around my waist, and everything explodes inside me. I need to get her inside before I blow my load right here. I tear my mouth from hers and, while still carrying her, head inside. She slides her mouth along my ear, my neck, my jaw as I shut the door behind us. Her teeth move along my skin, making each hair on my body stand to attention as I carry her through the living room. I need more space than the couch would provide.

Once in my room, I lay her down on the bed before I take the cider from her. With my free hand, I grab a coaster out of the nightstand and set the cider on it. I can't do water rings. They haunt me, and then I won't be able to do anything. So, as a safety measure, I keep the coasters in the nightstand. After I'm happy with the placement of the cider, right in the middle, I look down at her. She lies on my bed like she belongs there. Her hair is fanned out around her, her arms above her head, and there's this look on her face that is going to make it real hard to take this slow.

As I get onto the bed, I slowly move over her, pressing myself into her hot center as our mouths meet once more. I hold myself up with my elbows to make sure I don't crush her, but I don't think she cares. She moves her lips with mine with such heated need as she tangles her legs with mine. I run my hands up her sides and cup her breasts.

And that is when she goes still.

I open my eyes to find her watching me. I pull back and press my lips together. "I thought we were well past taking it slow. I'm in it to win it at this point, and that means I'm grabbing the boob. But if that's not okay, put the red light on now."

She swallows hard, and a look of pure horror covers her face. It's almost as if she's about to cry.

"Aviva?"

"I need to tell you something."

I lift up a bit more. "Okay?" She looks so unsure of herself as she glances away. I take her jaw, bringing her eyes back to mine. "Don't hide."

She presses her lips together as her eyes search mine. "Remember when I was talking about that guy I used to be with?"

"The one you changed the subject on?"

"Yeah. Him. Mike." Aviva's voice breaks a bit, and her face changes so quickly. Gone is the sex kitten that was about to rock my world, replaced by an anxiety-ridden woman. "He was around when my mom died from breast cancer, and he helped me through that."

I don't know what to say, so I don't say anything. I just watch as she struggles to find her words. "When I said I think he felt sorry for me, it's because after she died, like only about six weeks later, we found out that I carry the same cancerous gene she had. Then Jaylin was diagnosed with stage 2 breast cancer."

"Fucking hell."

"Exactly," she says, and when the tears gather in her eyes, I feel my stomach twist. "Well, Jaylin had to get her breasts removed, and since I didn't want to get cancer because I didn't want Callie to have to go through everything again, I did the same."

Her eyes search mine, and I must be an idiot. "Okay, I know this is a serious moment. But I must be super horny because I'm not following. I know that makes me a jackass, but goddamn, you're so hot. So yeah, what are you saying?"

She swallows hard, and then in the smallest, most shattering voice, she whispers, "I don't have breasts."

Nope, not horny. Just an idiot.

CHAPTER TWELVE

viva

NICO PULLS his brows together as his eyes search mine, and I see the confusion in his brown depths. My heart is jackhammering in my chest, so hard that my vision is shaky. I feel as if I almost can't breathe. I know I am, but each breath hurts as I draw it in. My chest is tight as I stare at him. I want to look away, but his fingers still hold my jaw, and I don't think he'd allow me. Since having my double mastectomy, I've never had to tell a man about it. I've never gotten close enough to a man to allow him to know. With Mike, he knew and we went at it. We never spoke of it, and most of the time, I wore a shirt to bed with him. I didn't plan on telling Nico, but here I am. I want to live, and for that to happen, I have to share this damaged part about me.

I'm just terrified he'll be disgusted.

"You don't have boobs?"

I press my lips together as I look down at his mouth. It's swollen from our kisses, and damn it, I want to kiss him again. I don't want to talk about this. "I had a double mastectomy a couple months after I lost my mom."

"That's where they cut off your boobs?"

"Yes."

"So, you have nothing?"

My lips quiver, and I feel the pain of loss all over again. "Nothing."

I glance up at him just in time to see him look down at my chest, and when he pokes my boob, I want to laugh. "What is this?"

"A fake boob. Rubber, so that it looks like I have something," I say in almost a whisper. I'm utterly mortified. Why I thought I was ready for this is beyond me. I was so ready to jump with him back at the pub. I wanted to live like Jaylin does, but I forgot what that entails. It means I have to show my whole fucked-up self, and I don't think I'm ready for that. "Maybe I should go."

He squishes his brows together as his gaze meets mine. "Why?"

"I don't know," I say, crossing my arms over my chest. But before I can lock my arms tight, he stops me. He pulls my hands away and laces our fingers together. "Aren't you grossed out?"

"No. Not at all," he says simply, his eyes burning into mine. "Do you want this?"

I swallow hard. I'm vibrating everywhere. "Yes."

"Then why the hell would you want to leave?"

I feel the heat all over my face, and I hate the tears that are gathering in my eyes. "I'm embarrassed."

"By what?"

I shrug, and I refuse to cry. I've cried enough over my misfortune, over losing my mom. While this moment, opening myself up to him, may be like ripping a Band-Aid off a wound that won't heal, I can't give that wound the power to own me. I meet his gaze with all the strength I can muster as I inhale shakily. "The situation and who you are. You can have anyone with boobs—"

"Stop assuming things about me."

I give him a look. "Nico, you were on Tinder. A place full of beautiful women."

"And none of them caught my attention. It was a beautiful woman who rammed her car into my ass who did."

I bite my lip. "I just feel you'll be disgusted by me."

Compassion fills his features as he gathers my face in his hands. "Aviva, I don't want your boobs. They weren't what drew me to you. It was you. All of you. I want you."

My lip quivers as a tear escapes. "No one has ever said that to me."

"Their loss, my gain," he whispers as he leans in, pressing his lips to mine.

I squeeze my eyes shut as our lips move together. When he pulls away, he cups my face and runs his thumbs along my jaw. He straddles my hips as he sits up before moving his hands up my arms to my shoulders. His fingers play with the string that holds my halter together, and I can feel every inch of him growing harder by the second. As he slowly unties the top of my halter, his eyes never leave mine. There is something in the way he looks at me and stares into my eyes. It feels as if he is looking into my soul. No one has ever looked at me like that or made me feel like this. As he slowly drags my halter down, I want to stop him, but something keeps me from doing so. I don't know if it's the kindness in his eyes, his sweet words, or my horniness. I'm not sure, but I am sure I want this.

I want to live.

I hold my breath as he reveals my chest. I watch his face, waiting for the repulsion as he uncovers my taped-on rubber boobs. I take a deep breath when he reaches for one of them, pulling it off with ease. I watch as he holds it in his hand, squeezing it before a smirk comes across his face. Is he laughing at me?

"Can I borrow this?"

I scrunch up my face. "What?"

"I want to beam Chandler in the face with it. It would be so funny."

If this was his way of breaking the tension, he succeeded. Within mere seconds, I'm laughing from the gut. He grins down at me before pulling off the other one and tossing them to the side of the bed.

"If they go missing, it wasn't me," he says, and I grin. That is, until he touches my scars. I'm holding my breath again as he runs his fingers along the scars. They're faded and only little white lines, but that isn't what embarrasses me. It's the sunken-in part of my chest where my breasts should be. He moves his gaze to mine as he whispers, "You're so strong, Aviva."

I shake my head, feeling the rush of shame. "I'm not. I was just scared. I didn't want to go through what my mom did. I didn't want Callie to live through two deaths from the same disease."

"I feel that makes you strong."

I shake my head once more, ignoring the sensation of his finger along my scar. No one, and I mean no one, has ever touched me like this. I feel so vulnerable but, at the same time, so safe. "No. If anything, I'm a coward because I didn't try to fight."

"You are not a coward, not even in the slightest," he says with such disdain on his face and in his voice. I've waited for the disgust, but it wasn't from how I looked; it was from what I said. "You are a fighter, Aviva. You went through this to protect yourself and your sister. I don't see that as cowardly."

He's got me feeling a certain kind of way, but I won't ignore the truth. "But I disfigured myself, made it so I can never breastfeed a baby, and then hid behind these scars for years to keep myself invisible to men. Because I'm a coward."

He narrows his eyes into slits, and I don't know why. He doesn't even really know me, but he cares so much. "Because no one was ever there to tell you that you are perfect just the way you are," he says with such ease, as if it was what he was born to say.

His words shake me to the core. No man has ever spoken to me like this, with such honesty. I've been lied to, cheated on, and stabbed in the back, but there is something about Nico that makes me feel as if he would never do any of that. What you see is what you get with him, and I admire that. He throws off his shirt before slowly lowering himself on top of me. His warm chest feels absolutely perfect against mine. I want to feel insecure that his pecs are bigger than my nonexistent chest, but it's hard when he is looking at me like this.

Like I'm beautiful.

Nico presses his nose against mine as his eyes burn into mine. I stroke my fingers along his back to his neck, wrapping them around it. "You say what you're thinking, huh?"

"Completely and with no control or cares." He looks down at my chin as my fingers dance along his neck. "Does it bother you?"

"Not at all."

"You don't think I'm weird?"

I smile. "No. Not at all. I wish I could be like that."

He pauses for a second, and his eyes…something flashes in them. It's as if he wants to say something, but he's holding back. "I've always been like this."

"It's refreshing."

"Funny, I was thinking that about you," he says, kissing the side of my mouth. "Aviva, you shouldn't be ashamed of your scars. You should be proud. They make you who you are. A strong, beautiful, intelligent, breathtaking woman. You can do and have anything you want."

Oh, I want to believe him so badly. Not the strong and beautiful part, but the "do and have anything" part. If that were true, I wouldn't be in debt. I wouldn't have a father who wants to keep me in the poorhouse, and I would have implants so I could feel like a woman. A woman who can attract someone like Nico. I know I am here, I know I'm in his arms, but I still feel like it's all a dream. That we'll go at it and it will be glorious, but then it'll be over.

"Can I be honest with you now?"

I meet his gaze as my fingers trail over his lips. "Do you know how to be anything else?"

He sends me a smirk. "True," he chuckles, but then his chuckle dies off. "I'm really weird about mess and fluids."

"Huh?"

"I don't like to come on you or anything like that. Chandler and Amelia said I need to be honest with the person I sleep with. And instead of freaking out on you when you wipe my come on my bed, I thought I'd be honest and let you know I don't like that. So, if you need a towel, I can get one now—"

"Nico."

He pauses, and goodness, he looks embarrassed. "Yeah?"

"I'm not a fan of come on me either. It's cool. If we can keep the come in the condom, that would be awesome. I can let you know when I'm about to if you go down on—"

"No. I love doing that. I just don't like mine all over you."

Never in my life did I think I would have this conversation. "Okay, that's no problem."

"I know it's stupid—"

I cup his jaw, and I press my lips to his to stop him from talking. I don't want to talk about it; I just want to do it. His mouth is downright dangerous against mine as it moves along my neck and down my throat. I feel him so hard against my leg, and God, I want him. He runs his mouth along my collarbone, sliding his tongue over the dip as his hands clutch my hips. I tense up when I feel him moving down my chest. I start to feel self-conscious, but when he rakes his teeth down the center of my chest, gone is everything but pure pleasure. I arch up, a guttural yell coming deep from inside me. Mike never kissed my chest—he always ignored it—but Nico does no such thing.

"Fuck, you taste good," he mutters against my skin, and my heart is out of control.

Desire swirls in my gut, and I feel as if I could come right here, right now. As he dips his tongue into my belly button, he unfastens my skirt and then pulls it off along with my thong. He throws my clothes to the floor with ease. I watch as he gets up on his knees, reaching over to his nightstand. I sit up, undoing his pants and unleashing a swollen cock that is bigger than any cock I have ever seen. I may be biased since he has been really kind to me, but holy mother of penises, Nico is hung. I blink twice, maybe four times, as I run my fingers along the engorged flesh. He's thick and long, a double whammy.

I lift him into my hand, and while I'm nervous since I haven't had a cock in my mouth in a very long time, I find myself wanting to please him. I want him to feel as good as I feel. He jumps when my mouth surrounds his head, and when he slips his hand into my hair, I slide my tongue around him.

I'm rewarded with a "Fuck yes" that has my toes curling against the bedspread. I hold him at the base before I move my mouth up and down him. I mix a little tongue and a little teeth, and by the sound of it, I think I've still got it. When my name falls from his lips in such a tortured way, my heart soars. I'd forgotten how much I like doing this. I really have a rhythm going, but then he stops me.

"As much as I want to blow right here, I really want to be inside you."

I lick my lips. "I want that too."

"Good, 'cause if we do it this way, I'm gonna need a sandwich and a nap before I'm ready for round two."

I grin up at him as he sheaths himself. "A sandwich, huh?"

He smirks at me before pushing me back onto the bed playfully. He takes me by the back of the knee, pulling me down the bed to him. "I'd rather have a sub than a sandwich, but I have something way better right now," he says before he pushes himself into me. I'm so wet, there is no resistance, and soon, we're both moaning loudly. He drops his head to my chest, inhaling deeply as I grasp his back. His cock fills me completely, and it's one hell of a tight fit. "I swear to God, if you ever make that noise again, I won't be able to keep from coming."

I kiss the top of his head. "Fuck me, Nico."

He looks down at me, his brow perked. "Are you trying to kill me?"

I lean up, kissing his bottom lip. "Yup."

His eyes darken, and then he is moving into me. With one hand behind my knee, pushing it forward into the bed, and the other at my hip, he's ruthless. He slams into me, his thighs hitting my ass, and the sound mixes with our own noises of pleasure. He pushes my knee back more, really opening me so he can go deeper. I feel my climax building. I know it's coming, and fuck, I want it. I look up at him as he thrusts into me, and I swear I've never seen such a beautiful man. His eyes are dark, hooded, and only on me. He looks at me as if I have a full rack and a perfect pussy. I mean, my pussy isn't bad by any means. I keep it rather trimmed up and clean, but his eyes, they make me feel like it's the best pussy he's ever had.

"I can't handle you," he mutters, and then he pulls out of me. I feel so totally empty without him that I whimper. To my surprise, he drops between my thighs and buries his face in my pussy. I cry out, squeezing my thighs against his head as he sucks me into that dangerous mouth of his. The amount of tongue he uses is mind-blowing. He sucks my clit, then fucks me with his tongue, and finally goes for my clit again. He's merciless, and when I come, I'm screaming so loud, I'm sure the whole city hears me. I would laugh at the fact that I sound like a yodeler screaming his name, but I'm too spent to give two fucks.

Nico enters me again with such force, and I feel it everywhere. I love it. God, I love it. He grabs on to my hips and slams into me. My body jerks up with each thrust, but hell, I want it. I need it. I feel another climax building, and soon, I'm wrapping my legs around his waist. He must have felt that I was almost there, because he presses his thumb into my clit, sending me right over the edge. I'm lost. Utterly lost. And I don't want to be found. He doesn't last too much longer before he comes, the sound loud and impassioned against my jaw.

He falls onto me, and I welcome the weight. I move my hair out of my face as I draw breath in deeply, and he does the same. He moves out of me and falls to the side, but his torso stays on mine. I'm covered in sweat, and so is he. I feel like I've run ten miles in Arizona.

"Please tell me that's how you always come," he whispers against my jaw, and I can't help but smile. "Fuck, that was so hot."

I move my lips into his hair and ask, "Which part? The convulsions or the yodeling?"

"I mean, the yodeling was pretty damn awesome."

"I should enter some competitions."

"I can help, put a curtain around us, and I'll get ya going."

I grin widely as his lips move over my jaw, and I close my eyes. "I haven't been with anyone in a while."

"Why? You should be loved on all the time."

"Because I didn't want anyone to see me."

"Don't hide this spectacular body," he whispers before kissing my left scar.

He then cuddles deep into me, leaving me feeling all kinds of things. I stroke my fingers through his hair and ask, "No sandwich?"

Nico kisses me once more in the same place. "I don't need it. I have you."

I glide my cheek along his hair and feel complete. For once, I feel like I did something for me. Nothing can touch what just happened in this room. Or on this night. It's all been perfect. Nothing can take that away from me. Not even the fear of tomorrow. I know I could ask what will happen next, and Nico would answer me. It would be a simple, "Will I see you tomorrow?" type of question, and he'd tell me exactly what he is thinking.

Problem is, I'm scared of his answer.

CHAPTER THIRTEEN

ico

THE SUN WARMS MY FACE, and I feel the sweet sea breeze as I stir awake. I opened the window before we fell asleep after our really fucking good night together. I wanted Aviva to feel the ocean air when she woke up. It's my favorite thing about living here. It's so refreshing, and I hope she likes it too. When she told me she wasn't a cuddler, I almost screamed out in relief. I told her it was because I get too hot, which is the reason she doesn't like to cuddle while she sleeps. But really, when I get hot, I sweat, and then it just sits there on us. Freaking me out. It's fucking gross.

I roll over, excited to see her, only to find she isn't here. I blink a few times. I know I went to bed with her last night. I sit up quickly, looking around. "Aviva?"

No answer.

And her clothes are gone.

And so are her rubber boobs that I had picked up and placed on the nightstand in the night.

What the fuck?

I throw the blankets off my naked body and head into the living room. My heart is pounding in my chest, and I'm utterly confused. Why would she leave? I thought we'd go to breakfast, hang out, anything other than her leaving.

"Aviva?" I call out, but no answer.

I check the bathroom, the patio, and finally, I accept that she's not here. I search the house for a note. Something telling me why she left or even her phone number so I can call. Sweat is dripping down my back and beading along my brow. I can't find any sign of her, and I don't understand. Did she not have a good time? Did I not satisfy her? Did she not like me?

My throat starts to tighten as I rack my brain, replaying the whole night. The hot touches, the sweet glances, and the talking. We talked a lot. She shared part of herself that she's never shared with anyone. Why would she do that if she didn't want to be here? If she didn't want to be with me? My heart is pounding in my chest to the point that I need to sit down. I lower myself into a chair as I inhale deeply. Did I let her see too much of me? Was I too honest? Was it the come thing? Did she want me to come on her? She seemed okay with it, didn't even laugh when I went to get a towel. She was understanding, cool, and even with the cuddling thing, she was good. Or at least, she seemed like she was. Fuck. Why the fuck did she leave?

No one has ever left. Usually I have to kick women out of my bed, but she left. Just left. No note, no number, no nothing. Gone. I realize I'm breathing really hard, and I sit back in my chair. I lean my head off the side as I draw in deep breaths and let them out. What if it was all a lie? What if she thought I was a head case? I had mentioned my therapist a few times. Did she figure it out? Fuck me... What the hell happened?

I feel like I'm suffocating. My eyes are crossing, and I feel my skin crawling. What if she figured it out and couldn't stand to be near me? What if she thought I was pathetic? What if she thought I was a weirdo? I swallow hard before I stand up quickly, reach for my helmet, and then sit on the floor. I slam it down over my head, needing the protection. I cross my arms over my chest, taking in deep breaths and trying to calm down. As the years have passed, I've learned how to cope when I get like this. As pathetic as it is, the helmet helps. Maybe Aviva figured that out, or she assumed so when I wouldn't let her touch it. It is my grandfather's, though. My safe haven. Through the cage, I stare at the wall as my vision normalizes. My breathing is still heavy, but my chest doesn't hurt. I take in deep breaths, forcing myself to let them out slowly.

"Is there a reason why you're sitting on the floor, naked, with your helmet on?" I don't even look at Chandler or acknowledge him. "Is this some kinky sex game you play? I mean, I get you're good on the ice, but I've never known someone to whack off while they wear their gear. Interesting, though I don't think I'm gonna try it. I get off just fine with my sexy woman."

I hear him moving around my kitchen. He is dropping off some food from his mom. She makes me dinners for the week because she spoils me. I lick my lips as I continue to stare at the wall.

I hear him lean on the counter. "Didn't you have someone over last night? When I went for my run, the lights were on, and I saw her."

Finally, I trust myself to respond. "Yeah."

I peel the helmet off and lay it in my lap, though Chandler has seen me naked plenty. Neither of us cares. "Are you okay?"

I swallow past the lump in my throat. "She just left."

"Who?"

"Aviva."

"Aviva? That's a really cool name."

It is. She is a cool chick. When she's not fucking leaving without a word or a note! "She just left. No note. No number. Nothing. Gone."

I look up at him as his eyes widen. "This is a first."

"It is."

He nods and then shrugs. "Dude, it happens. Sometimes it's good for you but not her—"

"No!" I roar, standing up and throwing down my helmet. "It was fucking good for both of us. We had a damn good time, and we clicked. For the first time in almost a year, I felt like I could click with someone else other than Shelli."

Chandler holds his palms up at me. "Whoa, dude. I didn't fuck you and leave. Don't take this out on me."

I grip the counter and take in a deep breath. My heart is jackhammering in my chest, and I hate this feeling. What did I do wrong? Nothing. I did nothing wrong. "I was honest, I was up front, and I told her what I did and didn't like."

"Good, but that doesn't mean that's why she left. Did she have something to do?"

"Probably, but why didn't she leave a note?"

"Couldn't find a pen?"

"Or she thought I was fucking crazy!" I yell, shaking my head and feeling stupid. "This is why I keep shit to myself—"

"But you don't. You try, but then things get messy and you freak."

He's right, but still. "Whatever. I just don't understand. I told her I didn't like bars, and that's how we ended up here—"

"Was it a line to get her here?"

I mush my brows together. "What?"

"Did she think it was a hookup?"

"No," I say, but then I'm unsure. "Well, I don't know. I mean, it wasn't a line for me. It wasn't a hookup for me."

"Did you tell her that? Did you two talk about it?"

I give him a dry look. "No, Chandler, we were too busy fucking!"

He rolls his eyes. "Then what do you expect?"

"Dude, you don't get it!" I yell, heading to my bedroom since my cock keeps slapping my thighs. I reach for a pair of shorts. "She shared shit with me, and I thought I meant something to her."

"What shit?"

"Personal shit. I'm not telling you!"

I walk back out, and he's staring at me. "Why, thank you so much. I know you think that thing is too big to contain, but it's not."

"Shut up," I grumble at him as I run my fingers through my hair. "I just don't get it."

"Why are you so upset? So, she left. Go find someone else. You're not hurting for females."

"No, it was different. She's different. Fuck." I inhale sharply as I crouch down, cradling my head. "I actually feel something when I'm with her. Like, I want to be myself. Damn it. What if she isn't into me? What if this was all a joke? But it doesn't seem like that."

I feel him staring at me. "Nico." I glance up, but I don't want to look in his eyes. "What in the hell is going on?"

I shrug, and I feel so small. I'm bigger than Chandler in every way, but right now, I feel like I come to his waist. "It's the same shit, different girl."

"What?"

"Shelli didn't want me and left me. Dumped me because I wasn't Aiden Fucking Cuntbasket Brooks. I thought maybe Aviva wanted me, that I was good enough. I mean, I'm not saying it was love at first sight, let's get married and have babies, but shit, I wanted her to like me."

I know this surprises my best friend and probably confuses him. I don't share feelings with him much. He's the touchy-feely one. I don't know how many times I listened to how much he loved Amelia and blah, blah, blah. Now it's me. Now I'm blah, blah, blah.

"Nico, who says she doesn't? Maybe she had somewhere to be?"

"Where is the note? The phone number? Dude, I mean, it's not that hard."

Chandler shrugs. "I'm giving her the benefit of doubt that maybe she got overwhelmed and bounced. Figured she'd see you sooner rather than later."

I didn't think of that. Probably because that's not how she rolls. When Aviva wants something, she goes for it. That's why I feel as if she may not have wanted me. Maybe I wasn't good enough, just like with Shelli. Whoa, am I a scorned man? Did Shelli give me a complex? Damn it.

"I don't know, but I think you should give her a second before you freak out."

I think that over. I don't want to give her time or space; I want to know what is going on. "Or I can go to the shop and see her."

"Or that," he says, pointing at me. "But maybe take a day. You were pretty freaked out two seconds ago."

I shake my head. "I can't. I need to know now."

* * *

WHEN I GET to the sub shop, I notice that the sign says closed, but I see Aviva at the counter. She's dancing around, cutting up stuff as she bobs her head. She looks happy. At least one of us does. I get out, slamming my door behind me as the front door to the shop opens.

Callie looks at me with a brow raised. "You look ready to fight."

"I might be. You leaving?"

"Yup, the gym calls."

"Good."

She scoffs. "A little reminder. She's a fighter too."

"I know," I say, pulling the door open.

Aviva doesn't even look back at me. "Forget something?"

"I didn't, but it seems you did."

She turns then, a knife in one hand and a cucumber in the other. "Nico."

"What the hell?"

"What the hell, what?"

"Way to leave me hanging this morning."

She seems a little taken aback. "I had to come home. I have this order for the IceCats I have to prepare." She holds out her arms to indicate where the platters and trimmings for sandwiches are set out, but I'm still not convinced. "I couldn't lie in bed all day, and I would have if I hadn't left."

"Bullshit. You couldn't leave me a note? A number? Anything? Just leave without even saying goodbye. Pretty fucked up."

She narrows her eyes a bit as she comes to the counter, leaning into it. "I didn't want to wake you, and before I could find a pad of paper, my Uber showed up."

"Likely excuse," I accuse, leaning my palms into the counter. "You could have woken me up. I would have driven you home."

"It was six in the morning," she says sharply. "And I don't like your tone at all."

"You don't like my tone?" I ask, my voice getting a bit higher. "Well, I don't like when the girl I went to bed with just runs out on me."

"I didn't run out on you! I figured you'd come in today and we could talk or whatever."

"And what if I didn't?"

"Then it would have been what I thought."

"Huh?"

"If you didn't, I would have assumed it was just a one-night stand."

"You thought it was a one-night stand?" I roar, and her eyes darken as she narrows them into slits.

She holds up a finger. "First of all, Nico, you need to lower your voice—"

"No. I never said it was a one-night stand, and neither did you. So why would you think that?" I ask incredulously. "That's the stupidest shit I've ever heard."

"Oh, I don't know, because we didn't talk about it? I didn't want to assume anything, and who knows... You're known for having fun."

I press my hand to my chest. "I'm known for having fun? What the fuck?"

"Tinder? Stalkers? I mean, shit, Nico, you don't scream one-woman man."

"Are you serious? I never said I was, but I also never made you feel like all I wanted was to fuck you!"

"Well, maybe I was just fucking you!"

I press my lips together. "Were you? Was that all it was? A mindless fuck?"

She looks away, placing the knife and then the cucumber on the counter. "I don't know."

"You don't know."

"No! Stop repeating what I'm saying!"

"Then make some fucking sense!"

"What do you want me to say? I was dreaming up our future life? No, I was freaking out because I shared my scars with you, and then I was coming out of my mind. So, no, I wasn't thinking of anything at the time. My day was going pretty fucking great so far, I was excited about seeing you, but now you've pissed me the hell off."

"And you don't think I'm pissed? You ran out on me—"

"For the love of God, Nico, suck up your pride. I didn't walk out on you! I had to work. I told you from the jump I'm one busy bitch and that I don't have time for this. I told you that."

"So, that's that?"

She blinks. "What?"

"I get that you don't have time. I don't either. But I wanted to make time for you."

She takes in a deep breath, her eyes locked on mine. Her eyes are watery, but I know she won't cry. She's too strong for that, but I've pissed her off real good. "I don't know what you want me to say."

I nodded slowly. "I wanted you to say that you wanted to try."

She rolls her eyes. "Nico, be real. I'm hardly your type."

"Hardly my type. How the fuck do you know my type?"

"Google shows all."

I'm disgusted. "You Googled me?"

"I did when I found out who you were, and I saw the girls you were with. I saw you with Shelli Adler. She's a fucking goddess compared to me."

"Google can kiss my ass, 'cause when I think of my type, I see you." I shake my head as I push off the counter. "And Shelli isn't even comparable to you."

Her cheeks fill with color. "Nico, you could do better."

"Stop it with this fucking pity party. You are perfect to me, even when you piss me the fuck off."

"Hardly."

"I don't agree." I start for the door. "Let me know when you find your confidence and realize that who you are is more than I could even fathom wanting me. When I say I want someone, I want them. And, Aviva, I want you. Only you."

As I slam the door behind me, I'm startled when Callie looks over at me. She lets out a long breath. "So, my sister found her match."

I scoff. "I don't think she'd agree."

"Well, she's an idiot."

Funny, I want to defend Aviva. "See ya, Callie."

"Bye, Nico. Hopefully not for long."

Hopefully.

CHAPTER FOURTEEN

viva

"VEE, THE GAME IS ON!"

I ignore Callie in the living room, even though she is only five feet away from me. Our living room and kitchen area are attached. It's old, but eh, it's charming. I can see the team on TV, and oh look, the camera is zooming in on Nico. I roll my eyes as I lean on my counter. Jaylin is sitting on the barstool in front of me with a glass of wine dangling from her fingers. There is a glass in front of me too, but I'm on a whole other level of annoyance. Which probably means I should be drinking it. I'm not, though. I still can't believe the phone call I just got. My car is totaled, and I have to get another one. And also, Nico is an asshole.

Someone pass the lube.

"I don't even know what I am going to do."

Jaylin, with compassion in her eyes, taps my hand. "I told you. I have an extra car. You can buy it."

I shake my head. "I don't take handouts."

"It's not a handout. I'm legit selling it to you."

I give her a skeptical look. "You're gonna sell it to me?"

She nods, looking prissy as all fuck in her beautiful, expensive suit. I should have gone to law school too. Maybe my life would have been different. "Yes, for the fair price of a hundred dollars."

I squint at her. "Isn't it a new car?"

She shrugs. "It's like a 2017. It's old."

Pain in my ass. "No, I'll figure it out."

"I'll have Kirby drop it off tomorrow."

I raise my brow. "No. And Kirby? You're still seeing him?"

She gives me a pointed look. "Yes, Aviva. I give my number to the guys I fuck, and I leave notes."

I glare. "Whatever. You weren't here when Nico came in. I just don't know who the hell he thinks he is. He was so upset, like I had kicked his dog or some shit. I just didn't leave a note!" I say in a yell-whisper because I don't want Callie hearing my drama. Since I've never had boy drama, it figures mine would involve the hottest dude in Carolina.

Jaylin shrugs. "I don't know why you didn't leave a note."

"You know why," I sneer at her, glaring. "I didn't know if he wanted to see me again. I wasn't putting myself out there."

"'Cause God forbid, he did and would call and things would be good." With an annoyed shrug, she says, "You sabotage yourself."

I gawk at her. "Do you even love me?"

She giggles around her wine before taking a sip. "Keeping it 100, sis."

I let out an annoyed sigh. "I don't self-sabotage things."

"No, like, for real. Shitty things happen so much around here that it's the only thing you know. So, why wouldn't this turn out that way? Which is why you self-sabotaged it."

I just blink at her, and before I can tell her she's stupid, Callie yells out, "Ooh, Nico is pissed. The other team scored in like two minutes."

I want to yell that I don't care. I don't *want* to care. Screw him! "You should have seen him, though," I say, waving my hands in the air.

"He was pissed, but not like an 'I'm gonna beat you up' kind of pissed, but a 'hurt' pissed. Like I'd really hurt him. It was one night!"

"You would know. You ride that hurt-pissed train a lot."

I hold out my hand to her. "Are you done? Can you listen without calling out all my faults?"

She shrugs, but that little smirk doesn't leave her full lips. "I think you should call him."

"No, I'm not calling him. I don't want to see him."

"Yous a damn lie."

"I don't," I say more sternly. "He probably won't want to see me either."

"There it is," she says, pointing at me and leaning on the counter. "For such a strong, beautiful woman, you sure are insecure as fuck when it comes to guys. It's the main reason you took Mike's bullshit for so long. You know you're better than this, right?"

I shake my head. "Whatever. I'm not insecure."

"Aviva, why did you let him see you the way you did?"

I gawk at her, confused. "'Cause he grabbed the boob. I didn't want him to yank it off. That would have been something. I would have been mortified."

She snorts, shaking her head. "That would have been the best story, though."

"Focus," I say dryly, and she nods.

"Yes, anyway...while I can understand that excuse, I know it's just an excuse. You told him because you trust him, because for once, you felt good. And you felt confident about someone."

I blink. "No way."

"Yes way. You were fucking Mike for how long? Fifteen years?"

"Why is Mike coming into this?"

"Oh no! They scored again! Look at him, Aviva! He is so bummed!" Callie yells, and both Jaylin and I look at the screen.

Aw. He does.

"He's a man. He's fine," I say offhandedly. My comment is not well received by Callie or Jaylin.

"You're a jerk."

"Why are you so mean?"

"What? I'm keeping it 100," I say, mocking Jaylin. She just laughs, though. "Back to Mike, please?"

She holds out her glass to me. "After your surgery, Mike never saw your chest. Never. Am I right?"

I really don't know why I chose her to be soul friends with. I look down into my glass, moving my fingers along the rim. "Yes," I mumble.

"And that was, what, after five years of knowing him before you had the surgery?"

"Yeah, so?"

"You've known this guy for like a month, and you showed him."

I press my lips together, my heart beating funny in my chest. "Doesn't mean anything."

"Oh, sis. It screams volumes, and you know it."

I swallow hard as I shrug one shoulder. "He's kind."

"Yup."

"And sweet."

"Yeah, his eyes were trained on you like you were a puck."

"Crap, they scored again!"

She jerks a thumb behind her. "Not tonight, though. Tonight, he apparently sucks."

We both look over at the screen as the announcer says, "I have never seen Merryweather let in this many pucks in a ten-minute span. He looks lost. He looks like he's not even in the game. I fully expect them to pull him."

Callie looks back at me, her eyes wide. "No! That will hurt his feelings."

"It's a game, sweetie. He's really strong," Jaylin says then, waving her off. "But I think he's good. Look at him. He's pissed. He'll bounce back."

Callie seems to agree with that as she sits back on her heels. She's newly obsessed with hockey, and if I'm honest, I may be as well. It's mainly the thing I have for the goalie.

Jaylin looks back at me, her eyes critical. "For the first time in, shit,

I don't know, nine years, I actually saw excitement in your eyes." She leans over, taking my hand in hers. "You had this smile on your face that warmed me from the inside out, Vee. I mean, it was beautiful. When you kissed him, I watched your whole body do it—"

"You sound like a stalker," I comment, but she doesn't care. She's going to tell me what I don't want to hear. What I already know.

That Nico means something to me.

"He makes you feel alive. And damn it, Aviva, I need that for you. I need you to live. If he has a way to make you want to live, then damn it, I'm Team Nico. All the way."

"You're supposed to be Team Aviva," I say softly.

"That's a losing team right now. I'm a winner." When our eyes meet, we both laugh. "You're a winner too." She laces our fingers together and squeezes. "I think he is wonderful, and you should call him."

Before I can even comment, Callie screams as she shoots up off the couch. "*No*!"

"What? What's wrong?" I ask, panicked. Did she hurt herself? Was she flipping off the couch again?

She throws out her hands toward the screen. "They scored again!"

Yup, they sure did. Beside the celebrated hug is Nico, his shoulders drooping as he stares at the bench. He looks like a statue, and then he nods. He smacks his stick to each side of the net and then skates toward the bench as another goalie comes on.

"Oh, they kicked him out!"

My heart aches as I watch him throw his stick down the hall and then his gloves. He kicks the door and then slams himself down. His helmet is still on, and when they hand him a hat, he throws it back at them.

"I have never seen this behavior out of Merryweather. It's as if I don't even know him," the commentator rambles on.

"For sure. He needs to regroup and come back strong on Wednesday. We need him. This game is over," the other jerk in a suit says.

When the camera pans off Nico, Callie turns, her eyes full of tears as she crosses her arms over her chest. Her face is red, and I think she's upset. I mean, I could be wrong, but she doesn't look pleased.

"You broke Nico."

I'm taken aback. "What? Who?"

"You!" she yells, pointing at me. "I know you think you don't deserve happiness, but you do. And so does he! He chose you, he likes you, so stop being an idiot and be nice to him!"

"Callie, be real."

She stomps away. "We all know you like him. You broke our goalie! I hope you know, I'm telling everyone so they can come and tell you you're an idiot."

The door slams, and I look at Jaylin. The asshole is laughing. "Freaking hormonal teenagers."

She shakes her head. "No, she's keeping it 100 too."

"Really? I didn't break him. Be real."

Just then, the camera focuses on Nico, and he looks so defeated. Even through his mask, I can see his dark eyes, and they are stewing with disappointment. He looks incredibly handsome but also murderous. It's hot.

"Shit. Did I break him?"

Jaylin nods. "You are the reason we lost."

I glare. "Whatever. But wait, am I about to have a whole fan base come for me?"

She shrugs. "I hope so. Maybe they'll be able to talk some sense into you."

I watch the screen for a second. I want to call him. I want to see him, but I can't. I won't allow some man to speak to me like that and then I just chase after him. If we need to see each other again, the universe will intervene. It has before, and it will again. Or we'll go our separate ways.

With a grin, I say, "I wonder if they'll want subs."

"You're such an asshole. You aren't gonna call him, are you?"

I bring my glass to my lips. "Nope."

No matter how much I want to.

CHAPTER FIFTEEN

ico

"How are you feeling?"

I don't even want to answer the woman who has been sent to fix me. There is no fixing me. I look down at my knees, watching them bounce. I can feel Dr. Jenkins's eyes on me. Even though I have no desire to answer or even participate in this session, I know I have to. "Like shit."

"Can you elaborate?"

I let out an annoyed sigh. I'm five seconds away from being a child and mocking her. "*Can you elaborate?*" No. Leave me alone.

"Well, I haven't been pulled from a game in almost a year, and then I got pulled Monday. I let in three goals Wednesday, and that fucking pisses me off."

I still won't look at her. I feel her staring at me. I know she wants more, but I just don't have it in me. While I've been playing like complete shit the last couple days, that's not what has me on edge. I'm pissed that I haven't heard from Aviva. She hasn't called, texted, or anything. I haven't been to the shop because I've had games and practice, but still, she hasn't made any attempt to see me. She ran out on me. She rejected me. And while I had been chasing her like crazy, I won't now.

Well, at least, I won't *right now*. I gotta calm down. I gotta figure out how I want to approach this. We went at it, and while I was pissed, I just wanted to kiss that angry little look on her face. I wanted to taste those lips, and damn it, I wanted to hold her. I wanted her to feel how much I enjoy spending time with her. Enjoy her. I really don't understand. How could she think I wouldn't want her? Fuck, if she doesn't make me crazy.

"Do you feel off?"

I shrug. "Yeah, I'm not focused."

"Why's that?"

I shake my head and thank God for player confidentiality. "I'm caught up on a girl."

"I didn't know you were dating someone," she says, her voice hinting at surprise.

Dating. Are we even dating? "I don't know if we are. I want to date her."

"Is she not returning the feelings?"

"She's wishy-washy. One second, I think she does want to. But the next, this fucking brick wall comes up." I shake my head, annoyed as I bring up her imaginary wall. "Like, fuck, I get that she's been through some shit and all, but I'm not a bad guy. She's making it seem like I fuck around a lot and don't commit. I tried to commit. It blew up in my fucking face."

Dr. Jenkins moves her pen against her notepad. "Did it really blow up in your face, or did you ignore the fact that Shelli didn't want to commit to you?"

I hate therapy. I mean, come on, I don't need this chick telling me the truth. Just lie to me. Smack a Band-Aid on me and tell me I'm good. I grind my teeth as I shrug. "Yeah, I ignored it."

"Are you ignoring it here?"

Am I? Does Aviva not want to date me? Was it really just a fuck? But if so, then why did she share all that shit with me? Why did she comfort me? Hold me so tenderly when I was nervous about her thinking I was weird. It doesn't make sense. Talk about some mixed signals. "I don't think so."

She gives me a small smile. Not just a kind one, but one full of sympathy. "With your diagnosis, Nico, you tend not to pick up on social cues. You see what you want. And it's my job—"

"No, it's different with her," I insist, my voice getting louder. "It felt different. She talked to me about things she's never told anyone."

"Okay," she says slowly. "But you have to remember, you feel differently from other people. You use sex as an outlet to feel things—"

"For fuck's sake, stop with the handbook!" I roar, slamming back in the chair. "I'm not a bad fucking guy."

"Nico, I never said you were."

"She made me sound like a whore. I like sex. What's wrong with that? I love women. But this one... This one is special. I want her."

Her eyes meet mine, full of compassion. "But Nico, she might not want you, and that's okay."

I look away, my throat getting tight.

"Have you told her—"

"Fuck no."

She pauses, and then I hear her writing something down.

Patient is a huge jackass.

I close my eyes, pinching the bridge of my nose. "I lashed out at her."

"Why did you lash out?"

I squirm in my seat, embarrassed. "Because I felt abandoned. I have never had a girl leave like that. Usually I have to force them to leave. But I felt like Aviva was rejecting me. And now I think I've ruined it with her."

"Have you spoken to her since that happened?"

"No," I say softly. "I've kept my distance, and she's kept hers."

"And you associate that with your bad playing?"

I nod. "I'm not focused. I'm too busy replaying everything over and over again. I want to see her again, but this nagging feeling inside me says she doesn't want to see me. Then, she is prideful as hell, so she'd rather cut off her arm than call me. I don't know. I really like her. She's spunky as all get-out and smart. Really strong, even though her confidence is shaken. So gorgeous and makes one hell of a sub." I smile, though I still don't look at her. "I miss her and her sister. I was helping her sister with math."

When she doesn't say anything, I glance up at her. Once I'm looking at her, she says, "I think that if you want to see her, talk to her, you need to. Or you'll stay in this funk."

I lick my lips as I look away. "What if she doesn't want to see me?"

"Then you know," she says softly. "But you need to see for yourself."

I know I need to agree or disagree with her, but I'm in my head. I was such an ass to Aviva. How do I go in and ask what she wants? What if she doesn't want what I want? And then…what do I even want? I want her. I understand my history and I know my track record, but I also know that the right woman could change everything. The one I want to work for. The one I want to see. The one I want to make happy. All of that points to Aviva. To Callie. I care for them both.

"Did you do your homework, Nico?"

Fuck me. "I didn't." I look up just in time to see the disappointment on her face. "But I was honest about what I liked and didn't like with Aviva. She almost touched my helmet, and I stopped her."

"Did you yell?"

I shake my head quickly. "No, I calmly asked her not to touch it."

"That's wonderful. Better than when you snatched it out of that girl's hand and screamed at her."

I nod. "Yeah, I don't know why that girl slept with me."

She smiles. "Why haven't you told anyone?"

The thought of opening up that part of myself honestly freaks me out. "Same reason as before. I don't want people to look at me differently."

"The right people won't."

I swallow hard as I nod.

"You could tell Aviva."

I scoff. "She'll think it's a line to get her to be with me."

She doesn't disagree. "I feel your best bet would be Chandler."

I think that over for a moment. I could tell him, but just as I think that, the fear consumes me. I've been best friends with this guy for a long time. We share everything and he's seen my neurotic ways, but can I tell him about that part of me?

* * *

I'M THINKING of Aviva and Dr. Jenkins as I drive.

Since Aviva shared what she did with me, I feel sharing with her would be fair. But something holds me back. I fear she'll think I'm using my condition to get her to like me. When, really, I'm terrified she'll run the other way. As much as I want to tell Chandler, I don't think I can. Not yet. He knows I'm phobic and anxious here and there, but he doesn't know the full extent of it. I don't want him to treat me any differently. I don't want him to feel sorry for me. I don't want things to change. I like how my life is now. I like that no one knows. It does worry me that when I have my episodes, people think I'm just a jackass instead of knowing the truth. That I'm suffering inside.

When my rental car signals a text, I hit accept, and then the system reads it aloud.

Hey. It's Callie. I need your help with this stupid equations crap. Can you come by? Please. Pretty please with a cherry on top?

Oh shit. Thankfully, I come to a stop at a stoplight to text her back quickly that I'm on my way.

Me: Is Aviva there?

Callie: Of course she is.

Me: Does she know I'm coming?

Callie: Yup.

Me: Will I be walking into the lion's den?

Callie: I can't confirm or deny that.

Little asshole.

Callie: One thing is for sure... She's been jerk since you left. So, if you can fix that so my sister smiles again like she did Sunday morning, that would be great.

I don't answer her. Instead, I drive off, heading toward the shop. I'd love to make Aviva smile again. I get giddy at the thought of making her laugh, but I don't know how to do that and not feel for her. She isn't the kind of woman I can be just friends with.

It's all or nothing.

When I arrive at the shop, Callie is sitting outside with her head in her book. I pull my truck in, and when I shut it off, she looks up. Relief fills her features as I get out, shutting the door and locking it. I peek into the shop just in time to see Aviva look away. And just like every single time I see her, she's beautiful. She has her hair up in a high bun, her bangs getting in her eyes. She moves around like she's working, but there isn't a soul in there.

"I hate this crap."

Callie's words pull my attention, and I chuckle. As I sit down beside her, reaching for her book, I ask, "Didn't I tell you, you gotta try to like it?"

"I don't like numbers. I have a calculator and Google. I don't need this."

I roll my eyes. "What if you don't have your phone?"

She gives me a terrified look. "Why wouldn't I have my phone?"

I shake my head. I pray for this generation. But truthfully, my phone is attached to me. That's how I know Aviva hasn't called or texted me. I don't answer Callie as I look over what she is doing. "Oh, derivative concepts? Easy peasy!"

I glance over at her to find her staring back at me like I've lost it. "Easy peasy? What is wrong with you? This crap is so hard!"

"It's fun," I say excitedly. "Pay attention."

For the next forty minutes, I make solid progress with her homework and her study guide. It doesn't take long for her to catch on. I love this kind of math. While angles are my jam, I love watching numbers work. It stimulates me. When she gets through the backside of her homework, I hold up my hand.

"Attagirl."

She smacks my hand, and the look of confidence on her face fills my happiness cup. I love helping her. I love helping anyone with math. "You should volunteer and help kids with this. It would really be great for kids like me who have no clue what is going on."

I laugh. "I actually do volunteer at the children's hospital."

"Aw, that's so sweet! You should do, like, Big Brothers or something. This guy I dated for a while was in that program, and he sucks at math. He could really use your help."

I nod. "Send me his info. I'll contact him."

She grins over at me. "How did you get so good at this?"

"I'm not sure. It's just easy for me. I always was in advanced math classes when I was growing up. If I hadn't loved hockey so much, I would have done something in the math field," I say with a shrug. "But hockey is life."

She leans on her hands, her eyes on me. "So, you were a nerd in school?"

I scoff. "Not at all. Math was the only thing I was good at. It has something to do with the numbers and how my brain works."

She's engrossed in what I am saying. "I have a friend in school. He's autistic. I think Asperger's, but he's like that. Everything else overwhelms him, but he gets lost in science and math. He loves it, but man does he hate gym and English."

My heart jumps up into my throat.

"He'll freak out, but it's understandable because he gets so overwhelmed. Super cool dude. He sits beside me in class and helps me a lot. He's so funny too, big IceCats fan."

I feel sweat drip down my brow as I breathe heavily.

She must have noticed the change in my body language, because she draws her brows in. "Nico? What's wrong?"

I stare into her eyes for a long time. Everything inside me is going crazy, firing up like mad, and I don't know what to do. Do I get up and leave? Do I ignore her statement and move on?

"I'm autistic too."

Well, I guess that's another option.

I tell a sixteen-year-old something I've never told anyone.

CHAPTER SIXTEEN

ico

CALLIE MOVES her eyes along my face, her brows furrow, and panic sets in deep inside me. Before I can try to say anything, maybe take it back or laugh it off as a joke, she asks, "Really?"

Lie. Lie. Nico, *lie*! "Yeah, I have a rare kind of milder autism. My mom calls it atypical autism. There is another big name for it, but I always forget. At first, they said it was a more regular form of autism, but as I got older and went to more doctors, we figured out what it really was. I didn't talk until I was four, and I was super freaked out by everything. Things overwhelmed me really fast, and if it weren't for hockey, I don't think I'd be the guy I am now."

So, I guess lying wasn't an option. Instead, I word-vomit on a child. A girl who thinks I'm cool and good at math. Now she's going to think I'm a crazy, weird person. Just like everyone else when I was growing up. Just how I didn't want anyone to see me.

"That's so cool," Callie says, her eyes wide and excited.

Huh? "What?"

"Like, you're a superhero," she gushes, pushing my shoulder back. It reminds me of the way Aviva does it. "Look at you. You came from not being able to speak to playing a position the people on TV say is hard as all get-out. I mean, you're amazing!"

I swallow past the lump in my throat. "I'm weird."

"No! Your mind works differently. That doesn't make you weird. I think it makes you awesome," she says, smacking me again. "That's so cool, and I know you. I'm so excited."

I don't know what to say. "Um. Okay."

"For real," she giggles, shaking her head. "Man, I know Camden is really awkward, but he has an excuse. Meanwhile, I'm just awkward and say things because people freak me out. They're so unpredictable."

I smile. "Yeah, I feel like that a lot."

"For sure," she says, smiling over at me. "So, you said your mom taught you?"

"Yeah, she was my teacher my whole life. She helped me learn in a way that worked for me."

"That's incredible," she sighs, leaning on her hand. "You know, when I Googled you, your autism diagnosis wasn't on there."

"I don't tell people. You're actually the first person I've told."

Her jaw drops. "Like, ever?"

"Yeah," I admit shyly.

"Why? Are you worried people will treat you and think of you differently?"

I nod. "Exactly that."

"But they won't. They'll think you're a damn rock star, and if they don't, screw them. You're awesome in my opinion. Man, just solve a problem or block a shot, though. Lately, you've been sucking."

I scoff; she's so much like her sister. "Please don't sugarcoat it."

She grins. "You should be open about it. You could help a lot of people."

I cock my head. "Why would me having autism help people?"

"Because," she says softly, "people with autism are treated like there is something wrong with them, when really, there isn't. There isn't anything wrong with any of us. We're all just made up differently. We all have paths that are meant for us, and you could show the world that you can do anything, no matter what, as long as you fight for it."

I hold her gaze. "You're very optimistic for everything you've been through."

She nods, her eyes sad. "It was hard watching my mom die, and then when Aviva got her diagnosis, I was terrified. But I watched my sister fight for us. We each only have one life, and I want to be happy. I want to change lives. I want to be what your mom was for you, but for another kid. All kids. I want to help them."

"You will."

"I hope so," she says, shaking her head. "I need to get a scholarship so that it takes the burden off Aviva, but she is freaking out about paying for gymnastics, and she won't take a handout from the gym."

"Does she take one from anyone?"

"Nope. She's too proud." She looks back at me. "She's *very* proud."

"I know."

"That's why she's an idiot sometimes."

"I think it adds to her charm."

She smiles, and I love how her eyes dazzle. "Does Aviva know?"

I shake my head. "Not at all. Please don't tell her."

"I won't," she promises. "I'm surprised you didn't tell her when she showed you her scars."

I press my lips together, eyeing her. "You know about that?"

She nods. "Oh yeah. I heard her with Jaylin, and then when you came into the shop the other day, I was listening in the back."

I shake my head. "She'd kill you if she knew."

Callie shrugs. "I don't care. She hides everything from me. If I didn't eavesdrop, I would know nothing."

"I guess not," I say with a laugh. "Still, that was our business."

"You're right," she says as our eyes meet. "But if I didn't know, I wouldn't have been able to tell her how much of an idiot she's being."

I bring my lip between my teeth. I'm about to ask what Aviva said to that when the door opens. Aviva comes out, looking as gorgeous as ever, carrying a tray holding a fountain drink cup and a sub. She looks from Callie to me, her eyes, those green depths, full of wickedness.

Wickedness I want to consume. She doesn't want me here. I can tell. She sets the tray down and pushes it toward me.

"You haven't been by in a couple days. Figured you might be hungry."

I pull the tray toward me. "Thank you. I have missed this." And other things. But from the way she is looking at me, she doesn't want to hear it. She taps her foot against the ground as our eyes stay locked. "You look really pretty today. I like that you pinned your bangs to the side."

She touches the pin, her face turning red. Her eyes are so dark and burning into mine. If Callie weren't here, I'd grab Aviva and throw her on this table. Kiss that pouty mouth of hers and make her cry my name. "Thanks. Um, er…" She pauses to look at Callie. I don't have to glance at Callie to know she's giving her big sister a look. "Thank you for helping her. I have no clue about that stuff."

I nod. "Anytime."

"I didn't want her bothering you, but Amelia said you wouldn't mind."

"I don't. She can call anytime," I say, opening the wrapper on my sub. "You can too."

When I wink at her, she presses her lips together and looks away. The color is creeping up her neck, and I want to trace it with my tongue. I've missed her. So damn much. As I take a huge bite of my sub, I'm in heaven. There is one thing that would make this even better, and that's if Aviva came and sat in my lap. I almost invite her to since she looks silly standing there, all unsure of herself. I don't care about our fight; I'm over it. I just want to see her. Be with her. Kiss that mouth of hers.

Around my bite, I ask, "Can I take you out?"

She whips her head back toward me. She furrows her brow as she asks, "What?"

"Can I take you out?" I ask again before I swallow. "I think we need a do-over."

"A do-over?"

"Yeah," I answer before taking a sip of my Cherry Coke. Aw, she remembered. "I think things heated up the other day, and we should go out. Maybe I was in the wrong for not showing you a good time."

Her eyes cut to Callie and then back to me. Once more, they go to Callie before she says, "Do you mind?"

Callie kicks her feet up on the table. "Not at all. I'm just listening as I work."

I snort, but Aviva is not amused. "Callie."

Callie waves her off and points at me. "Pay attention to him."

Aviva groans loudly as her eyes settle on mine. "You showed me the best time. I had a blast. First time in a while."

"Good. I was worried you hadn't."

She swallows hard. "I think we were both in the wrong, but I really don't want to talk about this right now."

I nod. "Which is why you should let me take you out."

"When?"

"Now."

"You're eating!"

"Yeah, but I'll be hungry again in a bit. Or we can get ice cream."

Callie perks up. "Oh! Can I go?"

"Sure," I say, just as Aviva says, "No!"

I point to her sister. "Or no."

"Rude."

"So rude," I say under my breath, and again, Aviva is not amused.

Her eyes look like they're about to pop out of her head. She crosses her arms over her chest and sighs deeply. "I have things to do."

"Then afterward."

She shakes her head. "I don't know. I think it's for the best—"

"Do you not want to see me?"

She widens her eyes, and her face burns with color. Damn it, if she isn't the prettiest woman I've ever seen. She licks her lips, setting me on edge, and I think I've almost got her.

"Come on. You know you do."

She looks down at the ground just as a car pulls up. It draws all of our attention, but since it's no one I know, I start eating again. I bring my focus back to Aviva just as she tenses up. What in the world? I look to Callie, and she's doing the same.

"Callie, get the hell inside," Aviva says quickly, but before Callie can even get up—though, I'm unsure she would have—the man who is getting out of the car says her name.

"Calliope, come here and give Daddy some sugar!" His thick accent is very Southern. Almost reminds me of Shelli's. I take in the man. He's tall, like Aviva, real skinny, and looks sick. Like too many hits of the crack pipe. I thought he was gone?

"Callie, don't you dare move."

Callie is torn; I can see that. I put my sub down and reach out, squeezing her shoulder. "Why don't you go inside?"

The man points his finger at me. "Who the hell is that?"

"None of your business," Aviva sneers. "Get inside, Calliope."

Callie gets up quickly and goes inside, leaving her books and papers outside. I look between Aviva and her dad. The resemblance is there, but so is a lot of disdain. Pretty sure Aviva may rip his eyes out.

"Why'd you go on and do that, sugar?"

"Because I told you, we are done with you. Why are you here? You aren't welcome," she says, her voice low and threatening.

I have to admit, I'm sorta turned on.

I find myself standing up and moving toward her. I don't think the guy is a threat, but just in case, I want her to know I am there. As I come up beside her, she looks at me, and I see the fear in her eyes. Her jaw is tense, and she looks like she might blow a gasket. I don't know what this guy did, but my heart shatters in my chest for her. Gone is the playfulness and teasing from before.

I have to protect her.

CHAPTER SEVENTEEN

viva

YOU'VE GOTTA BE KIDDING me.

I have been thinking nonstop of Nico all week. At first, I was pissed he came into my shop and started a fight. But the more I thought about it, the more I understood. I could have left a note that morning, but I ran because I was scared. I didn't want to know if he didn't want me. If he did want me, what was I supposed to do? I'm such a mess, and he's not. I've gone back and forth with myself about calling him and trying to figure things out, but my pride wouldn't let me. Plus, I told Jaylin I wouldn't, no matter how much I wanted to.

When I saw him get out of the car, all my anger from him yelling at me and losing his shit on me came back. I knew I couldn't say anything to him. Wouldn't say anything. But then I watched him with Callie. It wasn't the first time, but after being intimate with him, being in his arms and kissed gently... I don't know, but this time is different. The way he tended to Callie, made sure she understood while also making her laugh, pulled at my heartstrings. Next thing I knew, I was making him a sandwich and pouring him a big cup of Cherry Coke.

When I came out here, it was honestly to give him the sub and go. A thank you without saying the words. I didn't expect him to ask me out again. I figured after I went wild on him, he'd be bored by me. But he still stared at me with that look. That all-consuming look that sends me over the edge. I know I should resist; I know he won't want me for long, but I really want to say yes.

And then, of course, because life likes taking me in the ass, my dad shows up.

I just want one thing in my life to go well.

Nico's hand moves along the small of my back, and I know it's to let me know he's here. I appreciate it more than I can ever express, but it would be great if Nico could just leave. I look up at him. He doesn't look back at me. "You can go."

His eyes stay on my dad. "Nope, I'm good."

Why do he and Callie want to send me to an early grave? Dad points to Nico. "Boyfriend?"

"That's none of your business," I say sharply, my eyes cutting to his. He looks like absolute shit. All scraggly and dirty. I don't know where the car came from—oh, wait. Yes, I do. From the money he stole from me. Surprised he didn't use all of it on drugs. Would have been nice if I could have used it to do the same, but nope, I'm scrambling to make ends meet. "What do you want?"

"I think we need to talk. You're trying to get me off the damn lease of this place. I own this shop."

"You own jack shit. This is *my* shop. You gave it up when you decided to chase your next fix," I sneer. I swear to God, I have a few choice words for Dustin Sr.

"You can't take me off."

"I can, and I have. It's all legally complete."

"But it's not," he says, his beady brown eyes on me. "I want my share of this business."

I scoff. "I have run this place, by myself, for nine years. You get nothing."

He knows this; he's not stupid. Yet he has to say something to hurt me. "Then I'll fight you for Callie."

I laugh out loud. To the point where I bend over, laughing so hard, my stomach hurts. Probably to keep from crying. Nico's hand doesn't leave my back. When I stand up, my dad is glaring, but I don't care. I have no respect for this man. "Dad, who are they gonna give Callie to? A drug addict or a well-rounded citizen? Be real."

His dark eyes turn black as he shrugs. "I think they'd want her with her father, especially after losing her mother."

"I am her mother." I narrow my eyes to slits. "No one would give her to you."

"We'll let a judge decide."

"Yeah, when you get the money together, let me know."

With a toothy grin, he says, "I already have it. Came into some money a couple weeks ago."

My blood boils. "You stole it. But please, try me. You won't get shit. I have records, I have voice mails, everything. This place is mine. That girl in there is mine. You are dead to us."

He glares, and I can see the anger boiling inside him. I was always the one to fight with him when he was wrong. Mom never understood why we were oil and water, but I know. He's a piece of dog shit. "You've always been a real—"

"Before you finish that sentence, remember that I'm here," Nico says, and when I look up at him, I've never felt safer. "I don't do well with women being called names."

I look back at my dad, and he's fuming. He looks like he did when my mom died. He was pissed, hating everyone. We got into our biggest fight, the one that ultimately ended with him leaving us. I don't regret that fight. He was only concerned with getting his fix—not helping Callie or me, or settling Mom's affairs. He goes to turn around, but before doing so fully, he mutters, "I'll be back."

"And I'll be here."

Dad pauses, his eyes cutting to Nico's. But thankfully, he doesn't say anything. He gets into his car and drives away while Nico's hand continues to stroke along my back. I almost lean into him, but I'm completely humiliated. Out of all the people to be out here with me, it had to be Nico? He probably thinks my life is a pile of shit on fire. He'll want to run, I'm sure.

"So, he's fun." I close my eyes as his hand snakes around my waist. He pulls me back into him, and I allow him to. At my ear, he asks, "Are you okay?"

I'm shaking with anger. I hate to admit it, but I'm terrified of my dad. As much as I want to believe he can't do anything to ruin my shitshow of a life, what if he can? I swallow hard as I shrug. "I hate him."

"Yeah, there is nothing redeeming about him." He kisses my earlobe. "You're breathing so hard. It's okay. I'd never let anything happen to you." He kisses me again. "Seriously, Aviva, this isn't good for your heart. Breathe."

Tears rush to my eyes, and I close them tightly to keep them in. I refuse to cry in front of him. I know he thinks I'm a complete mess. He isn't wrong. I turn out of his arms. "Thanks. Listen, I've got things to do." I hook my thumb to the shop.

When a tear escapes, I hide my face, but I don't do a good enough job. Nico grabs my wrist instantly, pulling me to him. I don't know why I go; it's like I don't have control of my body. I find myself trapped in his arms, pressed against his hard chest, and I come undone. A sob bubbles in my throat, and soon, I'm clinging to him as it escapes. Callie could come out at any time, but I truly don't care. I can't keep this in. I'm so scared.

He kisses my temple, then the top of my head while whispering comforting words. "It's okay. Nothing is going to happen. I won't let it. It's okay, Aviva. Breathe."

"I hate him," I cry, and I hate how hard I'm clinging to Nico. I've never let go this completely. Never cried like this in front of anyone, but the thought of losing Callie or even this shop has me freaking the hell out. "I can't let him take her—"

"He won't. Aviva, he won't. It won't happen. Jaylin would freak and tear him a new one. Plus, Callie wouldn't go with him. She loves you. You are everything to her. You have nothing to worry about."

"Why can't just one thing go right?" I ask, rubbing my nose in his chest. "Just one thing. I feel like I'm always battling something to get ahead. My car—totaled—but since I only had liability, I'm fucked. But I didn't have the budget for full coverage because it gave me more money to buy supplies for the shop. Jaylin says I can buy her car, but it's almost a damn freebie for a hundred bucks. So, that's a no. I gotta figure out how I'm gonna get a car, and leasing one right now just seems impossible. I think I get ahead on my bills, but then my dad steals money from me. The gym wants money for Callie, and I have to pay them because I refuse to allow anyone to pay her way. But I don't know how. Callie's savings is diminishing, and damn it, I need one fucking thing to go right." He tightens his arms around me as his lips trail along my temple. "Ugh, I'm such a mess. Run. Run now."

He moves his lips along my hairline as he shakes his head. "I'm not going anywhere." His words are such a promise. A promise no one has ever given me. Everyone leaves. Well, except Callie and Jaylin. And so far, Nico.

I hear the door open, the bell chiming, and I freeze. When Callie's small voice reaches me, I cling to Nico.

"Everything okay?"

I don't even have time to answer before Nico says, "Everything is fine, Callie. Give your sister a few minutes, okay?"

"Yeah, no problem," I hear her say, but I know she hasn't shut the door. "Are you guys okay?"

I close my eyes, and I feel Nico's chuckles against the top of my head. "We're fine. Go inside."

Finally, the door shuts, and I hold Nico tighter. He kisses the top of my head, and I open my eyes. The sun is setting, turning the clouds an amazing pink color. I love nights here. I love this shop. I love my sister, and I really like Nico. I don't want to fight with him. I already don't have enough time for myself. The time I do have, I don't want to spend fighting with someone I like. Someone I want to be around. Someone who makes me feel so good.

I pull back to look at him, only to find him looking down at me.

His eyes are such a beautiful brown, and his smirk, it's breathtaking. "I'm sorry for how things went down that night."

"That night was great. It was the morning after."

I bite the inside of my cheek, and it thrills me that he thought it was great too. "Right. The night was perfect."

"It was."

"So yeah, I'm sorry for how I handled things."

He shrugs, moving his hand up my throat to my jaw. "I think we should have used better communication."

I nod, though I can't keep from smiling up at him. "Yeah. But I'm sorry I was an asshole when you came in here. Though, you were an asshole first."

His face breaks into a grin. "That's a very backward apology, but you're right. I was, and you were." He kisses my nose, and I lean into him. With his mouth moving against the spot between my nose and lip, he says, "I shouldn't have come in here acting all crazy-pants. I thought you didn't want me."

"I was scared you didn't want me."

He leans back as he slides his thumb along my lip. "So now we know we both want each other."

"That's really good to know."

"It is," he agrees, playing with my lip.

"What does it mean?"

"Mean?"

"For us."

"It means I want to be with you."

"In or out of bed?"

He chuckles. "Very much in the bed, but also out of it. I think we could have something here."

Could we? I want it so badly, and that has to mean something since I haven't wanted a relationship in a long time. I felt as if that part of me wasn't available. But since meeting Nico, that's changed. I could revert back to questioning my worth to him, but as I look into his eyes, I feel like the most prized jewel. It's absolutely ridiculous how he makes me feel, and damn it, I love that feeling. So, does that mean we could have something here?

"I think so," I answer out loud, and his grin takes over his beautiful face. "I'm insanely busy."

"I'll work for your time. I'll make subs if I get to see you."

Oh heart, be still. "That's super sweet."

"It's true," he says with a shrug, a little color filling his cheeks. "I'm busy too."

I shake my head. "I can't stop a puck, and I sure as hell can't skate."

Man, if I don't love his smile. "Well, I know what our next date will be."

Yup, I walked right into that.

"But before that, let me make one thing go right for you," he says, leaning into me.

Between his eyes, his mouth, and his cologne, I'm dizzy. Gone are thoughts of my dad or anything that has to do with him. Nico consumes me, and I have to admit, I'm okay with it.

"What's that?" I ask, breathless.

He moves closer, his lips touching mine. "Let me make you come."

Shit, I think I just did. As I gaze up into his eyes, I rise to my tippy-toes and press my mouth into his jaw. "That would make this day a whole lot better."

"Good," he says, kissing my nose. "So, I'll take you and Callie for dinner and then get Callie her ice cream." Yup, he gets my heart for how he cares for Callie. "Do you like baths?"

I chuckle at his randomness. "I haven't taken a bath in years."

He nods. "Then I'll draw you a bath and then take you right to bed once you're good and relaxed."

I swallow hard as I gaze up at him. "Do you know how sexy I find you right now?"

He grabs my butt, pulling me closer, and I can feel the length of him. "Pretty damn sexy. I'm a good-looking dude."

I snort but just for a second before he captures my mouth with his. As he glides his lips over mine, gripping my ass with his hand, I realize

I want this to be real. I want to know everything will work out and fall into place. Problem is, this is my life, and things never fall into place or go well.

I just hope that doesn't apply to Nico.

CHAPTER EIGHTEEN

viva

"ANYWHERE IN THE WORLD—WHERE would you go?"

I watch Nico's face as he thinks. Callie is grinning from ear to ear as she eats her cookie dough sundae. Nico took us to a fancy dinner, and it excited Callie to get to dress up. I'm pretty sure Nico did it to see me in a skirt, and I don't mind. I actually like being all snazzy. Makes me think of Jaylin and how perfect she looks all the time. Nico, well, he's a heartthrob. He pulled out all the stops in a sexy blue suit that hugs him in all the right places. His hair is brushed to the side, and his grin...well, it doesn't stop for anything.

Me, I don't think I've ever smiled this much.

"Iceland."

Callie looks surprised. "Really? It's cold."

"Duh, ice, so I can play hockey."

I laugh along with her. "You're such a hockey nerd."

"I am, hands down," he laughs as he takes a bite of his ice cream. "Where would you go?"

"Barcelona."

"Really? Why?"

I shake my head. "She wants to go because Ed Sheeran sang a song about it."

"So?" She holds her hands to her chest. "I want to dance in the streets to it and then eat all the food. He makes it seem so magical."

I roll my eyes. I want to take her, but I just don't know when.

Nico grins. "I've been. It's pretty awesome."

She smacks him playfully. She gets that from me. "Oh my God. Is it? I want to go so bad."

"Do you have a passport?"

She nods. "Yup. It's just waiting for the stamp."

He grins, his eyes cutting to mine. "We should go."

I shake my head. "Please. I can't afford that—"

"I can," he says simply. "I have a plane we can use too."

Callie is practically slapping me at this point. "Oh my God, Veev! He has a plane we can use. That's most of the cost. Please!"

I shake my head, sending a glare to Nico. "When, Callie? I work all the time, and he's doing hockey."

"Doing hockey?" he asks, and I shrug.

"Playing, whatever. You're busy, and so I am."

Nico's eyes are playful. "You could close for a weekend."

I scoff. "Not right now. I gotta get ahead, and then maybe."

"This summer?" Callie asks, almost climbing into my lap. "This summer, Vee. Say you'll let him take us in the summer. No one wants subs in the summer, and he'll be done with hockey. Please!"

"Calliope, please. This," I say, moving my hand between us, "is so new. He might hate us come summer."

She trains her big beautiful green eyes on him. "Promise me you'll still love us then."

Nico looks over at me, that shit-eating grin on his face. "That's the plan."

Both of them are thorns in my side.

Thankfully, though, that satisfies Callie. She sits back, grabbing her ice cream. “Okay, then it’s a plan. Don’t mess this up,” she says, pointing her spoon at me.

I laugh as I meet his gaze. “That was your plan the whole time, huh? Lock the kid in so I can’t go anywhere.”

He nods, slipping his hand into mine. “Basically. I know how to get what I want.”

He sends me a sneaky wink, and I shake my head. Oh, I’m playing with some dangerous fire here. He is too much. After making sure Callie is engrossed in her ice cream, I run my tongue along my lips and very seductively drag it over my ice cream.

He looks away, shaking his head. “I see how you’re gonna play this.”

“Torture me, I’ll torture you.” I feel Callie’s gaze, but I ignore it. “You too.”

That sends them both into a fit of laughter. When the laughter subsides, he points his spoon at me. “So, this car thing. Can we talk about it now?” He jerks his head at Callie, and I nod.

“Yeah, she knows.”

“I think I want to buy this truck I’ve been renting, not the actual one but one like it. You can have my other car since it’s not totaled.”

I scoff. “Your red sports thingy? No way.”

He grins. “Why? You’d look hot in that car.”

“So would I when I drive it,” Callie mentions, but there is no way.

“Absolutely not. I think I might just buy Jaylin’s. It’s a Honda.”

“Boring,” they both singsong, and I laugh.

“It’s just fine for me.”

“How about you buy that for her and take mine?”

I hold his gaze. “You can use that death trap as a trade-in.”

He draws in his brows. “Hey, it’s only a death trap when crazy women slam into it,” he teases, and I snort with laughter.

“You got me there.”

He grins. “Take it.”

“No. I swear, I’m good. I’ll take Jaylin for the low price of a hundred bucks and be on my way.”

He holds my gaze, and I think he knows I won't budge because he nods. "Fine. Can I pay Jaylin?"

"No way. Why would you even ask?"

"'Cause I want to make you smile."

My heart flutters, and of course, I do smile. "You're just pissing me off."

"Your face doesn't look pissed off," Callie observes, and I glare over at her.

"You're about to walk home," I throw at her, and soon, she is giggling as she gets back on her phone.

When Nico laces his fingers through mine, I hide behind my ice cream to keep myself from giggling like my sister. His eyes are so dark, and he's so damn smooth. I'm holding a guy's hand while eating ice cream. I think this is a first. "You're working tomorrow?"

"All day long. You have a game or practice?"

"Practice, but I'm free Sunday before we leave for two weeks."

My stomach falls. "You're leaving for two weeks?"

"Yeah, we have games in Canada and then against the California teams," he says around his mouthful of ice cream.

"That's why I don't have orders for two weeks," I say, all of it clicking in my head.

"Yeah, sorry. I'd bring you with me, and you could make subs during the day. But at night..." His words fall off since there is a teenager beside us. Unfortunately, my sister doesn't understand that he was trying to be discreet.

"He'll want in your pants," she announces, not even looking at us. She's on that damn phone, and I want to toss it.

"Callie," I say sternly, and she shrugs.

"We're all thinking it."

I look back to him, and he nods. I roll my eyes and think it's time for a change of subject. "Well, that sucks," I say, and I mean it. That is super disappointing. I don't want him to leave.

"Don't worry. I'll call and text."

"You better," I say, stroking my thumb along his. "So, I'm closed Sunday. We can do something then."

"Yes, like go skating."

I make a face. "I was thinking Netflix and chill."

That makes the phone drop and Nico's eyes widen. "Talk about me speaking the truth. Listen to you."

I draw in my brows. "What? I need to catch up on *Stranger Things*, and I wanted to eat my weight in Sour Patch Kids. Netflix and chilling with him and my Sour Patch Kids. Not you. You're not invited."

Callie looks at Nico, who is laughing—hard. What am I missing? "Thank God! Vee, Netflix and chill means the guy comes over for a hookup."

My jaw drops. "No way!"

"Get off the damn bread recipe sites and pay attention to reality, please," she says, and I feel stupid.

I press my hand to my chest as I look back at him. "Did you know that?"

He nods. "Yeah."

"I'm so old," I cry out playfully, and Callie nods.

"So old."

Nico's brow perks. "How old are you?"

"Thirty-two. You?"

He grins. "Twenty-seven."

"Mmm, my sister is a cougar."

"For the love of God, I am not. It's only five years."

"Cougar," she says, and then she rawrrs like the child she is. Lord help me. Nico, he thinks it's hilarious. "Anyway! Can I stay with Amanda tonight? We're gonna train for a couple hours and then go to her house for the night."

I'm still pissed about the cougar talk. I should say no, but I really want that bath and Nico. "That's fine."

"Are you going to go skating with us on Sunday?" Nico asks, and she nods.

"Yeah," she says.

This all feels very right. Like this is supposed to happen. There has never been a third person, but it's nice to have one now.

When Nico looks over at me, he grins. "What?"

"You fit in."

"Damn right, I do. I'm awesome."

Callie nods. "He is."

Yeah. Yeah, he is.

* * *

WE DON'T EVEN MAKE it up the stairs before Nico has his arms around me. I laugh loudly as he turns me in his hold and presses me up against his front door. He cradles my head in his hands before his mouth captures mine. God, he tastes so damn good. Feels so good. His body envelops mine, holding me so close I can feel his heart pounding in his chest. I know the cadence of my heart matches his. He moves his tongue along my lips playfully, teasing with his teeth and driving me absolutely insane. I have wanted this since he showed up at the shop.

Shit, since I met him.

He somehow gets the door open and walks me inside, guiding me in before kicking the door shut. He holds me in his arms, still kissing me as he locks the door before dropping his keys into a bowl by the door. He pulls his mouth not far from mine. "I am going to undress you, taste every single inch of you, and then put you in the tub where you will relax and not think of anything but how hard you will come when I get you in my bed."

I draw in a deep breath. His eyes are something wicked for sure. "I think I'm gonna like all of that."

"Oh, I'm gonna make damn sure you do," he says against my mouth. "And if I think you don't, I'll just bury my face right here." He cups my pussy, and yup, I'm pretty sure I'm going to die from coming at this man's hands. It will be a really great way to go. No fucks in the world. Flying on a cloud of desire.

"I think that's a fantastic idea."

He grins against my mouth. "I do too."

He wraps his arms around my waist and picks me up off the ground. I wrap my legs around his waist as I hold his face in my hands and our lips meet once more. He carries me into his bedroom and slowly lays me down on the bed. I feel my eyes roll up in the back of my head as he kisses down my jaw and neck. When he hovers over me, I meet his eyes with mine in a fiery connection. Jesus, his eyes are hooded, dark, and I'm ready for all the naughty things they promise me.

He runs his hands down my dress, grabbing the fabric at the bottom. "I can't rip this, can I?"

"No, I will legit bite you if you do. Right in the jugular."

He looks over at me with a disturbed look on his face. "That's violent."

"Don't rip my favorite dress."

He grins as he pulls it up, exposing my thighs. He moves down my body, running his tongue along me as he reveals more skin. I moan from my soul. He follows the fabric of my dress up with his tongue, not missing a spot with his tongue or teeth. When he pulls the dress above my head, I lie there in my bra, rubber boobs, and a very revealing thong. He licks his lips as he looks me over.

"You are by far the most gorgeous woman I have ever seen," he murmurs against my skin, making it really hard to believe otherwise. He pulls me up and unhooks my bra, throwing it along with the boobs to the floor. I thought it would be weird, but I'm so far gone, I don't even care. The refreshing thing is, I don't think he cares either. He kisses down the center of my chest, yanking at my thong with his hands as he licks and bites. I'm freaking lost in the feel of his mouth, arching so I can feel it even more. His fingers bite into my skin, and I cry out when he traces his tongue along my left scar.

"Does it hurt?"

I cover my chest with my hands. "Not at all. I don't even feel anything. Still a bit numb after all this time."

He kisses my scars again. He then kisses up my throat, my jaw, before meeting my gaze, and he pulls my hands away. "Why are you so embarrassed by them?"

"Because I'm not fully a woman, in a way. The only thing that makes me different from a preteen boy is my vagina."

He presses his palm into my other breast. "Well, with a great pussy like yours, you really don't need anything else."

I smile against his lips. "I want to get implants, but I never had the money to do so. And then there's Callie. I have to make sure she is set before me."

He brings in his brows. "She has the gene?"

I nod, my eyes welling up with tears. "Yes, and it kills me on a daily basis that I couldn't protect her from it."

His eyes change. Gone is the heat, and I feel stupid. I wipe away my tear, shaking my head. "Way to ruin the moment, Aviva."

"No," he says sternly. "You didn't ruin it. You just made me want you more."

"Nico…" I don't even know what I was going to say. I just had to say his name.

"I think you are so damn hot, so damn womanly, and everything I want."

I close my eyes. "You're unreal."

"I know, but I feel like I've been thinking that about you since I met you."

Before I can say anything, his mouth takes mine, and slowly he slides my thong down my thighs. He sits up, pulling it down and off me before standing up at the side of the bed. I watch as he drinks me in, and I wonder what he is thinking. His look is so hot and wanton, but after putting myself down for so many years, I find it hard to believe he really wants me. He grabs me by my ankles, pulling me to the edge of the bed, and I laugh. He takes my wrists, lifting me up and into his arms. I slam into him, but it doesn't hurt; it only makes me burn from the inside out. He snakes his arm around me, lifting me so that our lips meet as he carries me into the bathroom.

The bathroom is bigger than I expected, but it's hard for me to take it in when his mouth is moving against mine like that. He sits me on the side of the tub, kissing my nose and then the side of my mouth before standing back up. He sighs hard, and I grin.

"What?"

"I'm so damn hot for you. I just want to take you right here, but I also want you to relax." He struggles to get out the words as he throws some Epsom salts in the tub. "You are beyond sexy, Aviva."

I bite my lip as he starts to fill the tub. Man, I want him, and damn it, I should take what I want. I reach out, grabbing him by the legs of his pants, pulling him to me. He comes, a sexy smirk on his lips before he cups my face.

"What are you doing?"

"Not what I'm doing. What you're about to do to me."

I undo his pants as he drops his mouth to mine. As I quickly push down his pants, along with his boxers, he throws off his jacket. I pull away, gripping his cock in my hand, moving my palm up and down the velvety skin. He groans loudly, and I look up at him in awe. I let him go and stand up, his wild eyes watching me. I turn and bend over, holding on to the tub, my ass right there for his pleasure.

The groan I'm answered with has my mouth watering. Nico takes my ass in his hands just as I feel his mouth on me. He licks up my pussy, and I cry out as I squeeze my eyes shut. He dips his tongue to rub against my clit, sliding up until he finds my entrance. Using just the tip of his tongue, he licks it ever so slowly along me, sending me into fits. He gives my pussy openmouthed kisses, and his name falls off my lips in a needy tone.

"That's right, baby. Fuck, this is so right," he says, and then his hand smacks my ass, making me cry out. He rubs his palm across the spot he just smacked and takes me by my hips. He jerks me back against his cock, my wet center gliding along his long, engorged flesh. He guides my hips up and down so that I slide along his cock, and I'm lost.

Gone. I might have died. I'm not sure.

His fingers clench into my hips, and then he moves away. I look over my shoulder to see him opening a drawer and pulling out a row of condoms. He tears one off and then opens it quickly. His hands are shaking, and a grin moves across my face. I'm driving him crazy. I did that. He sheathes himself and then grabs me by my hips once more. With the next breath I take, he fills me completely. I let my head fall as his groans fill the bathroom. His fingers squeeze my hips as he starts to move in and out of me. His thrusts are hard, but I welcome them. I crave them. Each one has me jerking forward, taking every single breath I have in my body. He slides his hand down my spine, and he wraps my hair around his fist before pulling my head back.

"Oh… Oh, Nico," I cry, and he turns my head so his mouth can take mine. He stills for only a second to kiss me, and I'm shaking with lust. When he tears his mouth from mine, he grips my hair while he holds my hip with his other hand as I shatter into a billion pieces.

"Fuck," he groans out as he starts to slam into me.

I ride out my orgasm, squeezing him like a vise, and it feels so fucking good. He clutches my hip as he yells my name in a heated, broken voice. It doesn't take long until he is coming just as hard as I did. He jerks into me, his body quivering against mine as his mouth drops to my back. My legs are about to give out, but I don't dare move. I feel as if I could fall face first into this water and drown, but I couldn't care if I tried.

Because I have never felt more alive in my life.

CHAPTER NINETEEN

ico

CALLIE IS a natural on the ice. For someone who hasn't ever been skating, she's pretty damn good. I only had to help a bit before she caught on and took off. I love how big she is smiling and how much fun she's having. She left her hair down, so it's flying behind her as she races across the ice. In my oversized hoodie since neither she nor Aviva brought a jacket, she's having a blast. I want to put a stick in her hand, but I'm currently making sure her sister doesn't die.

Aviva is not a natural.

I'm unsure how this girl walks on a daily basis.

"I'm going to die. *Oh my God*, Nico, I'm going to die."

It's hard not to laugh. I hold her by her waist—she is hardly even putting pressure on the ice—as I say, "Babe, I got you."

"No! Ah! Oh my God, how the hell do you do this? Nico! Ah!"

She swings her arms out, and I can't even see straight, I'm laughing so hard. "Aviva, you aren't even touching the ice. I'm holding you up."

She stops flailing her arms and looks over at me. With a forgiving smile, she shrugs. "I'm kinda scared."

"No?" I say sarcastically. "You got this. One foot at a time."

She tenses up. "I don't want to die."

I give her a pointed look. "Would I let you die?"

She searches my eyes. "No...?"

"No," I repeat, slowly lowering her to the ice. With my arm still around her, I push off. "There you go."

"Ah, I'm skating! Look, Callie! I'm doing it!"

Meanwhile, Callie is spinning on the ice like a damn figure skater. "You mean Nico is pushing you across some ice?"

Man, I want to laugh so hard. I kiss Aviva's ear. "You're doing great. Don't listen to her," I encourage as I loosen my grip. "Okay, slide your skates. Yes. Good. Attagirl! You're doing great."

She's still digging her nails into my arm, but she's actually somewhat moving on her own. I could probably let her go, but I honestly don't want to. The last two days have been great. We spent Friday night going at it. The whole night. We couldn't get enough of each other. While I was at practice on Saturday, she was running the shop. When she was done, she and Callie came over for a bonfire on the beach. The cops came over, which Chandler warned me about, but I'm not paying some bitter asshole to keep from calling the cops. I'll deal, and we had fun anyway. I've never laughed so hard in my life. They are both a blast to hang out with. I didn't want Aviva to leave, but I don't want Callie getting the wrong idea. I don't want her thinking I'm just in it to get her sister into bed. I want her to know I respect them both.

I don't know where this train of thought came from. I think it all stems from when Callie told me she Googled me. If she did that, then she saw me with all the women I've been with. Since Aviva assumed I wasn't a one-woman man, I'm pretty sure Callie must think the same. I'm out to prove people wrong; I live off it. Plus, I want Callie to know her worth. Aviva has an issue with that, and I don't want that for Callie. I care too much about her. I care way too much for both of them given the amount of time I've known them. It worries me, these overwhelming feelings, but I wouldn't want to feel anything else. They both make me happy. But Aviva, man, she makes me feel things, real things.

I kiss her jaw at her excitement of not falling. I'm not sure if her delight is from the endless orgasms I keep giving her or if it's me. Or both. I'm not sure, but she hasn't stopped smiling. Every time I see her, she seems like she's glowing. I thought getting the car from Jaylin would piss her off, but she actually took it in stride. It's probably because Callie's competition season is coming up, and Aviva will need a car for that. I wish she'd let me help her, but I wouldn't dare offer. She'd probably claw my eyes out.

When I notice that she is actually skating, I loosen my grip. "I'm going to let you go."

She starts falling as she cries out, "Don't you dare!"

I hold her close to me and laugh. "I'm starting to think you're doing this so I won't let you go."

I can see her grin as she leans into me. "Maybe."

I kiss her cheek. "Good, I don't want to let you go either." She exhales harshly, and I perk my brow. "What's wrong?"

She shrugs, and if I could see her face, I know she'd have her brow furrowed. "I feel stupid saying this, but I don't want you to leave."

"Why does that make you stupid?"

She looks up at me, and like I thought, her brow is all puckered. "Because we've only been seeing each other—"

"Seeing each other?"

She eyes me. "Yes, it's where I see you and you see—"

I press my lips to hers to keep her from talking anymore. "Shut it, smartass." She grins against my lip as we glide across the ice. Callie is just dancing to the music that is playing, and I'm starting to think maybe she needs to be a skater. The girl is awesome. "We aren't seeing each other."

She scoffs. "I'm legit staring at you right now."

I roll my eyes, and then without thinking, I say, "I want you to be my girlfriend."

She seems surprised, but then she curves her lip at the side. "You do?"

"Yeah," I say softly. It's the truth. I don't want to date her or see her; I want to know that she's mine. That when I call, she is waiting to hear from me. The person I can talk to about a bad day and a good day. We stayed up until two last night talking about our days, and it was great. We talked hockey and subs, and I never thought I could love talking about two things so much. I might be rushing this—I probably am—but I think the biggest mistake I made with Shelli was that I didn't lock her in. I just kept fucking her and being around when she wanted it. I didn't ask her to be mine. I won't make that mistake again. I won't let someone take Aviva from me.

"I don't want to leave and think that you could find someone else better."

She reaches up, cupping my face. "That's my line."

"I mean, I deleted my Tinder account yesterday. I'm serious here."

She grins. "Aw—"

"Aviva."

"Yes. Sorry. I hear you."

I smile. "I know it's kinda early. Like you said, we've only been doing this dance for about a week, but I know what I want. I've known for a while, and I want to be your boyfriend."

"It is kinda rushed," she drawls, her eyes burning into mine. I feel the rejection wash over me, but then she smiles. "But I've never wanted to be wanted by anyone the way I want to be wanted by you."

I exhale in a rush before dropping my mouth to hers. She cups my face as our lips dance, and everything inside me fires off like mad. I press my forehead into hers, and I know she feels how hard I am against her sweet ass. She does this to me; she drives me absolutely reckless, and I crave it. I love this feeling. I pull back to look down into her face, and man, she has me in my feelings.

"Um, guys?"

I can't pull my gaze from hers. Her green depths are swirling with such heat and sweetness. I can't believe this girl is into me. I'm just a weirdo hockey player, and she's perfection. I open my mouth to tell her that, but before I can even get the words out, we smack right into the boards. I fall back on the ice with her on top of me, and within seconds, our sides are splitting with laughter. She falls to the side of me, our legs tangled together as our eyes meet. She's crying from laughing, and I know I mirror her. I wipe her tears as she sets me with a frisky look.

"I thought you said you wouldn't let me fall," she scolds playfully, smacking my chest.

I gather her up in my arms, kissing her nose. "Not my fault. All yours."

"How?"

"You distracted me!"

Her lips turn into a smirk as she cups my jaw, running her thumb along my lips. "What am I going to do with you?"

"Everything," I answer, and I don't want anything but that.

To do everything with Aviva.

WHEN AMELIA OPENS THE DOOR, her eyes widen a bit as she takes us all in.

"Coach!"

Amelia and Callie embrace as she looks over at me. "Hey, girl. How are you?"

"Good. Where are the babies?"

"They're on the floor," she says, hooking her thumb behind her, and Callie rushes past her to go in. I watch as she glances from me to Aviva and then back to me. She looks genuinely surprised, and that pleases me. I love keeping her on her toes. After Amelia saying Aviva doesn't have time for me, I like that she is seeing Aviva's hand in mine and grins on our faces.

"Boom. She likes me."

Amelia rolls her eyes. "Shut up! When you said you were bringing someone, I didn't expect to see my favorite gymnast and her sister."

I shrug. "I'm full of surprises."

"I hope it's okay—" Aviva starts, but Amelia quickly waves her off.

"Of course it is. You're always welcome! Dinner is almost done. Come on in."

We follow her in, and the aroma of tacos fills the house. It smells damn good. For the last six months, we've been having dinner together before we leave on road trips. I don't know how it happened, but I just started showing up before I packed, and Amelia would feed me. She wasn't that great of a cook when we met, but she's getting better. Tacos are her specialty.

As I walk in, I notice the house is actually clean, which means Amelia is finding her footing. That pleases me since she was struggling for a bit there. "Looks great in here."

Amelia grins over at me. "Yeah, I've learned to clean when they're sleeping."

Callie is on the floor with the twins and Sadie. She's their guard dog; those are her babies. At least that's the running joke.

Aviva drops to her knees to gush over the babies. "They're getting so big, Amelia," she says as Sadie demands attention.

I rub Sadie's back as Amelia agrees with Aviva. "I know. I feel like they're growing every second."

"They are," Aviva says, and I bend down to my buddy Carter.

He's a chubby little thing and so damn cute. "Hey, fat man, come here." I pick him up, cradling his head before pressing him to my chest and standing. "He's a sack of potatoes. What are you feeding this kid?"

Amelia shrugs. "Formula. He's hungry."

Aviva glances up at her. "You're not breastfeeding?"

She shakes her head. "My milk didn't come in. My boobs are worthless," she says with a shrug. "I don't care, though, as long as my kids are healthy and happy."

I watch emotion slip over Aviva's face as she cups Hannah's little hand. I want to know what she is thinking, but not here. Not now. I rock Carter back and forth as Chandler comes into the room. "Hey, man. Oh hey, Callie!"

His brows are at his hairline as he looks from Callie to Aviva and then to me.

Callie, none the wiser, grins back at him. "Hey, Chandler!"

It's like it all clicks in his head. "Aviva is Callie's sister."

Aviva waves. "Yup, that's me."

"And you guys came with Nico."

They both nod, and Aviva asks, "Is that okay?"

"More than okay. Just putting together the pieces," he says, heading toward the kitchen. "It's great to have you guys."

Aviva makes a face as she looks up at me. I shrug and follow him into the kitchen. "Dinner almost ready?"

Chandler nods, stirring some rice. "So, Aviva?"

"Aviva."

"I see it worked out."

"Yeah," I say against Carter's temple. He's starting to fall asleep. "We're together."

He gives me a sideways look. "Together? You've only known her a month."

"Yeah, and I think you and Amelia got together quicker."

He scoffs. "We hooked up in college."

"And you only knew her for a little bit then."

He holds up his palms at me. "Not judging. Just saying."

"Saying what?" I ask, and he glances back over at me.

"Don't use her to fill the void that Shelli left."

I scrunch up my face. "She has nothing to do with Shelli."

Chandler nods. "I hope not, 'cause I hear she's a good woman. She loves that girl so damn much. And you gotta remember, you're not dating just Aviva. You're dating Callie too. That's two hearts that will break if you decide—"

"I'm not gonna decide anything like that," I snap, holding his gaze. "Don't do that to me. I like her. A lot. And I love Callie. I wouldn't hurt them."

"Good," Chandler says softly. "I want this to work for you. I want this to be it, because I want you to be happy, bro." He clutches my shoulder, holding my gaze. "You're a damn good dude, my best friend, and that's all I want for you. If she's it, then I'm nothing but supportive."

I swallow hard. I feel guilty all of a sudden. This guy has been my best friend for years, and I told Callie before I told him. This guy cares for me. Cares for my happiness as I do his, and I'm too much of a coward to tell him the truth. I'd rather he think I'm an asshole who fucks around than that there is something not normal about me. But what if Callie is right? That everyone will believe it's my superpower? That's silly. I'm not a kid. I'm an adult, but the guilt is real.

"I love you, dude," I find myself saying, and Chandler grins.

"I love you too, man." He smacks my arm and goes back to stirring the rice. I feel a hand slide up my back, and when I look to the side, it's Aviva.

"You guys having a bro moment?"

Chandler snorts. "Totally. We have the best bromance."

She smiles. "That's wonderful," she says before leaning up to kiss my jaw. "Does he approve of me?"

I scoff as Chandler laughs before he speaks. "It's not you who needs the approving. It's him. He's wild as all get-out."

Aviva's face brightens. "Yeah, but he's also great."

Chandler looks between us and then nods. "Yeah, he's okay."

He leaves the kitchen, and I roll my eyes. "He's a pain."

"I just got the third degree."

"From Amelia?"

"Yup," she says, still smiling, so it must have not bothered her. "She said you're a handful. I didn't disagree."

"Why does she hate me? I love her," I say in a teasing matter, but Aviva smacks my arm.

"She just wanted to make sure I was happy."

I lean my head on Carter's and ask, "What did you say?"

She sighs slowly as she places her hand on Carter's back. "Very much so."

As our lips meet, my eyes drift shut. Yeah, it's new and sparkly, this relationship of ours, but damn if she isn't the beginning to my happiness.

CHAPTER TWENTY

viva

"WHY AM I NERVOUS?"

Jaylin looks over at me from the table where she's sitting. She has paperwork spread out, and her brow is furrowed. Dustin Sr. is coming in to discuss why my rent is now two hundred dollars more and why he told my dad. I don't know why my stomach is churning, but it is. I knew never to trust that man, but I had no choice. My mom rented the place way before I knew anything about business. If I had my way, I'd buy the building outright and flip him the bird.

"I don't know. You have no reason to be. I'm going to ruin him."

I sigh as a smile pulls at my lips. My best friend is a badass.

"How's the car doing?"

I cover the olive bin and grab the cucumber one. "Good, thank you. I love it."

"Awesome. It's a good car."

I nod. "Nico thought he was gonna give me his red sports car."

Her eyes widen. "You should have taken it!"

"No way. I can't imagine myself in something like that. Callie, though... She already decided she would look fabulous."

Jaylin laughs. "That girl is a mess. Why did he want to give you that?"

"I guess he's getting a truck. He says he'll be better protected from crazy women drivers," I say dryly, and she snorts with laughter.

"So, things are going well?"

I'm beaming, and I don't even try to hide it. "They are. He's wonderful. Direct as all hell, but wonderful."

"What do you mean, direct?"

"I don't know. He doesn't think. He just does." I shake my head, a grin on my face. "He goes on these big stream-of-consciousness bursts of stuff that don't even make sense, but he's telling me. Like, last night, I guess his cup thing shifted during the game, and his ball fell out?" I start to giggle, remembering how silly he sounded. "So he goes on this long ramble about how he was worried he was going to lose it, and then he wouldn't be able to have kids, and then he would be known as One-Nut Buck, and I wouldn't want to sleep with him because he only has one ball. I swear, he is so silly."

My face hurts from grinning, and I know Jaylin notices. "Aw, someone is smitten."

I shrug. "I guess. I don't know."

"You do know. You like him."

I bite my lip. Should I admit it? "I do. A lot."

"Good. You need someone who makes you feel good," she says sweetly, and I know she means it.

I think she's my biggest cheerleader when it comes to my bliss. For so long, I haven't cared, but now I do. I feel like I'm chasing it now. Craving it. Since Nico is gone and we only have the phone to communicate, I look for things around me to make me feel good. Usually after a long day of work, I go to bed. But the past couple nights, I've gone to watch Callie at the gym. We made cookies last night and had our version of Netflix and chill. *Stranger Things* and cookies. It was the best, and it was what I wanted to do. I wished Nico were there, but I was still happy. It's all so crazy. All it took was for someone to come along and show me that I can be happy even with this shittastic life of mine. I don't know how it all happened so quickly, but it has.

I'm smitten.

"He asked me to be his girlfriend," I say, and she looks over at me, her brow perked.

"Let me guess. You said no?"

"No. I actually said yes." I pause. "Well, I didn't disagree or agree. I just said I like being wanted, but that was my way of saying yes."

She rolls her eyes. "Because being direct is so hard."

I scoff. "Not for him. I wish I could be like that. I always second-guess myself."

She gives me a look. "If you treated your personal life the way you do your business life, you would have found someone a long time ago."

I make a face. "But then I wouldn't have found Nico. Or better yet, run my car into him."

"True," Jaylin laughs, shaking her head. "How long has it been?"

"We've been together for over a week now."

She nods. "Yup. He's the one."

My face twists. "What?"

She looks over her shoulder at me. "I'm telling you, Aviva. You may have crashed into him, but that dude crashed into your life and turned it upside down. You haven't quit smiling since I've been here. You keep checking your phone, gushing, and being so girly. You've never been like this. This all means something."

I hold her gaze. "I can't even disagree with you, but I'm terrified that it's not the case for him, which is why I will keep my guard up."

She lets her head fall onto the table with a loud groan. "I'm gonna start calling you Self-Sabotage Sally."

"I'm not sabotaging myself!" I throw back at her, but her face is twisted in disdain.

"You are just waiting for that shoe to drop. Aviva, listen to me. Sometimes, things happen for the good."

I swallow hard. I want to believe that. My track record, though, it's a doozy. The front door opens, the bell signaling, and we both look to see Dustin Sr. walk in. He looks at Jaylin, and I know he wants to turn right back around.

"Why is she here?"

Jaylin stands up, straightening her skirt. "It's so *wonderful* to see you, too."

Well, here we go.

* * *

"Do not, and I mean do not, pay the whole month. Make sure you subtract that hundred," Jaylin says to me sternly as I sign the new papers she drew up. She grabs them from me as I sign, and my heart is still beating hard in my chest. Dustin Sr. does not like Jaylin and crumbled like a cookie when she went at him. He didn't fight her on anything and claimed the rent amount was a mistake. If I knew this was how he was going to act when Jaylin was around, I'd have her around all the time. Still, though, I'm nervous. Things like this don't work out like that.

"And I think we really need to look into buying this place."

I look at her with a deadpan expression. "Yes. I'll reach up my ass and grab the extra wad of cash I have stored up there."

She sends a look back at me that says she's tired of my sass. "I'll help you get the loan—and I know, no handouts." She mocks me with hand movements and all; it's quite disturbing. "But it wouldn't be a handout. It's to help you. If we offer him a price he can't turn down, then we'll be done with him and your dad."

I swallow hard, the thought of my dad making my skin crawl. "Do you think Dustin Sr. will follow through on the nondisclosure?"

The look on her face doesn't bode well for Dustin Sr. "I wish he wouldn't. I'll take him to court so damn fast." After packing up her briefcase, she reaches for my hands. "You have nothing to worry about. Everything is taken care of, and I really want you to think about what I offered. I'll help with the loan—hell, we can get a bigger one to pay off your mom's stuff. It would help a lot. Consider it." She leans over, kissing my cheek. "And hey, keep smiling."

I send her a small smile. "I will. And thank you."

She smiles. "Anything for you."

She sashays out of my shop, and I exhale roughly. I glance at my copies of the paperwork we all signed. I want to be excited about this. I know for a fact, though, either my dad will walk through that door or Nico will call to tell me he's moved on. I gather the paperwork and go to the back to file it in my mini office as I consider what Jaylin said.

I would love to own this place. I could change a few things, but the best part would be I would never have to look at Dustin Sr. or Jr. again. Problem is, my mom always said, "Don't lend money to friends." Jaylin isn't just a friend, though; she's family. My mom used to call Jaylin her daughter all the time. She's a sister to me, but could I allow her to do this for me? I just bought her car for a hundred bucks, and that is already giving me an ulcer. I just hate the feeling of owing someone something.

I hate the feeling of being helpless and needing someone to save me.

A few minutes after I step out of the office, a customer comes in, so I get to work. It's almost an hour before it slows down enough for me to check my phone. As I lean into the counter, I grin since there is a missed call from Nico and a text.

Nico: Can you stop being a sub superstar and call me?

I laugh as I push his name, and when his voice fills the line, I want to sigh with contentment. "Hey."

"Hey. How'd the meeting go?"

"Good, actually," I say as I lean over the counter, watching the door. "My landlord is completely scared of Jaylin, so he basically did whatever she wanted."

"Well, she is a badass."

"She is."

"I'm glad it worked out."

"Yeah, me too." I inhale and go back and forth with myself on whether I want to tell him the next part. I decide I do. "Jaylin asked if he'd sell the shop, and he said for the right price. So now she is trying to convince me to let her help me get a loan to buy it, but you know how I am."

He's quiet for a moment, and then he says, "I know how you are, but I think it would be for the best."

"I know, but I just don't feel right about it." I tuck my hair behind my ear. "I am going to think about it, though."

"Good. You should. It's a good idea, unless..." he starts, and I already know what he is going to say. "I can buy it outright, and you can just pay me monthly. I'd be the best landlord."

I grin. "Oh yeah?"

"Oh, hell yeah. I'd basically do whatever you want, in the shop and in the bed."

I giggle, my face filling with heat. "You're impossible."

He laughs, but then his serious tone is back. "Seriously. I'm loaded. I can buy it."

I roll my eyes. "I am aware of your loaded status, and I don't care. I don't want your money."

"But you still want me?"

"Very much so." Ugh, I miss him. "How many more days till you'll be home?"

He chuckles. "Miss me?"

"I do," I admit. "I've been watching the games while I watch Callie at practice."

"I like that you watch me. I'll have to play even better now."

"You've only lost one game."

"I do not want to talk about that."

I bring in a breath. "So, we don't talk about hockey?"

"Nope."

"Cool," I say, but his voice is stern. "I'm sorry."

"Don't apologize," he says quickly, clearing his throat. "How's Callie doing?"

"Good. She's flipping way more than I like, but she seems happy. Oh! She passed that test, thanks to you. Thank you for FaceTiming with her the other night."

It was the sweetest thing ever. She was almost in tears, she was so nervous about her test. When I told Nico that when he called after his game, he FaceTimed her to help. He had just finished putting up a shutout, and he still made sure Callie was good. I swear, I think it chipped at my walls a bit.

"Great! Man, I was worried. I'm glad." He clears his throat, and I hear his bed move. "So, I need to ask you something."

"Okay?" Why is my heart kicking up in speed? What will he ask?

"So, you know I go to therapy, right?"

"Yeah, you've mentioned it." I've wanted to ask why, but I wouldn't dare. If he wants to tell me, then he will.

"Well, I have this thing about interviews and large crowds. I don't do well in those situations, and well, there is this foundation thing the whole team is going to. Usually, I can get out of it, but this year, they're really pushing me to go because they think it's time. I need to force myself to get past my issues. Well, my therapist suggested that I take you. To help. 'Cause I feel comfortable around you."

My face breaks into a grin. "You talk to your therapist about me?"

He groans. "Aviva."

"I'm teasing. Of course I will. I'd love to."

He exhales hard. Did he think I would say no? "Okay, I'm freaking out, and it's like three weeks away."

"Why are you freaking out? You'll be fine."

"Yeah, I don't think so. It makes me uncomfortable."

I bite my lip. "Is it like a phobia?"

He hesitates. "Yeah, something like that. I don't know. It's weird, I get really overwhelmed very quickly."

I can hear it in his voice, and it makes my stomach hurt. "It's okay. We'll be together. I'll protect you," I say sweetly, and he laughs.

"That's my job."

"Eh, I'll take the reins for one night."

I can hear his smirk in his voice. "And I'll take the reins once I get you to bed."

"I really like the sound of that." I feel like lying in my bed and rolling around, grinning like I did when I was a teenager. He gives me that fluttery, girlie feeling. I love it.

"Another thing."

"Wow, you have a lot to say today."

He chuckles softly. "So, don't get mad, okay?"

I groan. "That means I will."

He laughs some more. "No, really. Hear me out."

"Okay…"

"I have a friend who used to play for the Nashville Assassins. He just retired, and he used to help with my travel team back in the day. Anyway, his wife is a breast cancer survivor, and she runs this bomb-ass lingerie company for breast cancer survivors." I'm breathless as he continues. "She called the other day, and we were chitchatting because I bought you like the whole site."

My heart stops dead in my chest. "What?"

"Yeah, I want you to feel like I see you. Fucking sexy. And this stuff is awesome. It should be there tomorrow or the next day. I don't know. I gotta check my shipping confirmation. So we were talking, and she was telling me she is coming to Baybridge next month for a breast cancer conference. It's women only, and I really think you and Callie should go."

My mouth goes dry, and I don't know what to say.

"I won't be in town. I have games, so I can't drive you guys. But I got you both tickets for this thing, a hotel, and a car to take you since it's a forty-minute drive and I don't want you to put the miles on your new car. I know you have to work, but her talk is Sunday, which works out perfectly. You guys leave Saturday night and come home Sunday night."

Tears rush down my face as I close my eyes. "Nico."

"Shit. You're mad?"

"Not at all," I say as I inhale shakily. "I can't believe you did this."

"I think you need this. I go to conferences and therapy, and it helps me. I want to help you," he says simply. "And I think you and Callie need it."

I can't agree because I'm holding in a sob. "Okay."

"So, you'll go?"

"Yes, I'll go."

"Awesome. You're going to love Lacey King. Check out her site. I'll send you the link."

"Okay," I say, wiping my face. "I'm going to suck you raw when you get home."

He pauses for a moment and then starts laughing uncontrollably. I can't help it; I'm laughing just as hard. He makes me extremely happy. "I'll take you up on that for sure."

We continue to laugh as the door flies open, and Callie comes running toward me. "Aviva!"

I stand up, alarmed. "What?"

"You're never gonna guess it, but someone called the gym and paid off my bills. Like, for the next two years. We owe nothing! Can you believe it?"

I blink. "What?"

"Yeah! Look!" She hands me a paper that says we're paid in full, and then it shows a credit for what I assume covers for the next two years of her career at the gym. "Amelia was stunned. They didn't even know the person. They just called and paid it!"

My heart is pounding in my chest as I read the paper over and over again.

"What's going on?" Nico asks, and I clear my throat free of emotion.

"Someone called and paid Callie's gymnastics bill."

"Oh, that's cool."

"I don't know who would do that," I say, staring at the paper. "Was it you?"

"Nope," he says matter-of-factly. "I'm not stupid."

I want to laugh, but I'm stunned. It couldn't have been Jaylin; she knows better. But then, who? Who would do this for us? "Do you think it was Dad?"

Callie shakes her head. "No, he wouldn't spend the money he stole from us on me."

She isn't wrong. But who?

And there's that shoe. I think it's about to fall.

On my face.

CHAPTER TWENTY-ONE

viva

"I don't know why you're making such a huge deal of this."

I flash Callie a dark look as we cross the parking lot. "I don't know why you're not. Two years of tuition and back pay? That's a down payment on a Lexus. That's insane. I need to know."

"Why? So you can yell at them?"

Yes. "No. So I can tell them to take their damn money back!"

"Ugh! This is great for us, Vee. Let it be!" Callie yells at me, trying to keep up. She's a shorter gymnast, so it's hard for her to match my steps. "Why can't you just accept this?"

I reach for the door handle of GymMasters. "Because good things don't happen for me."

Callie slams her palm into the door to stop me. She holds up her other hand and, counting off on her fingers, says, "Not getting cancer. Me. Jaylin. And Nico. All good things that have happened to you."

Why is she such a pain in my ass? "Other than that," I say, pulling hard on the door and going inside. The place is packed with their rec classes, so I pass people and move around them to get to the offices. I can see Dominica is in her office, and I go straight for her. I knock, and she looks up.

"Oh hey, Aviva." She looks worried but not surprised. She probably knew I'd come in. I was going to come last night, but by the time I had closed, the team coaches were gone.

"Hey, Dominica. Listen, I need to know who paid off Callie's account."

She shrugs. Fucking shrugs. "I don't know. They called, I ran the card, and they hung up. They didn't give me a name."

"You didn't need it to run the card?"

She shook her head. "No. I just needed the numbers."

I make a face. "So, you just take random money from strangers over the phone?"

She smiles. "If it results in me getting paid, yes."

I can't blame her there. "Will you please send it back? Refund it?"

"You want me to refund that amount of money so you can *maybe* pay it?"

I press my lips together. When she puts it that way, I feel this conversation won't end the way I want. "Yes."

"No," she says simply. "I asked three times if they were sure, and they were demanding to pay this money."

"I don't want it. I can pay her bills."

"Aviva, I know. But this is wonderful for Callie. No stress on you, and she can train. There will still be a balance toward the end of her career with us, but right now, you guys are solid."

Oh, my blood is boiling. "Male or female?"

"Huh?"

"On the phone. Was it a male or a female?"

She doesn't want to answer me. She hesitates but says, "A female."

I bite my lip, confused. I don't know any other females who would do this except Jaylin. "Okay, thank you."

I turn on my heel and head out.

Callie is waiting by the beam. "Did she send it back?"

"She wouldn't."

"Good. Bye."

"Bye," I throw back at her as I head out of the gym.

I slam the door for good measure as I pull my phone out of my back pocket. I dial Jaylin's office number, and she answers right away. "Hey you."

"Hey. Did you pay Callie's gym bill?"

"No way. Do I look dumb?"

I groan loudly. "Someone paid her tuition for the next two years, and I want to know who."

"Was it Nico?"

"He said no."

"Could he be lying?"

"I don't think he is capable of lying, for one. And for two, Dominica said it was a woman who called in."

"Huh," she says. "I mean, who cares? This is a blessing."

"That I'm sure will come at a cost."

She makes a sound of frustration. "Why do you do that? Just be happy."

"I can't. I know how this will go. Everything is going so well. I'm happy, I'm having orgasms, and I'm getting somewhat ahead. Which means, bam! Something will go wrong."

Jaylin sighs, annoyed. "Okay, whatever. I wish you wouldn't do that to yourself. Just be happy."

"I don't want anyone paying my bills."

"I get that. But sometimes it's nice to know someone cared enough to do it and move on."

I pause mid-step. "Who the hell cares about me? There is you, Callie, and Nico. That's it."

"Aw, Nico made the list."

I roll my eyes. "You annoy me."

She snickers. "Kirby told me last night that Nico is always talking about you. I thought it was cute."

"Man, you're still talking to him? It's been over a week. I'd thought you'd move on by now."

She sighs. "Well, we aren't talking, talking."

I pause. "Huh?"

"Well, funny story that I guess I've forgotten to tell you," she says, but by the tone of her voice, I don't think it's going to be very funny. "I was wondering why we hadn't hooked up yet. Like, that night, we made out, but then I was trying to play hard to get, so I didn't go home with him—"

"You? Hard to get?"

"Hey, he's super sexy with the mouth of a god. I wanted the first time to be savage, so I only gave him my number. He said he'd call me and he did, but we just talked, no plans for a date. He's been doing this dance with me for about two weeks now. So last night, I told him I wanted to get together when he got back in town. I mean, I've been getting off to pictures of this guy. He's gorgeous. But he then informed me that he's in an on-again, off-again relationship, and they just got back on, which was why he was calling. To tell me he can no longer see me because things just got complicated."

I blink. "Complicated?"

"He wouldn't go into detail, but she's back in his life."

"What a douche."

"Eh, in his defense, they were off when we made out. And then they started talking again, and he wasn't sure what was going to happen. He says he does like me, a lot, but things are a bit messy with the other girl, so he needs to see what happens."

"Did you tell him thanks but no thanks? Fuck off?"

"No, I politely said, 'Have a nice life,' and hung up."

"Oh, you took the high road."

"I did," she says softly. "It was so hard."

"I bet," I say, a grin pulling at my lips. I'm almost to the shop when the brown delivery truck pulls up.

"But before all that, he went on and on about how Nico is all caught up on my best friend, who is gorgeous and smart."

I giggle. "He said that?"

"Yes, and I thought it was sweet. Meanwhile, the guy I thought could have been the one...well...isn't. So, there is that."

That makes me gloomy. "Oh, you liked him, liked him?"

"Yup, and he was a sexy white man who would off piss my mom. It was going to be glorious."

I chuckle at her as the deliveryman walks up to me. "Ms. Pearce, here you go."

He hands me a signing thingy, and I sign it as I say, "Hey, my box of stuff Nico ordered me just came in. Can I call you later?"

"Oh! The Lacey's Lace stuff? If you don't like something, can I have it?"

I roll my eyes as the man places the huge box at my feet. "He ordered it for my size chest, not your Pamela Anderson, *Baywatch*-size tits."

She scoffs. "Girl, I'm going for Queen Latifah. Get it right."

I laugh as I hang up. I tuck my phone into my back pocket as I look down at the gold and black box. I'm beyond excited to open this. I pick it up and head into the shop. I closed a bit early so I could go figure things out over at the gym since we were super busy all day. I can usually gauge my dinner customers from my lunch rush. If we're popping for the day, then the night is usually very slow. I don't know why, but I'm right because no one was waiting around outside. When I get into my bedroom, I set the box down and then open it. I pause for a second and check my watch. Did Nico have a game tonight? Shit, I should know this. After a quick Google search of the IceCats schedule, I see he doesn't. Great. I hit his contact for FaceTime and set my phone up on my dresser. When his beautiful face comes on the phone, I grin.

"Hey there, gorgeous."

My heart flutters in my chest. We have spent almost every night on the phone. It's weird, but in this short time, I feel closer to Nico than I ever did to Mike. I grew up with Mike, like next-door kind of thing, but we never talked. It was all physical, all the time. But with Nico being gone, all we have is talk. To say I enjoy it is an understatement. I love it. But man, I want him home.

"Hey, whatcha doing?"

"Lying in bed. I had therapy and then tapes, and then we had to get settled into the new hotel. I am ready to be home. I miss my bed."

I make a face. "I bet. I'd hate to travel like that. The bed bug thing would freak me out."

His face turns serious. "Aviva, I shit you not. I make them come up, spray my bed, and change the sheets in front of me."

I grin. Of course he does. "Hey, I can't hate, but since I'm just a mere sub maker and nothing like a hockey god, they won't do that for me."

He gives me a look. "I bet they will when you go to Baybridge."

Oh, he knows what to say to chip at my walls. "You'd make them do that for me?"

"Yup. Consider it done."

"Aw, you've made my shitty day twice."

A perplexed look covers his gorgeous features. "Why is it shitty?"

"Dominica won't tell me who the hell paid Callie's gym bill."

He gives me a dry look. "Who the hell cares? Let it be. This is a good thing. You can focus on getting a loan for the shop, or even getting ahead on your mom's medical bills."

I shrug. "That's what Jaylin said."

"Have you talked to her about the loan? Is she still willing to do it?"

I shake my head. "I don't know. We didn't talk about it today. Apparently Kirby kind of called it off with her." He makes a face, and I raise my eyebrow. "So, you know?"

He brings his shoulders up and then his palms in a very I-don't-know way, but guilt is all over his face. "Yeah. It's messy."

"Is it?"

"Yeah, the girl he was in a long-term relationship with came up pregnant. She's saying he either stays with her or she's giving up the baby. Kirby comes from a really bad family, kind of like our fucked-up dads, but his was both parents. So he wants to try for the baby's sake. So it can have two parents. And if that doesn't work, then I don't know. His girl, she's a fucking shitshow of a disaster." He scoffs. "If you think your life is a mess, hers is worse. And she causes it."

I scrunch up my face in horror. "Good Lord."

"Yeah, but he's bummed. He liked Jaylin a lot."

"That's what she said, and she liked him."

"Sucks, but life."

"Exactly, which is why I think this thing with Callie's gym is not good."

He perks a brow. "Huh?"

"Life hates me."

"Then love life more," he says simply, and that gives me pause. "Just go with the flow."

"The flow gives me anxiety."

He chuckles. "Embrace the flow."

I roll my eyes, but he's right. Jaylin's right. Hell, even Callie is right. This is good. This can help a lot, and I really needed that load taken off me. There is just this nagging feeling in my soul that way too much good is going on. I'm actually happy. To be honest, I'm waiting for Nico to take off and/or my dad to walk in with papers suing me for custody of Callie. Or maybe I went through the bad to get to the good.

Who I am kidding? Good doesn't come easily for me.

I should take what I can get.

"Fine. I'm embracing."

"Attagirl."

I grin. "So…are you alone?"

He laughs lightly, his face breaking into a wide grin. "I am, actually. Why? Did you get my package?"

"Not the one I really want, but a really nice black and gold one," I say, moving out of the way so he can see the box. "I thought maybe I could do a little show for you? Let you see them in action."

He groans. "But I can't touch you."

"I know." I smirk. "Get you all hot and bothered so when you get home, you'll come straight for me."

He's breathless. "Aviva, I was already coming for you. You're my first stop."

"Aw. I feel special."

"You are," he says. "I can't wait. I'm gonna hold you so close when I get there."

"Yeah?"

"Yup, and I'm pretty sure I won't let go for sixteen minutes."

"Sixteen? That's odd."

"It's how many days I've been gone, and it's not nearly enough. But sixteen hours…we'll start getting sticky and shit. You know how I am."

I hold in my laughter. "I do, and I can't wait."

"Me either. Now put something on."

I flash him a sexy look as I open the box and start removing the pieces of beautiful lace. Lacey's Lace has high-quality pieces, and they're stunning. She has won so many awards for her designs and also for all the work she's done for survivors. I don't think I've ever paid this kind of money for something that will cover my ass. "Oh, Nico, it's all so gorgeous."

"I'm glad you love it."

When I pick out a strappy black number that feels like butter and looks like a million bucks, I hold it up. "I'm so putting this one on first."

"Aviva, shut up. That's my favorite one." I giggle as I start to take off my clothes. "Aw shit, I get to see you undress. Hell yeah, let me see that sweet ass."

I laugh as I turn around so all he sees is my ass. "Maybe I'd eat that ass like a damn yogurt cup."

I look over my shoulder at him, my eyes wide, and all he is doing is grinning like a cock in a henhouse. I have never heard someone say that in my life, but the image of it has me falling onto the bed, laughing.

I have never felt so damn good in my life.

CHAPTER TWENTY-TWO

ico

I'M NOT a fan of the Shark Tank.

It's loud. Super loud.

Usually I can handle the crowds, but these fans are something on a Saturday night when their team had a good run last year. They're ready for the Cup, so they need the points, and it's my job to crush those dreams. My team just has to score and take the crowd out of it. I will keep the pucks out of the net and completely ruin everyone's night except ours. I swallow hard, zoning in on my boys as they skate around while the Sharks' starting line is announced. I outline their numbers with my eyes. Memorizing who's on the ice and what their plays look like. I look up at the clock, and I wait till there are only .49 seconds until the game starts. When the number shows, I smack my stick twice on the left post, and then three times on the right. I inhale deeply, then exhale through my nose. I do this four times. I move my thumb in my glove, squeezing the stick before tapping my leg as the time expires and the puck is dropped.

Game on.

I'm ready.

I am so focused on the puck that soon the noise falls away, and all I see or hear is the puck. It's cool how this works for me. I can hear the way puck moves when it is hit. When it's slapped, I know it's gonna come in hot but with a little bit of a wiggle to it. Wrist shots are sorta silent, but they move like lightning when they come toward me. All I see is the puck, but also, I see the fucker who tries to mess with me. Everyone always wants to take an extra poke at me when they can. They hate how good I am. How I can ruin their night while lying on my back like a turtle. I can still block their shot, no matter what. I will. I'm that damn good.

Seventeen minutes have already passed, and I've blocked all nine of their shots. My boys are throwing pucks at their net with no accuracy at all. They didn't put up high shots last game, and while we won, it took the whole night to score that goal. Coach ripped into them for being too clean. He wanted grittiness. He also said that if it weren't for me, we would have lost. He's the best for stroking my ego. He and Aviva. After my shutout the other night, which she called a "shutoff," she kept saying how impressed she was by me. It made me feel way too much.

I think I've fallen for her.

But I can't think of her right now. I have a game to win. I focus in just as Chandler gets the puck. He holds it, his eyes moving like crazy as he tries to set up the play. A forward comes toward him, so he passes it out to his partner, Kurri, who holds it once more. He sends it back to Chandler, who shoots...but misses the goal completely. I don't know why he does that. He was drafted early; shouldn't he know how to hit the net by now? The puck moves up the boards and Kurri tries to stop it, but the bugger jumps over his blade. One of the forwards is in the right place at the right time, and he's off.

Coming right for me.

Bring it.

I square up, watching every single inch of his body. I can usually tell if they'll go top shelf by the positioning of their back leg. By the looks of it, this dude has no clue what he is going to do. He's coming in hot, though. I watch the puck, ready, and when he pulls his stick back, I think he's gonna slap it. What an idiot. Like I expect, he slaps it, and I block it with my blocker. Unfortunately, the damn thing rebounds right back on the asshole's stick. I guess he was hoping for that because his back leg slides, and I know he is going top shelf. When I swallow the puck with my glove, I stand up, towering over the guy as the few IceCats fans cheer.

The Sharks guy is not happy. "Fuck."

"Maybe next time," I call, and then I chuckle. "But probably not."

I mean, not to be cocky, but I know I'm that good.

* * *

I LET in two power play goals, but in my defense, our defense was sucking. I don't know what is going on with our second defense pair, but they need to get their shit together. Thankfully, our boys put up four goals, so we won. Yet, those two goals haunt me. I sit at the front of the plane, my legs stretched out toward the wall with my head hanging over the back of the seat. Usually, the front is for coaches and media, but the first row is mine. They know I don't do confined spaces, and the guys… I love them, but there is too much stimulation back there. If they aren't talking about the game, they're talking about hot chicks. And then the video games —I shudder at the thought. Way too much stimulation. Don't get me wrong, I love me a game of *Mario Kart* or even *Call of Duty*, but with the full plane, and then the lights… Yeah, it messes with me.

I exhale heavily, and when I feel someone fall into the seat beside me, I open my eyes.

Chandler is staring at me. "Hey."

"Hey."

He hooks his thumb to the back. "I think we're gonna play some cards if you want to join."

I shake my head. "I'm good. Decompressing from the game."

"I hear you," he says, nodding. He stretches out his legs. "Going to see Aviva when we land?"

"Yeah, it's late, but she wants me to come by."

"Nice. I'm ready to see Amelia and the kids."

I grin over at him. "I bet. It has to be harder being away."

His face says it all. He'd give up everything to be home with the kids and Amelia. "Yeah, but the nice thing is my mom is helping a lot. She traded me in for the kids."

I laugh. "It's weird not having her on the road."

Chandler nods because he knows I'm right. His parents used to go all over with us. He comes from some insane blue-blood money, and they do what they want, when they want. They travel with us, rent houses where we are, and enjoy life. It's awesome. Since the twins came, though, Mama and Papa Moon have not been seen. Instead, they're home with Amelia, spoiling the shit out of those babies. I find it sweet since they couldn't have kids biologically.

"Yeah, but it's nice to know that the kids and Amelia are cared for," he says. I love how happy he is. He deserves it. "Though, my mom is on my last nerve."

I laugh. "How? She's awesome."

He gives me an exasperated look. "She wants us to get a bigger house. Says the beach house isn't good enough for the kids. I mean, she's right, they don't have their own rooms, but they're little. It doesn't matter right now."

"Yeah, I can see both sides."

"Amelia says she'll do what I want, but I don't want to leave the place where we fell in love."

God, he's so mushy-gushy. "I hear you."

"I think I might build on to it instead."

"That's a good idea."

"Yeah," he says, and then he turns to look at me. "So, things are good with you and Aviva?"

"Real good," I admit.

"I thought being on the road would be hard for you. Usually you'd already have been through a few girls by now."

I would have. It's how I handle being on the road and losing, or hell, even winning. I love sex, but I guess it's different now. I don't want to jeopardize what I have at home. "Don't need them when I have my baby at home."

Chandler seems impressed. "That's awesome, dude. You seem happy."

"I am. Really."

He nods as he looks away. "Listen, I need to talk to you."

I sit up, crossing my legs. "Yeah?"

"We both know how much I love Amelia," he starts, and I just give him a dry look.

"No! You love her? I'd never suspect that."

He snorts, and I grin over at him. "Yeah, and I know we were waiting to get married so that we can have a huge shindig. But last night, we were talking on FaceTime, and I was watching her with the babies, holding them, and just looking like an angel. I decided I didn't want to wait."

"No?"

"No. So I told her I want to get married. Now."

I jerk my head back. "Did you marry her without telling anyone?"

He laughs. "No, but we decided that during our little game break, we're gonna have a small wedding on the beach."

My heart warms. "No shit."

"Yeah, and I want you to be my best man."

I swallow hard. I know I should just say yes, but I find I'm starting to sweat. I'll have to stand with no gear on in front of how many people? I know they'll probably only be looking at Amelia and Chandler, but I'll be up there. "It'll be small?"

"Yeah, my family, hers, you. Fifteen people max," he promises. "Everyone who will be there will be people you know."

He thought this through, and I swear, I don't know what I would do without this man. He's my brother, and my love for him is soul-deep. Just acknowledging that brings the guilt back. I should tell him. Right now, right here—tell him the truth. He loves me, cares for me, yet I can't. "Yeah, of course."

He cups my shoulder. "Awesome, but just a heads-up, Shelli will be there. With Aiden."

I wait for something. A feeling. Sadness, anger, resentment—anything. But nothing comes. I shrug. "That's fine. Can I bring Aviva and Callie?"

He nods eagerly. "Absolutely."

"Awesome. Yeah, I'm there for you, bro."

"Fantastic. I was worried. I know you don't do crowds."

I slowly nod as I bite my lip. "Yeah, but I'll do this crowd to watch my two favorite people tie that knot."

Chandler is excited; it's radiating off him. "We're gonna head to Barcelona after the wedding for a few days just as a mini-honeymoon."

I laugh. "No shit. Callie wants to go there."

"Really? Barcelona? That's weird."

"Has something to do with some Ed Sheeran song. I don't know. But she really wants to go. I said I'd take them in the summer. But shit, since you're going, you should take her."

He gives me a deadpan expression. "I'm gonna be banging my brand-new wife the whole time we're there, not caring for a sixteen-year-old."

I chuckle. "I didn't think of that. Maybe I'll take her since I can't get Aviva to shut the shop down."

"She won't let you."

"Why?"

"Because it's her sister, and you are the boyfriend. People don't just hand over their sisters to their boyfriends of a few months to go to foreign countries."

I shrug. "You're probably right. She's a helicopter sister, for sure," I laugh, and he smiles.

"Hey, after everything they've been through, can you blame her?"

I can't. I actually support it. I couldn't imagine. Losing her mom, having the gene for the same cancer that killed her mom and then could kill her sister. It terrifies me just thinking about it. "Maybe I can get her to go too. Share a plane."

He shoots me a look. "I wanted to bang my wife on the plane too."

"Who said you couldn't do it in the bathroom?"

He flashes me a smirk. "I forget who I'm talking to."

He holds out his hand, and I slap it, but before I can pull away, he holds it. "This look looks great on you."

"What look?"

"Relationship look."

"I gotta keep up with my brother."

He grins. "I hear that."

But I don't think he does. I don't think he knows how much he has inspired me. How much I have learned from him and how much he means to me. Which is why the guilt is eating at me from the inside for not telling him. He meets my gaze, and then he brings in his brows. "What's up? You look like you've let a puck in. And by the way, those goals weren't your fault."

I can't even smile as I nod. "I know."

"Then what's up?"

I lean toward him, and he leans in too.

"Did you cheat?"

I give him a dry look. "Fuck no. Shut up."

He lets out a long breath. "Thank God. I was nervous for a second there."

I clear my throat and then bite real hard into the inside of my cheek as I search his eyes. "I need to tell you something."

He immediately seems concerned. "You okay?"

"Yeah," I answer quickly. "I'm fine."

"Okay," he says slowly, trying to read me with his eyes. "You know you can tell me anything."

I can. Damn it, I can. "You know how I'm a bit odd about things?"

He shrugs. "Yeah, so?"

"When I was three, I was diagnosed with autism." I say it so low, I wouldn't be surprised if he couldn't hear me. "I am an autistic adult, and that's why I do the things I do. Why I can't do crowds or interviews, and apparently, I use sex as an—"

Chandler covers my shoulder with his hand, cupping it hard. "I know."

All the breath leaves my body. "What?"

His face is so kind as he nods. "I've known for a real long time. I overheard Coach talking to your therapist."

I can't breathe. "What? You did? Did anyone else?"

"No, man. It was an isolated incident, and your therapist lit into Coach for saying the word. I was the only one in there. No one else heard. I promise."

I still can't catch my breath. "So, you knew? Why didn't you say anything?"

"Because it doesn't matter," he says simply, shrugging. "You're Nico Merryweather, my best friend, my brother. Everything else doesn't matter."

I look away, closing my eyes as he moves his hand, cupping my neck. Emotion is taking over and I want to fall apart, but I probably already look pathetic.

With his voice low, Chandler whispers, "You're the best person I know. And I love you, bro. Don't ever feel like you're not the fucking awesome dude you are. Okay?"

I look back up at him, and I feel like I'm naked in front of him. He knows me. He's always known, yet he never, ever treated me differently. He's loved me for me, and I couldn't ask for a better friend. "Thanks, Chandler."

He squeezes my neck. "No need to thank me. What are brothers for?"

I never knew until I met Chandler. And now that I have him, I can't believe I went through life without him for so long.

CHAPTER TWENTY-THREE

ico

AVIVA IS WAITING for me when I pull into the parking lot of the shop.

It's almost three in the morning, but there she is, standing in the doorway. A wide grin is on her face, and I know it's all for me. I get out of the truck as she pushes the door open and comes toward me. Shit, I want to swallow her up. She's wearing a huge shirt and a pair of shorts, and she might as well be in one of those lace numbers I bought her. I reach for her, pulling her in close as our mouths connect instantly. God, she tastes just as good as I remember, maybe even better. I gather her in my arms, holding her so tight I worry she can't breathe, but I can't stop. Not seeing her like this, not being able to touch her, has been torture. But now I have her, and I refuse to let go.

Her fingers glide up my cheeks and into my hair as our kiss deepens. I squeeze her in my arms, lifting her off the ground so we're closer. Her fingers thread into my hair, the tips of her fingers digging into my scalp as she kisses me passionately. I don't even have to question if she missed me. I can taste, feel it. Man, she drives me absolutely wild. I pull back as she rests her nose against mine, breathing just as heavily as I am.

"Hi," she whispers, and I grin against her lips.

"Hey." I kiss her top lip and then her bottom. "I missed you."

"I missed you."

She leaves me breathless. "Is Callie sleeping?"

"Like a rock."

"Good." I capture her mouth once more. She wraps her legs around my waist, and I carry her into the shop, locking the door behind me. She kisses down my throat, moving my shirt over so she can kiss my chest the best she can reach. I can't go far; I need her. I lay her down on the table, and I'm about to cover her body with mine when I realize people eat here. Her legs squeeze me in closer so my hard cock presses into her. She doesn't care, so I shouldn't care.

But I care.

I lift her up, and she laughs. "What are you doing?"

"Can't do you here. People eat here."

She giggles more as she kisses up my jaw. "I can clean it. I did clean it."

"Nope," I say as I carry her into the back. I look around for a surface, but soon I'm getting overwhelmed. I can't do her on the counters because she makes food there. The floor? I think I just threw up. The wall? Yeah, wall.

I press her into the wall, pinning her with my hips while I devour her mouth. Her fingers press into my neck as she draws the kisses out of me. She pulls away, and I open-mouth kiss her down her jaw, her neck, before pulling back to yank off her shirt. She's wearing the bra I just bought her. The lace looks incredible against her soft skin, and it's making it real hard to see straight.

"Fuck, I want to rip this off you, but it's so pretty."

She arches up into me. "I want you so bad."

She doesn't need to say more. I undo her shorts and put her on her feet to yank them down as she unfastens mine. I reach into my back pocket for my wallet just as she falls to her knees, taking me in her hands. She licks up my cock, swirling that naughty tongue around my head before taking me in her mouth. I fall back into the wall, holding myself up with my palm. As she moves up and down my cock, each time taking me deeper and deeper, I feel everything getting tighter. I put the condom between my lips and grasp her hair in my hands, guiding her up and down my cock. I thrust into her mouth, pressing to the back of her throat, needing this. Needing her. She sucks me hard, sending a chill down my back.

I don't want to come here. I want to be inside her, but she has other ideas. I try to stop her, but she won't. Her lips are so thick, her tongue perfect against my hot skin. She cups my balls, squeezing them as I thrust back into her throat once more, unable to handle it. She picks up speed, her head bobbing on me just the way I love it. I feel my toes curling in my dress shoes, and there is no stopping the train that is my orgasm. I rise up on my toes, exploding into her mouth as her name leaves my lips.

She sucks me dry while she watches me, quivering under her mouth. I take in a jerky breath as I look down at her. She removes me from her mouth, kissing the head, making me jump, but that sneaky grin on her lips lets me know she did it on purpose. I reach down, taking her face in my hands before shaking my head. I pull the condom out of my mouth and wave it at her. "I had this ready."

That sneaky grin hasn't moved. "I told you I'd suck the skin off you."

Desire rolls in my gut. "Fuck if you don't make me crazy."

She stands up, wrapping her arms around my neck. "Why don't we go upstairs, where there is a sub for you? We can nap and carry on when you're ready."

I grab her ass, squeezing it hard. "I'm always ready when it comes to you."

She kisses my nose. "Then come on."

She couldn't stop me if she tried.

Her place is pitch dark when we go upstairs. She's still only in a bra and panties, while my shirt is untucked and my pants hang loosely on my hips. She grabs the sub for me and then two Cokes before we head back to her room. After she shuts the door, she holds up a finger at me. "Don't eat in my bed. I'll be right back. Let me go brush my teeth."

Thank God. I really want to kiss her some more.

My hands are full as I look around her room. It's a soft blue with gray accents. Her headboard is white, and her bed has gray sheets. I like the contrast of it. I walk over to her dresser that has a mirror attached to it and set everything down. She doesn't have much in here, just a bed, a night table, a chair, and the dresser. There is a bathroom that's attached and then a closet, but the door's closed. The box from Lacey's Lace is in the corner, while the pieces are laid out on the chaise. I open my sub as I take in all the pictures that are tucked into the sides of the mirror. They are mostly of Callie, but there are also a lot of her and her mom. The only reason I assume it's her mom is because it's like looking at an older version of Aviva. Same eyes, same smile, and same hair. Stunning.

When she comes out of the bathroom, she throws her washcloth in the laundry basket. I point to the pictures. "This is your mom?"

She comes to me, grabbing a soda and nodding. "Yup, that's her."

"She's beautiful."

"She is," she agrees, taking a long drink of her soda.

"Do you not have any other family?"

She shakes her head. "My mom's parents were older when they had her, so they passed before I was even born. We grew up with my dad's parents, but when Dad went rogue, they blamed us, saying we didn't love him enough to help him. Total bullshit, so we haven't seen or spoken to them in years."

"That's crap."

"Yup, cancer tore this family to shit," she says softly, leaning into me. I wrap my arm around her back as I take another bite of my sub. "Do you have grandparents?"

"I do. My mom's parents. Don't know my dad's."

She shakes her head. "I knew that."

"Yeah," I laugh, and she smiles up at me as she slides her hands under my shirt, holding me close.

"When do you have to leave again?"

I exhale loudly. "I have two home games, then leave for two, and then come back for two."

"Hockey plays a lot of games."

I nod. "We do."

She pouts up at me. "I don't want you to leave again. I've missed you."

I gather her in my arms. "Same here, baby."

She kisses my jaw and cuddles into my chest. "Did you have a nice flight?"

"I did," I answer, Chandler's confession heavy on my mind. "Actually, I'm gonna need your date services again."

She perks her brow as she looks up at me. "What am I, an escort?"

I laugh loudly. "My bad. No. I mean I want you to go somewhere with me."

She eyes me playfully, sending my heart into fits. "Oh, really? Where?"

"Chandler and Amelia are getting married. I'm doing the best man thing."

Aviva's face lights up. "Aw, how sweet. Where?"

"Oh, the beach by my house, actually. It's not for a month, but I need to lock you in. Make sure you don't get any other dates," I tease, and she grins.

"I'm yours."

"Damn right, you are," I say, pressing my lips to hers. She leans into the kiss, her fingers stroking my collarbone.

When she pulls back, I kiss her bottom lip before going back to my sub. "I'm jealous of the attention you're showing that sub."

I smirk. "Don't worry. I'm going between your legs next." She beams up at me as I hold her close to my side. Around my bite, I say, "They're going to Barcelona."

"Who?" she asks, drawing her brows in.

"Amelia and Chandler."

"Oh, don't tell Callie," she says dryly. "I'd never hear the end of it."

"Well, I was going to see if you wanted to go."

She shakes her head. "I can't leave the shop."

"Sure, for a weekend. Leave late Thursday, come home Sunday."

"I can't," she says simply. "This summer, I will try. I gotta get ahead."

I bite my lip. "Can I take Callie?"

She gives me a serious look. I suspected her to yell no or even snap at me, but her eyes just look so sad. "I really want to go with her."

"Then we'll wait," I say automatically. "I'm sorry. I didn't think that through."

"I know. You just want to make Callie happy."

"I do, but I want the same thing with you."

She moves her hand up to my mouth, wiping away some mayo.

"Don't be mad."

She shakes her head. "I'm not. Promise. I just really wanna go, and maybe with whoever paid Callie's gym bill, I can catch up. I actually had a great two weeks, and when I add in the IceCats money, I've been able to refill Callie's savings—" She pauses, and then she presses her lips together.

"What?"

"I forgot to tell you."

"What?" I ask, a little on edge. I don't like the look on her face. "What's wrong?"

"We went to the doctor for Callie. They said they'll do the total mastectomy if she wants it now, which is crazy because they usually want the patient to be eighteen. But I think the doctor knows Callie is freaking out."

"Wow. Is she going to do it?"

She nods. "Yeah, after competition season."

My stomach aches for her. "All right. Are you okay?"

"I just wish I could have saved her from this."

"You're doing everything to make her the best version of herself, and I really think the conference in Baybridge is gonna be great for both of you."

She slowly nods her head as she smiles up at me. "Jaylin is going to go with us."

"That's awesome. I feel dumb. I should have invited her."

She waves me off. "Don't you worry. She invited herself."

I chuckle, and then I remember something. "Did you tell her about Kirby?"

She shakes her head. "Not at all. That's not my business to tell."

"Good. Don't. He's pretty worked up about it."

"I wouldn't doubt it. That's a lot to deal with," she says, unbuttoning my shirt.

I set my sub down, and without much thought, I ask, "Do you want kids?"

She meets my gaze. "I do." She takes in a deep breath, looking a little embarrassed. "It's funny you ask, because when we went to Amelia's and I saw her feeding the babies formula, it actually made me feel better about having kids."

I raise my brow. "I'm confused."

She points to her chest. "I can't feed a baby, and I thought, how could I have a kid and not be able to give them a mother's milk? It would make me a bad mom, I thought. But Amelia couldn't, and she is an amazing mom. I hope I can be like that."

I cup her face, kissing her nose. "Boobs or not, you'll be a great mom. Look at Callie."

She curves her lips. "She is pretty wonderful."

"Perfection."

She beams up at me, covering my hand with hers. "Do you want kids?"

"I do," I admit, and I'm surprised I was so open with that statement. I've always wanted them, and having them with Aviva would be so damn cool. I'm scared that when I tell her my diagnosis, she won't want to have them with me. Not that we're doing that now. That's crazy talk, but still, just saying.

"You're so good with Carter and Hannah. I don't even know why I asked."

I shrug. "Because we're getting to know each other."

Something flashes in her eyes, and it sends desire straight to my gut. I want to know everything about this girl. The insides and outs. Every nook and cranny. I want it all. "Are you done yet?"

She then pushes my shirt and suit jacket down my arms. I allow them to fall to the floor before gathering her in my arms once more. "I can be."

"Good, because we have over two weeks to make up for."

"We absolutely do."

CHAPTER TWENTY-FOUR

ico

"How is your goal list going for the month?"

I unfold the paper that usually hangs on my fridge. I read them over and nod. "Good. I've met all of them."

Dr. Jenkins beams. "Nico, that's wonderful." She leans over and nods. "Yes. You have bounced back from those two bad games."

"Yeah, but I'm a little worried."

She leans back in her chair, recrossing her legs. She's wearing a shorter skirt than normal, with these red tights. I don't know who she's trying to impress, but it's obvious she is. "Why is that?"

I scratch the back of my head. "Aviva and I got together, and then I started playing well again. I don't think anything bad will happen. I really feel good about us. I worry that if it does, I'll go back to playing like shit, and I don't like that. It's actually giving me anxiety, and there is no reason for that."

Through her black-rimmed glasses, she eyes me. "So how do you think we can make sure that doesn't happen?"

"I don't know. That's your job."

She smiles. "Yes, but we're a team. I want to see what you want to do to make sure it doesn't happen."

I shrug. "I guess I really gotta separate my personal life and game life."

"Yes, and how?"

"Coach always says 'leave your shit at the door.'"

"I think he's right, so why don't we try that for the next couple weeks? Before you walk into the locker room, you leave everything but hockey outside. Don't think of Aviva or your mom...anything. It's only hockey. How do you feel about that?"

"I don't know," I admit. "Because I really love how Aviva makes me feel. My mom, she lifts me up before games, and I remind myself of her praise."

"Okay, praise is good, but don't think of them. Think of the praise. What I mean is, think of what they're doing—"

"I don't really do that. I'm usually focused."

"Okay," she says happily. "But what made the last time different?"

I press my lips together. "I don't know. I've never had that happen to me before, and even with all the shit that happened with Shelli, I didn't get like that. I played my best hockey. I mean, we were only one goal away from winning the Cup against the fuckbag who stole her from me."

I know she wants to shoot me an exasperated look. She's a professional, though. "He didn't steal her, remember?"

I roll my eyes. I'm not a professional. "Whatever. She wanted him, not me. It's cool though, 'cause I wouldn't have been able to be with Aviva if it had worked out with Shelli."

She nods. "Do you think of Shelli still?"

"No, not really," I admit. "Sometimes things will remind me of her, but overall, no. Chandler is getting married, and she's coming in for the wedding since he's marrying her cousin, and I didn't even care. I only cared if Aviva would be my date. Even the fuckbag is coming, and I don't care."

"You know you have to stop calling him that."

I scrunch up my face. "Why?"

"Because if he's a fuckbag, you still care about the situation."

"No, I don't. I don't hate him for taking Shelli. I hate him because he's a fuckbag."

She doesn't believe me. "Do you truly think that?"

Why is this so exhausting? "Fine, maybe I do because she chose him. But it doesn't matter. Aiden. There. Or hell, Brooks. I can call him Brooks."

She doesn't seem convinced, but why are we even speaking of that guy? They don't matter. "Let's move on," she sighs.

"Thank God."

Her gaze seems annoyed, but hey, she signed up for this. I know they pay her good money to deal with me. "Do you feel maybe it was a fluke? The bad games?"

I move in my seat, trying to readjust. "Could be. But I know I wasn't focused."

"Okay, so we've learned from that?"

"Yeah."

"Good. Let's move on," she says, tapping her pen to my folder. It probably reads that I'm a huge asshole. "So, things are going well with Aviva?"

"Yes," I say, and I look her in the eye. "Really good. I love every second with her, and we have a blast."

"Has there been anything that you second-guessed yourself about or felt you shouldn't have said?"

I laugh. "I say a lot of things, but she goes with it."

A small smile pulls at her lips.

"But not really. Well, I assumed she would let me take her sister to Barcelona, but Chandler told me she wouldn't. I didn't really see anything wrong with it, but apparently it's weird. Plus, Aviva wants to go."

"Did that upset you?"

I shake my head. "No, I kind of felt bad. I didn't mean to hurt her feelings."

"You hurt her feelings?"

"I think so, by trying to leave her out."

"And you realized that?"

I nod. "I did, actually, which now surprises me." I kind of feel proud of myself.

She grins. "I think that's the first social cue you've picked up on since we've been working together. I'm very proud of you, Nico."

I grin back at her. "It's easy with her, if that makes sense. I try to be in tune. I want her to be happy."

"That's wonderful, Nico," she says softly. "Have you told her about your diagnosis?"

I let my head drop back. How'd I know she was going to ask that? "No, but I did tell Chandler."

I sit up, and she looks as if she won the lottery. "You did?"

"I did," I say on an exhale. "He already knew. He overheard it a while back."

"And he never said anything?"

"Nope. He says it doesn't matter." Still, it doesn't seem real to me. It all seems like a dream. I wish everyone would react like Chandler and Callie have, but I know they won't. Which is why I haven't told Aviva.

"That's fantastic. I'm glad that worked out," she says, and she's marking some stuff down. "Can we create our next goal sheet to have 'Tell Aviva' as goal one?"

Why does my throat hurt? "I don't know if I'm ready for that."

"Why is that?"

"I don't know. It puts this fire in the pit of my stomach. We were talking a couple weeks ago, and we got on the subject of wanting kids. And all I could think was would she want them with me if she knew?"

"Kids? That was fast."

I shrug. "I don't think so. It was in passing. Do you want kids? And she asked me. It wasn't a big deal."

"It didn't freak you out?"

"No," I say simply. "Except when I realized, what if she doesn't want to have them with me because our child could have autism and it could be worse?"

She exhales heavily. "Okay, that one sentence brings up a lot of questions for me, but we're running out of time."

"What?" I ask, needing to know. "We can go over."

She meets my gaze, probably surprised since I'm almost always running for the door. "Okay. When you thought of having kids before, did your autism worry you?"

I shake my head. "No."

"So, why now?"

I think that over. "I think maybe it's because I don't want to lose Aviva, and my diagnosis could make me lose her."

"Nico, she is a breast cancer survivor. Do you think she's thinking you wouldn't want to have a baby with her because the same thing could happen to your daughter?"

I think about that for a moment and then nod. "Actually, she probably is."

She smiles. "Okay, that doesn't help."

I laugh. "I get it. I shouldn't fear the future. I should embrace it."

"Absolutely." She holds my gaze. "I come from a long line of alcoholics, and I broke that chain, but that doesn't mean my children won't have it as a vice. But you better believe I'm gonna have a baby, and I will love that baby no matter what. The same goes for you and, I'm sure, Aviva."

Dr. Jenkins has never spoken about herself. I nod slowly. "Okay."

Her eyes haven't left mine, and it's making me itch. It's almost like she's challenging me to look away, and that always makes me uncomfortable. "Next, Nico, do you feel you love Aviva?"

Talk about my heart skipping a beat. And like I always do, I speak without thinking. "I do."

"Do you think she loves you?"

"I think she cares deeply for what I let her see."

She nods thoughtfully. "Exactly. How can she love all of you if you don't show her? She's shown you. Now show her."

I press my lips together. I want to agree, I want to say I'll do it, but I don't see that happening anytime soon. "Maybe after she meets my mom."

Her eyes widen. "Your mom is coming to town?"

I want to laugh. "Yup. She can't wait to meet you."

She groans. "I might be sick that day."

I laugh now, and she shakes her head. "Okay, before you go, though, how do you feel about the gala tonight?"

Man, I was doing well not thinking about that damn gala. Within seconds, my flight sense is screaming. I have been trying to prepare for this stupid gala for the last three weeks, but I am freaking the fuck out. I don't want to go. I don't care how hot my girl looks in the dress she got or that she promised not to wear panties—I don't want to go.

"My chest hurts thinking about it."

She nods. "Remember to breathe. Hold Aviva's hand. Take it easy. Don't throw yourself into it. Ease into it."

I try to swallow past the lump in my throat, but it's basically suffocating me.

"It will be okay. It's such a small event. Only players, with their dates, staff, and the donors. This is a wonderful event for you to try. You will be okay, and if not, then leave. But I truly want you to try for at least thirty minutes."

My skin feels clammy. "Okay."

"And remember, no alcohol. You do not need a vice."

"Damn it, I forgot that part," I say, groaning loudly.

"You can do it. I know you can. You're so ready. You're doing so great, Nico."

I don't think I am, but her encouragement makes me feel a little better. Like, two percent better.

"Does Aviva know that this is a big deal?"

I shake my head. "I told her I'm freaking out, but she doesn't know that I may not make it past the thirty minutes."

"Tell her. Please."

Yeah, because that's gonna be easy.

Hey, Aviva, I probably won't make it past the thirty minutes because right now, I'd rather rip off my left nut than go.

Damn it, the thought of all those people. Standing around me, wanting to make small talk. Able to touch me and look at me without my gear.

Shit. I don't think I'm gonna make it.

* * *

MY HANDS ARE SHAKING against the steering wheel as I head to get Aviva. We have to be there at seven and it's already ten minutes till, and I'm driving like a turtle. I don't want to go. It's that simple. To make matters worse, my mom decided to call and talk me to death.

"Why are you being so short with me?"

I want to groan loudly, but she wouldn't appreciate that. Especially since she's been dealing with it basically since I was born. I've always been a pain in the ass. "I have that gala tonight, and Dr. Jenkins says I can't drink."

"Oh," she says softly. "I forgot that was tonight. I have it written down, but I forgot."

"It's fine."

"You can do this, Nicolas. I promise. I have noticed such huge progress since you've been with this new therapist."

"I thought you hated her."

"I do. She sucks, but you're doing great."

"Because that makes sense."

"Don't question me," she says sternly. "Listen, you know you have this."

"Eh, that's spotty," I say with my face all twisted in annoyance, fear, and a wee bit of anger. I don't know why I have to do this. Why can't I be the player who just doesn't do shit but win hockey games? I think I'm doing what I'm paid for. "Aviva is excited, though."

"Is she? Send me pictures."

"I will." I probably won't, though. "Are you bringing Mimi and Papa when you come?"

"I am."

"Fantastic, Aviva will get to meet all of my crazy family."

She chuckles happily. "For as much as you talk about her and her sister, I'm sure we'll all love her."

"Are you going to give her the third degree?"

"Yes, and this could all be done before I arrive if you'd give me her number."

I roll my eyes. "I wouldn't subject her to that. I want her to like me."

"How could she not? You're absolutely perfect."

I love my mom. "Thanks, Mom."

"It's the truth. You know I love you more than anything in this world."

"I know."

"And if a woman is going to come in and replace me—"

"No one can replace you," I say quickly. "Aviva wouldn't even try."

She pauses. I want to say I feel better, but I don't. I'm terrified. I swallow hard as I turn onto Aviva's street.

"I'm very excited to meet her, and I hope I am able to go watch Callie do flips and stuff."

"Callie's pretty badass. Great girl."

"It pleases me that you care for her. It has to be hard to raise a young girl and date."

I scoff. "I think I'm the first boyfriend Aviva has had since she lost her mom."

"Because who can say no to you!"

"Aviva. She can say no. She did…a lot," I laugh, and my mom gushes.

"I love her already."

My laughter subsides as I pull into the parking lot. "Hey, make sure before you come, everything is taken care of on your end."

"It will be. My lawyer is doing everything we ask and is also handling the will."

My nerves are making my words come out jerky, and I wish I could focus on what she is saying, but I'm all kinds of screwed up. "Just make sure everything is done and right. Send my lawyer the paperwork."

"Please."

"Please. I'm sorry. I'm freaking out."

"You're going to be fine."

I just wish I believed her.

CHAPTER TWENTY-FIVE

viva

"I'll Be There for You" by the Rembrandts is blasting through the shop.

Even though I'm wearing a very expensive—and completely out of my comfort zone—evening gown, I help Callie prep for tomorrow as we sing at the top of our lungs. She's actually a decent singer; then again, there's not really much Callie isn't good at. When I asked her to prep for tomorrow after Nico invited me to go to this gala with him, I was nervous to hand over the reins. I'm discovering, though, Callie is a lot like me. She is smart and quick on her feet. I'm very proud of the woman she is becoming.

"I told Amelia about the surgery."

I glance back over at her as I pull the bread out of the proofer. "What did she say?"

"She said she understood but that I can't get lazy on her."

"Well, of course not," I say, putting in the next batch. "You know we can just do the mastectomy now and then do the reconstruction and augmentation when you're older."

She shakes her head. "No, I'll be like you and put it off."

She's got me there. I shift uncomfortably in my bra. I wish I'd had an augmentation now; a real set of breasts would have given me better options for a dress. Also, a lot more confidence. Since I don't have cleavage, I went with a sparkly, midnight-blue halter-top gown that shows all of my back. I was kind of nervous about my little bit of back fat, but Nico promised the dress looked great on me. He says he sees no back fat, but I know it lives there. I left my hair down in big, wide curls with a small braid around the crown of my head. Callie did my makeup all classy-like, with a dark red lip. With a pair of strappy-backed heels, I feel like I look sexy, and I actually feel somewhat sexy. I just hope Nico thinks so.

"Whatever you want," I answer as I move to get another batch of bread going. "I just don't want you out of the gym long."

"I know. I don't either."

"And I'll be pissed if you pop a boob."

She snorts. "Me too!"

She moves past me to grab the big stack of onions. I really should move away. I don't want to smell like onions when Nico gets here. "So, things with Nico are going very well."

I nod as I side-eye her. "They are."

"How long has it been?"

"Almost two months now."

She gushes, "I'm just so happy for you two. You're, like, the best together. I like him way more than Mike."

"Me too," I agree. I feel all gooey inside.

Things have been great with Nico. I've never had a man do everything to spend time with me. He'll sit in the shop just so he can talk to me between customers. He keeps me laughing all the time, and we have a great time. He went to Callie's gym practices twice last week, and while he didn't want to sit in the crowd, standing by the wall with him was worth the numb legs at the end. He's just great, really great, and I'm so damn happy.

"Do you love him?" she asks, and I laugh loudly.

"Callie, I don't know. It's still early. You can't tell this early."

"Yes, you can," she says quickly. "And you do. You're just hiding behind your walls."

She might not be wrong, but I don't want to acknowledge what I am feeling yet. I don't want my mind to fuck with what we have. I could fall, completely and wholeheartedly, for Nico, but the fear that he can't fall for me is there. I don't want to keep beating a dead horse, but he could do so much better than me. So much. Yet he's here almost every day, and when he's not, my phone is blowing up.

It gives me some inconceivable feels.

"Well, I love him. He could be my brother-in-law any day," she says, and I smile, my heart bursting in my chest.

"He'd love that."

"Yeah, he's great. Really, I love him for how much happier you are now. Who knew all you needed was for someone to get in your pants?"

For the love of God. "Calliope, come on!"

She snorts with laughter just as the door opens and in comes my super-hot date. He's wearing a black tux with pants hemmed to the ankles to show off his fancy blue suede shoes. Every time I see them, I want to sing the song. I don't want to sing now, though. Not that I can with my tongue hanging out of my mouth. With his hair slicked back, Nico is one fine man.

And he is all mine.

"Hey!" I call to him, excited to see him. When he comes in closer, though, I notice his body language. He's not happy, more nervous. I come around the counter and go to him. "Hey, you okay?"

He shakes his head. "Nope. Don't want to go." I thread our fingers together as he comes down for a kiss. "You look incredible, babe."

I want to swoon, but I'm worried about him. "We don't have to go."

"I do," he says on an exhale. "They're making me."

I feel awful for him, but before I can try to help, Callie says, "Nico, you're a rock star. You got this."

He doesn't seem convinced. "I don't know about that."

"You do. It's a party. Just think of everyone as Vee, Chandler, Amelia, and me. You got this."

He exhales hard, looking down at me. "I could just stare at you."

My heart warms. "You could. I won't leave your side, even if I've got to pee."

"Man, that's real right there. She always has to pee," Callie teases, and thankfully, finally, he smiles the smile I adore.

I squeeze his hand. "We'll have fun."

He shrugs. "I don't know. But just a warning, I don't know how long I'll last, and I don't know how I'll act. This is a first for me."

I'm so confused. "You don't go to parties?"

"Not without a lot of alcohol, and my therapist is not letting me drink."

I agree with his therapist. "That's good. You don't need to drink."

"I beg to differ. It's how I get through shit like this."

"We got this," I say once more, kissing his jaw. "Come on, let's go."

He hesitates, but then he lets out a sigh. "Fine."

Well, I wasn't nervous before, but now I am.

* * *

THE GALA for the IceCats foundation is in a ritzy hotel ballroom. I've never been to this hotel, but from the outside, I can tell it is fancy. Nico didn't speak one word the whole way here, and I felt he needed a moment, so I didn't speak either, just listened to the music. But when we come to a stop at the valet and my door opens, I glance over at him. He's holding the steering wheel with white knuckles, and I don't know if he'll get out of the truck. I hold up my finger to the valet. "One second, please."

I pull my door shut and then reach out to Nico, covering his hand with mine. "Nico, it's okay. One thing at a time."

He swallows hard. "Just let me be for a second."

I pull my hand away and lean back in my seat. Seconds turn into minutes, and when I notice the line behind us, I clear my throat. "Nico—"

"Just a fucking minute."

Okay then. I press my lips together because I really want to snap back at him. I know that he is struggling with this, though, so I will be patient. Finally, and without a word, he throws open his door and gets out.

"Okay," I drawl as I pick up my bag, but before I can grab the door handle, it's open and Nico is standing there.

He holds out his hand to me, and I take it. He isn't looking at me, though. He's looking around us. When my feet hit the ground, he wraps his arms around me, and I can feel him shaking. What in the world is causing this? I did some research, and OCD can trigger this kind of reaction, not being able to control the situation. But I worry it's more. I want to ask. Man, I want to ask, but I feel that's something he should tell me.

As we walk toward the entrance, his body is rock hard, and I see the sweat dripping down his neck. I'm really starting to get nervous. "I'm glad you asked me to come."

"Yeah," he says sharply, and I bite the inside of my cheek. He's never this abrupt with me, and I don't like it one bit.

I try to ignore it though as we head toward the ballroom. When we enter, I'm amazed by how gorgeous everything is. The team's colors, red and silver, cover every inch of the place. Big white flower arrangements line the tables, and a huge chandelier hangs from the ceiling. It's stunning in here.

"Wow."

"What?"

I look up and hate how taut his jaw is and how wild his eyes are. I want my carefree, fun Nico, and it kills me that I can't fix whatever he is feeling inside. I reach up and press my hand into his chest. "Look how beautiful it is."

"All I see is people."

It's a good two hundred people, and I can tell it bothers him. "Hey."

He doesn't look at me. "What?"

"Nico."

Finally, he does, and I smile. "I'm right here."

He looks away. "You just don't understand."

"Then help me to. What can I do?"

"Nothing," he says but not as sharply as before. "It's my burden."

"Let it be mine. Let me help."

He sighs deeply. "Unless you can get into my head and make these fucked-up feelings and the need to run go away, there is nothing you can do," he bites back, and my heart hurts for him.

"Hey, bro!" I look up just as Kirby comes toward us.

Nico slaps hands with him, but it's not a fluid motion. He's forcing himself. "Hey, what's up?"

"Nothing much. This is my girl, Lilly."

I look to the bleach-blonde woman standing beside Kirby. She's gorgeous, but she's not Jaylin. She doesn't look like a mess; she looks like a beauty queen.

Nico nods to her. "Nice to meet you. This is my girlfriend, Aviva."

She grins at me. "What a neat name!"

"Thanks," I say with a curt smile.

"What does it mean?"

No one has ever asked me that. "It actually means springtime. I was born in the spring, and my mom was all about meanings."

"That's so cool."

"Thanks."

"You want a drink?" Kirby asks Nico, but he shakes his head.

"I'm not drinking tonight."

Kirby's brow shoots up. "Really? You always drink when we go out."

"I'm good," he says, and then he looks past Kirby and Lilly. "Excuse us."

He takes my hand and guides me away. When I see that we're heading toward Chandler and Amelia, I pray maybe they can help him calm down. Chandler's eyes widen a bit when he sees us.

"Hey, guys," he calls, and Amelia walks over to me, hugging me tightly. I watch as Chandler pulls Nico to the side. I try to ignore them, but I really want to know what he is saying.

To distract myself, I gush over Amelia. "How you are so gorgeous and skinny after twins is unfair to us mere mortals who eat cake and blow up."

She scoffs. "Please, Aviva, I'd kill for those curves. Your ass is so damn round."

I grin. "Thank God for Kim Kardashian."

"Right?" she laughs, holding my wrist. "You look beautiful tonight. I love this dress. Where did you get it?"

"Macy's. Nico picked it out."

She beams. "Of course he did. I've never seen him doing that kind of thing before. But with you, it's different. He is really into you. It's so sweet."

I bite my lip as I search her eyes. "He's not doing well tonight."

Amelia shakes her head. "No, he won't be. Please be patient with him. He doesn't do crowds."

I start to ask why, and I know that's shitty of me, but I need to know. Before I can, though, Nico takes my waist in his hand and pulls me close to him. He kisses my temple and then moves his nose to my ear. He stays like that for a minute, breathing me in, and my heart is pounding. I don't know what to do. I turn my face to press my lips to his. "You okay?"

He nods, though I know he's lying. "Sure."

When "River" by Leon Bridges starts to play, I slide my nose along his. "Will you dance with me?"

Something changes in his eyes, and then he nods. I back away from him, pulling him by his hand to bring him to the dance floor where no one is dancing. I love this song, and when I first heard it, I wanted to dance with Nico to it. I pull him toward me, and he grins as he gathers me in his arms. His hands rest at the small of my back as my hands press into his chest. I lay my chin on my hands, looking up into his beautiful brown eyes, and all my anxieties wash away. He leans his head down, pressing his forehead into mine, and slowly but surely, the cadence of his heart slows down.

I want to cry in relief. "Feeling better?"

His eyes fall shut as his nose touches mine. "So much."

"What did you talk to Chandler about?"

Nico opens his eyes, meeting my gaze. "He told me to calm down and do what makes me happy. Ignore everything around me but that one thing that makes me happy." He kisses my nose. "So, I wrapped my arms around you and kissed my favorite spot."

As we sway to the music, I can't stop staring into his eyes. They're so beautiful, so perfect. I am falling for this complicated, wild man.

And I want to believe it's okay.

I want to believe it's for the best.

But what if it's not?

CHAPTER TWENTY-SIX

viva

After a weird midafternoon rush and celebrating with Callie about her A in math—thank you, Nico Merryweather—I reach for my laptop. I have a stack of mail I need to look through, but after last night, I'm worried about Nico. Since I like to know what I am walking into, I find myself on WebMD a lot. When I get to the doctor and they tell me it's only a rash, I've already convinced myself it's cancer, so I'm good. Same thing here. I figure out what I think is ailing Nico, he tells me something that doesn't even come close, and boom! Things are great. I just need somewhere to start.

I think it's a phobia, but I don't know. It made me so nervous. Nico didn't eat, he didn't talk, and when people tried to talk to him, other than Chandler or me, I felt as if I had to save him. I learned so much about why you should make a donation if you're a business owner that now I feel like I need to start donating. Problem is, I would probably qualify for a donation myself. I was stricken with worry for Nico, but I learned a lot from those amazing businesspeople, and I made some contacts. I didn't have fun, though; I was too concerned about Nico. To make matters worse, he didn't even come in or invite me over at the end of the night. He went home, and it killed me to see him drive away.

In the Google search bar, I type in "phobias." For the next hour, I read every single phobia known to man between making subs and answering phone calls. I search levels of anxiety, and somehow, I find myself reading a piece about depression, which is a huge mistake because then I start diagnosing myself. I quickly click away from that, and just as I'm about to type "sensory issues," Callie comes up beside me.

"Why are you searching sensory things?"

"I'm worried about Nico," I say, but before I can hit enter, Callie turns the computer around to herself. "Hey!"

"Hey back," she laughs, but I notice her jaw is a little taut. "I need to look up some stuff for school before I head over to the gym. You can wait. Plus, if you're worried about Nico, ask Nico. It's not like he wouldn't answer you."

I put my hands on my hips. "I don't like the way you just take things from me."

She shrugs. "Hey, you're the one who claims me."

I lean over, kissing her cheek. "Always will, too, you asshole."

She giggles as I reach for the stack of envelopes. "But for real, what are you worried about?"

I start to look through the weekly coupons. "He was so off last night. He didn't eat. He didn't speak. He was just there. I could feel the fear coming off him in waves. He told me he didn't think we'd stay the whole night, but we did, and honestly, I think it was because of Chandler. He has a way of speaking to Nico."

"Made you jealous?"

"So damn much," I admit as I tear out a coupon for toothpaste. We always run out of toothpaste since Callie uses it on the rips on her hands from the gym. Crazy person. "But it bothered me. I mean, I know there is something wrong—"

"No, there isn't," she snaps, and when I look over at her, she's glaring at me.

"O…kay. No need to get defensive. I'm the one dating him."

"There is nothing wrong with him. And you definitely can't be like, 'Hey Nico, what's wrong with you?' That's shitty as hell."

My jaw falls open a bit. "Whoa." I hold up my palms to her. "I am well aware of how to speak to people, and what is up with the language?"

She slams the computer shut. "I don't want you saying or thinking there is something wrong with him just because he doesn't handle things like we do. He's different but in no way wrong!"

Tears are gathering in her eyes, and I'm truly so confused, I don't know what to say. "Callie, relax—"

"For real! Promise me you won't use that phrasing with him."

"I won't."

She storms out, taking my computer with her, and I'm left totally baffled. What the hell just happened? I shake my head and go back to my mail. Hormones, man, they're out to get me. I don't know if I'll make it with her. Holy Grilled Cheese Jesus.

When I come to an envelope from the medical billing company that holds my mom's account, I draw in my brows so much, they practically touch. Before I open it, I think real hard. I sent in that payment. Yeah. Yeah, I did. I tear the envelope open, praying it's only a statement and not another bill. I pull out the letter, and my check falls out. Now, I feel not only my brows touching but my whole face folding in. What in the hell? I look at my uncashed check and then quickly open the letter.

Ms. Pearce,

Your check, #2809, was not cashed, as your account was paid in full on the ninth of the month. We thank you for paying off your account sooner than we had discussed, and we are returning your check to you so you can destroy it. We wish you well.

Account #18083: PAID IN FULL. ACCOUNT CLOSED.

. . .

I THINK I'm having a stroke. My heart is in my throat, closing my airway and suffocating me. My mouth is dry, and soon, my vision is blurry.

"What in the ever-loving fuck!"

"What? I live here."

I glance at Callie, and she's still clutching my laptop while glaring at me. I turn the letter toward her, crumpling it with my hand. "The account is paid in full."

She looks at me like I've lost my mind. "I need more than that."

"Mom's bill. Paid." I'm hyperventilating. I lean on the counter as she snatches the paper from me, and when I hear her gasp, I assume she got to the paid in full part. I keep blinking, trying to make sense of how this happened. After I recover…somewhat, I stand up straight and pull my phone out of my pocket. I dial the company's number and, when they answer, demand to know who made the payment. Callie watches as I yell into the phone. "I need to know who paid this."

"Ma'am, it says the account was paid in full with cash."

"Cash!" I screech. "Who in the hell has $300,000 lying around? I sure as fuck don't!"

"Ma'am, I don't know. We took the money and applied it to the account they requested."

"Who was it?" I roar. "I want a name."

I hear typing, and I just know the lady is about to hang up on me. "There was no name left."

Why do people just take money without getting a fucking name?

I slam my phone down, and before I slam my head too, I make sure I didn't crack the screen of my phone. One of these days, I will, and then I'll be really screwed. Or probably not… My fairy godmother from Walt Disney World will just buy me a new one! Or hell, Santa will bring me one. Easter Bunny might have one up his ass! "What the hell is happening?"

"I mean—"

"No, ma'am. I don't want you to be all 'this is great' or a 'this is a blessing.' This kind of shit does not happen!"

Callie's eyes widen, and slowly she shuts her mouth, looking away. I don't snap at her often, but right now, I can't help it.

"I need to know who is doing this."

The door opens, and Callie turns just as I cut my eyes to the entrance. "Oh, you've got to be fucking kidding me." My sperm donor crosses his arms over his chest, and I let my head drop to the side while staring at Callie. She looks back at me, and I hold out my hand to him. "See? Do you see?"

Without being asked, Callie heads toward the back, but I know she's not gone. She's within earshot to hear everything since she's a spy disguised as a gymnast. Hell, I might as well send her out to investigate; she could figure out who is sending this money.

"Listen, I don't have time for this—"

He holds up his palms. "Just want to talk."

I exhale very dramatically. I don't want to talk. "What?"

I hadn't noticed he was holding a manila folder until he hands it to me. "Here."

I take it, and my hands are shaking. Here it is. The papers that take Callie from me. I open the folder reluctantly as he says, "I talked to Callie a couple days ago."

My eyes widen, and I'm about to fly off the handle when Callie's voice comes from the back. "I didn't tell you because I didn't want you to kill me."

I close my eyes to keep in the tears. I can't lose her. I take a few cleansing breaths before I reopen my eyes to focus on the paperwork.

"I'm leaving town for good this weekend, and I asked if she wanted to go. She told me no—she wouldn't and couldn't leave you."

I stop reading to meet his pain-filled eyes. He looks clean and sober, and that surprises me.

"I haven't done right by her or you since losing Willow, and I apologize for that. There is nothing here for me anymore. I've realized that, and all I do is hurt you two. So, I'm leaving, and those are the papers to make it official that I'm not Callie's dad anymore. She's better off as yours than she ever was being mine. She's the one who said that. She's the one who said if I wanted to apologize, this was how to do it."

Talk about emotional overload. A sob leaves my throat, and I bend over, pressing my hands into my knees as I try to draw in breaths. This can't be happening. Is it real? I look up, and he's still standing there, watching me with no emotion whatsoever. I want to think this man loved me, us, at one time, but it's hard to believe he did. Ever. I feel Callie come up beside me, wrapping her arms around me, and I cuddle her hard into my chest. I cup the back of her head, holding her as I cry.

"What the fuck?" The deep, throaty sound of Nico's voice makes me look up quickly. He's staring at my dad as if he will rip his head off without notice, but then he comes over to me, wrapping his arms around Callie and me. "Are you okay? What happened? I'll kill him if he did—"

"We're fine," I somehow get out, and he studies us. He looks us over, and I continue to shake my head. "I promise. We're fine."

He looks back at my dad, and I follow with my gaze, but my dad isn't there.

He is gone.

And hopefully forever.

* * *

JAYLIN STANDS AT MY COUNTER, looking over the paperwork as I pace angrily in front of her. Nico is sitting on a barstool watching me and probably thinking I'm a crazy person.

"This is insane. All of it. I mean, I'm ecstatic to have that man out of our lives and not having to worry about him stealing my money or Callie, but come on. Insane, right?"

Jaylin doesn't look up at me. Instead, her eyes move over the paperwork as she nods. "Callie asked for this?"

"She said she told him this was the way he could apologize to us for treating us like garbage."

She looks up at me through her lashes and seems impressed. "Did she now?"

"Yeah." I want to take great pride in that, but there is a lot going on right now.

Later, I'll be proud and happy that my sister chose me over a drug addict.

I'm anxious out of my mind, so I keep pacing. The paperwork could be bogus, and he could be using it as a way to get us to beg him to stay. Not that it would happen, but I don't know, it's a theory. I feel like I have to keep moving. My whole body is shaking.

"Aviva, it's okay. No matter what, Callie loves you," Nico reminds me.

"I know, and I swear, I'm good with that. But I don't trust him. You know how he is. All those times he stole from me, all those times he threatened to take Callie from me, how he blamed me for my mother's death..."

"'Cause you are cancer," Jaylin says sarcastically, and I hold out my palms to her.

"Exactly!"

"I know," Nico says, reaching for me. And of course, I go to him. He draws me between his legs, kissing my temple before he wraps his arms around me tightly. "I don't trust him either, but I've got you and Callie. Jaylin and I won't let anything happen to you two."

Jaylin continues to read as she nods. I look back at Nico, cupping his jaw in my hand. "Thanks."

"Listen, I don't want you two staying here tonight. Since the shop is closed tomorrow anyway, come stay with me. You and Callie can stay in my room, and I'll sleep on the couch."

My breath catches. "I can't kick you out of your room."

"I'm kicking myself out. Clearly I should have put furniture in my guest room. But I need to break in my couch. I don't even sit on it."

I smile. "You'd do that for me?"

He strokes my cheek. "I'd do anything for you."

I lean in, pressing my mouth to his. He eagerly accepts my kiss and basically steals my breath. When Jaylin clears her throat, I pull away, looking back at her.

I can't read her face, but I know I'm okay. No matter what, like Nico said, they have my back. I'm strong. I've got this. But still, I squeak when I ask, "What?"

"The papers are legit. A cheap, shitty lawyer downtown did it, but they're legit. He's relinquished his rights to Callie, giving them solely to you."

I almost faint, I feel it, but Nico's arms tighten around me, holding me close to his chest.

"It's all real, Vee. She's yours if you want her. I can get the paperwork started."

My lips quiver and I nod. "Yes. Please."

"I thought you'd say that, so I'll get that in the works. It shouldn't take too long."

I wipe away a tear. "Can we make sure she names her first child after me?"

Jaylin snorts as Nico chuckles against my jaw. "Nope. She's naming it after me. My name goes both ways," she says with a wink. "Like I did in college."

I laugh out loud as Nico whistles, impressed. With a grin on her face, she picks up her phone, typing something, and then looks up at me. "As for your mom's account, there is no paper trail whatsoever. Whoever did it wanted to make sure you didn't know. No contact info, nothing. Just the money, to the cent, was deposited." She holds out her hands, dropping her phone. "I couldn't find who did it if I wanted."

"Can you usually find out?"

Jaylin looks at Nico, a smirk on her face. "I can do anything. I'm that good."

He nods. "I've always liked you."

She grins as her gaze meets mine. "I won't stop looking, but... I mean, I know you don't want to hear this, but it's not a bad thing. It's actually a great thing. Imagine how much you'll be able to save now. If you think about—"

"I know, it's a blessing," I say dryly, and she laughs.

"Please don't go around saying it like that. People will think you're ungrateful."

"I didn't want it! I can pay my own damn bills."

She gathers her things. "Well, you don't have that one anymore." She holds up the folder. "I'm taking this with me. I'll call you as soon as I know a timeline. And if you do get a call from your fairy godmother, let her know I'm in serious need of a dude like Nico but a whole lot whiter."

Nico scoffs. "I'm Canadian."

"That *is* pretty white," she teases with a wink, and I lean into him.

"Love you," I tell her.

Her loving gaze meets mine. "You too."

She goes out the door, shutting it behind her, and I sigh deeply as Nico glides his lips along my jaw. "Are you okay?"

"I am. Just a little overwhelmed."

"I can tell." He kisses my cheek. "Anything I can do to help?"

"I like where we are right now."

"Me too."

I cuddle into him, closing my eyes. "How do you feel today?"

"Fine? Why?"

"After last night—"

He quickly shakes his head, holding me closer as if to keep me from asking. "Oh no, I'm fine. Last night was nothing. Let's forget that."

I take in a deep breath, and the words are right there.

Tell me why you acted like that.

But I can't right now. I don't know if it will start a fight, and where I am right now, deep in his arms, protected from everything, is right where I want to be.

Everything else can't matter.

Or I'll ruin it.

CHAPTER TWENTY-SEVEN

ico

Callie is highly upset.

"It's unfair!" she complains from the back seat. "Amelia gets to go to Barcelona, and I want to go to Barcelona! She is going zip-lining, and she gets to dance in the streets. I am so very jealous."

If I weren't a little nervous, I would tease her. Thankfully, Aviva has it covered. "Oh no, are you? I couldn't tell."

"It's not even fair, Vee! She gets to go, leaving me to train by myself while knowing she's in the one place I want to go. She wouldn't even have known it existed if it weren't for me!"

"Yes, because Barcelona didn't exist until Ed Sheeran sang about it," she says sarcastically, and I chuckle as she strokes her thumb along my palm.

"Exactly!"

Aviva glances over at me, annoyed, and I smile. I can tell she's nervous about meeting my family, but she has nothing to worry about. They'll love her, and they'll absolutely adore Callie. I've been worried about her since the whole thing with her dad happened, but like Jaylin said, it was handled quickly. Callie is legally Aviva's now, and it thrills me as much as it thrills her. Callie hasn't known it any other way, so she's just being Callie. Which, right now, means driving us crazy about Barcelona.

"We can go. Like, with them. She said Chandler said we can go as long as we don't talk to them. I am totally okay with that."

I snort. "Chandler would be the main one talking to us."

"Right?" Aviva laughs, and I bring her hand to my lips. "That's enough, Callie. Let it go. We aren't going yet, but maybe we can get some cool suggestions from them."

I hear a loud and very dramatic sigh before Callie mutters, "Fine."

"Don't act like that in front of Nico's family. We want them to like us."

I give her a side-eye as Callie says, "Who cares if they don't like us? Nico does."

"Motherf—" Aviva mutters, and I laugh. "Calliope, don't make me kill you."

"I think you're supposed to ground me before you jump to murder. I think there is, like, a stepladder with the whole parenting thing."

Aviva turns in her seat. "Are you trying to piss me off?"

"I want to go to Barcelona!"

I look in the mirror. "Are you on your period? You're being a whiny brat."

Callie snaps her mouth shut, but Aviva points at me. "Yes, what he said."

"I hate you two," she mutters, and I reject that.

"That's untrue. You love us. You want to hang with us and make cake and watch TV and all the other things we do. Stop acting like this, and be the joy we all love."

She doesn't have a response to that, but there is peace.

I glance over at Aviva to see if I said too much, but she looks content as we ride out toward the restaurant by my mom's hotel. She was going to stay with me, but there is hardly room for everyone. When Callie and Aviva stayed over a week ago, it was tight. I didn't realize how much crap a teenage girl needs to get ready. She basically wears a leotard and high ponytail every day, but she had more shit in my bathroom than I could fathom.

But I loved every second of it. I'd almost begged Aviva never to leave. My house was full and happy, and we had the time of our lives. We cooked, we made a cake, and then we watched movies until we all fell asleep on the couch. When I woke up because I was hot, it was from Aviva and Callie leaning on me as they slept. I felt so damn loved, so damn complete, and I've never felt like that in my life outside of my mother's love.

I love these girls, and I want my family to love them.

I want my mom to know that I have found what I needed. That she doesn't have to watch over me and protect me. That I actually do it myself and for others.

I think I might have grown up.

Didn't take as long as I thought it would.

"So, we're sitting right behind you at the game?"

I nod as I turn downtown. "Yeah, I bought the tickets off one of our shareholders. We're playing the Caps, so it should be a great game."

"The Caps?"

"Washington Capitals," Callie says, annoyed, from the back.

Aviva shrugs. "And we have to wear those oversized shirts?"

"Jerseys, and they're meant to be big."

"They're like dresses."

I flash her a toothy grin. "I mean, you don't have to wear anything under it."

She chuckles lightly as Callie groans. "Gross."

"Hush, you," I throw back at her, and I swear she mumbles something along the lines of me being an asshole. I'm not sure, so I let it go. "I think you guys will have a blast. I think Amelia is going to go to show you the ropes and buy you all the bad food."

Aviva's brow perks. "Bad food?"

"Oh yeah. Stadium food is life. Get the pretzel, right? With the cheese. And then get a thing of popcorn. Dip the pretzel in the cheese and then dip it in popcorn. Boom. It's like a tree of popcorn. I mean, basically a party in your mouth."

When I look over to see her excitement, I find that she isn't as enthusiastic as I am. "That sounds absolutely disgusting."

"Well, that's rude," I tease, and she laughs.

"Actually, I think it sounds amazing," Callie says, and I glance back at her.

"Thank you. That's why you're my favorite."

That makes them both laugh, which was my end game. When we arrive at Surf House, my mom's favorite place to eat when she's in town, I do valet since we're kind of late. I didn't realize how slow I was driving until we got here. After making sure everything is set, I take Aviva's hand and head inside with Callie beside me. The loud sounds of the place, the clashing and clanking of plates, smacks me right in the face when we enter. I go straight to the hostess and tell her my name.

"Of course, Mr. Merryweather. This way."

"We are so cool," Callie gushes as we head toward the back where there are private dining rooms. "Yes, Mr. Merryweather. This way, Mr. Merryweather. Would you like high tea?" she says in the worst British accent I've ever heard. Aviva smiles and laughs along with her, but I gotta get to the back. When the hostess opens the door, a feeling of relief washes over me. I step in, not saying anything to my mom before ushering Aviva and Callie inside. I shut the door behind them before the hostess can and press my hand to the cool wood. I take a deep breath in, letting it out through my nose as Aviva's hand comes to my back.

"You okay?"

I nod, breathing in once more. "It's just so damn loud in this place."

"But it's my favorite," Mom says, and I turn just as she approaches me. She takes my face in her hands, kissing me loudly on the cheek. "Ah, my Nicolas. I've missed you so much. Thank you for coming. I know it's hard."

I wave her off. "It's fine. I just wish they had a back way in."

She pats my face, kissing me again. "I agree." She studies me critically. "You look skinny."

I make a face. "I seriously eat, like, nine subs a day. Carbs galore."

Callie snorts. "For real. I've never seen someone eat so many subs."

My mom drops her hands and looks over at Callie. She points to her. "Callie?"

"Yes. Hi. It's great to meet you."

"It's so wonderful to meet you. I'm Myra." Mom smiles widely. "I have heard so much about you. Nicolas talks constantly about you and how talented you are."

Callie beams at me. "He's a good guy. We like him."

I smirk as Mom turns to Aviva. She's standing beside me, not her usual self due to the nerves. She holds out her hand, and my mom takes it. "It's nice to meet you. Nico speaks of you all the time. You've raised an amazing guy."

"He is my favorite. It's great to finally meet you, Aviva," Mom says before letting go of Aviva's hand. "I've never heard him talk so much about two people in my life. You guys have a nice little thing going for you."

We all move to sit down. As Callie falls into her seat, she nods. "We're basically a family."

My heart warms as I sit down beside Aviva. Before I can agree, Aviva adds, "They're close. Two little troublemakers, these two are."

Does she not think we're family? I feel like we're family. I look around the table to see that we're missing some people. "Where are Mimi and Papa?"

"So, they were supposed to come," Mom says before sitting across from me, beside Callie. "Plane tickets were bought, but then Papa had some tournament he got called in to do, and you know Mimi doesn't travel without him."

I grin. "He's still reffing?"

She nods. "Yes, at seventy-one, on skates."

"That's cool." Callie glances over at me. "That's gonna be you."

I laugh along with everyone as the waitress comes in. After ordering drinks and an appetizer, my mom meets Aviva's gaze. Aviva seems to tense up, but I can't get over how gorgeous she looks. She put her hair in a high bun with her bangs covering her forehead. She's wearing a flowy, flowery dress that hugs that ass of hers in all the ways I like. She has those stupid rubber boobs in, and I almost want to throw them away. I hate that she depends on those to feel like a woman. She's gorgeous no matter what.

"So, you own your own business?"

I slip my hand into Aviva's as she goes on and on about her sub shop. I love listening to her talk about it. She's full of so much pride and loves telling the story of how her mom opened it. "She was obsessed with the 90s since touring with all the artists and all. We used to talk about how we would open a shop with funny sub names. It was fun and still is. I won't change a thing, I love it."

Mom smiles as she nods. "When did you lose her?"

"Nine years ago."

"I'm sure that's not easy."

Aviva presses her lips together and shakes her head. "No, but I've got Callie, and she keeps me on my toes."

Callie scoffs. "I'm a joy and a delight."

I snort at that. "A pain in the ass and snarky like your sister, is more like it."

"Hey!" Aviva laughs, and Callie nods.

"I do get it all from her."

Mom laughs as she leans back in her chair. "Sounds like these two keep you busy."

Aviva nods, and the smile that covers her face hits me straight in the chest. "Yeah, but it's a good busy. They gang up on me a lot, though. Both so extravagant."

Mom laughs. "Oh, Nicolas has always been like that." She looks over at me, and I smile. "We grew up poor, so he's all about blowing the money he's worked for."

"I don't see a thing wrong with that," Aviva adds, leaning into me. "He works very hard."

Before anyone can agree, though they don't need to since I know I do, our appetizers are brought out.

We order dinner before Callie asks, "Has *Nicolas* always wanted to be a hockey player?"

Mom beams, while I want to give Callie the finger. Little shit. "Yes. He didn't talk when he was younger. I don't think he started until he was four. His first words were 'hockey glove.' My father played and used to play with Nico. He'd run around with the helmet on his head, and that's the only time he would speak to us."

My heart kicks up, and I look over just in time to see Aviva furrow her brow. Shit. I look to Callie and say, "Tell my mom about that double back hand twist thing you did."

Callie must have caught my drift, but before she can utter a word, Aviva says, "You didn't talk until you were four?"

Mom nods. "Oh yes. We were worried he'd never talk."

"Why—"

"Probably because I talk way more than I should now," I say quickly. "Mom, Callie did this awesome twist double back thing. Don't you have the video?"

"I do," Callie gushes, pulling out her phone, but my mom is staring at me.

I try to tell her with my eyes to shut up, but apparently the social cues that I lack come from her. "Nicolas. Do they not know?"

I feel Aviva's gaze on me and can see the worried crease in Callie's forehead.

"No."

Mom's eyes widen as she looks between them both and then me. When she starts to speak in French, I close my eyes. Because there is no way they won't think we're talking about them.

How do you claim to love this woman, but she doesn't know?

I don't want her to know. I don't want her to think differently of me.

That is ludicrous. If she loves you, then it will not matter.

I am aware, but what if she doesn't? I can't chance it. I will tell them.

"Nicolas," she warns, but I shake my head.

When my gaze falls on Callie, she gives me a look of pure horror. "I didn't know you spoke French."

I nod. "Yeah. Well, I'm French Canadian."

Callie nods and then points to Aviva. "She knows French."

Well, fuck me sideways. I ignore my heart that has jumped into my throat before grabbing my water. I drain it as Aviva's gaze burns into the side of my face. Mom, though, she doesn't seem to care that Aviva could understand. She's staring at me with such a disapproving look on her face, and I don't know what to do.

"Well, since no one wants to say anything, I will. What haven't you told me?"

Callie covers her face, and I want to mirror her. "It's nothing," I mutter.

"It appears it is something," Aviva says sternly. "Nico, look at me."

"Oh, Aviva honey, he doesn't look people in the eye."

"He looks at me," Aviva snaps, and when I look over at her, her eyes are searching mine. "What is going on?"

I shrug and look away once more. "Can we please talk about something else?"

Callie is all for it, but not my mom. "I don't know why he has not told you, and it upsets me because he shouldn't be ashamed—"

I slam my hands onto the table, making everyone jump. "I'm not fucking ashamed." I feel Aviva's hand on my bicep, and I suck in a deep breath. "Let's drop it."

"Nicolas is autistic."

Everything stops. I love my mom. I love her so much, but right now, I might hate her. I hadn't even realized I'd closed my eyes until I opened them to look at her. She isn't even sorry, but that's my mom. She is never embarrassed by my diagnosis, only proud of me. Right now, though, I want to rip her head off. How could she do this to me?

"That was not your place," Callie says, very low and dangerous. I look over at her, and she's glaring at my mom. "That wasn't your truth to share."

"Excuse me, little girl, but—"

"I am sixteen years old, and even I know that it's his choice who knows what about him. You are his mother, but you don't get to choose that for him anymore. He's an adult."

"I am well aware—"

"If you were aware, you'd know not to speak his truth. Nico is a wonderful man. No one would know unless he told them. Is he quirky? Yup. But his heart is so big, it doesn't matter. He will sit with me for hours, helping me with whatever I ask. Aviva says 'Jump!' and he's like 'How high?' even when it gives him anxiety. He came to my practice the other day, in a crowded room, and I knew it bothered him, but he stood there, proud of me. He fights that label daily, and it does not define him. And I am disgusted that you took it upon yourself to tell my sister."

"Young lady, I have never—"

"Stop calling me anything but my name. I'm not calling you old lady, later-age lady, or Nico's mom. I've called you Mrs. Myra!"

My mom's jaw actually drops, and Aviva flies off the handle, leaving my skin prickling. "Calliope, what in the world!"

But Callie's eyes are on my mother. "Would you have done that to anyone else? Just a guy you knew? Would you tell his business? Being his mother doesn't give you that right."

Oh, I think I might throw up. But then Callie's tear-flooded gaze meets mine, and I can't worry about me. I have to worry about Callie.

"I want to go home."

I stand instantly. "Okay, let's go—"

"Nicolas."

"I love you," I say, still not meeting Aviva's gaze. I feel my anxiety boiling inside me like that monster thing on that show Aviva made me watch. I still don't understand why that girl's nose was bleeding the whole time. Hell, she might have been as overwhelmed as I am right now, and that's what caused the bleed. I don't know, but Callie wants to go, and I don't blame her. She's shaking, she's so upset. "But Callie wants to go home, and I drove."

"Nico, she is fine. We all just need to calm down," Aviva says to me, but I shake my head.

"Fine, then I need to go." I still won't look at her, but out of the corner of my eye, I see her grab her things.

Aviva stands as I pull out her chair for her. "I'm very sorry, Ms. Merryweather. I don't know—"

"Do not apologize for me, Aviva. She needs to apologize to Nico," Callie sneers.

And one thing is for sure, I gotta get this kid out of here. I go to her and wrap my arm around her shoulder to pull her with me as we walk out. "It's okay, Cal."

"It is not," she says, tears streaming down her face. "That is your label to share. Not hers."

I kiss the top of her head. "Thanks."

She leans into me, and I hug her tightly. "I love you, Nico, and you did not deserve that. You should have been able to tell Aviva when you wanted."

I lean my head into hers. She's right, but none of that matters now. "I love you too, Cal."

She pushes through a side door, and I automatically feel free when we are met with the outside air. No people, breaking dishes, or loud noises.

Freedom from everything.

But not for long, because Aviva is going to want answers.

Answers I'm terrified to give her.

CHAPTER TWENTY-EIGHT

viva

THE RIDE back to my place is silent.

My mind is running like mad, and I really don't know what just happened back there. There are three things that are screaming in my head and causing my whole body to shudder in confusion, a touch of betrayal, and anger.

One, Calliope acting like a fucking fool to the one person I wanted to like me since I'm pretty fond of Nico.

Two, Nico apparently telling his mom he loved me.

Three, Nico is autistic.

Oh, and four, his mom probably hates both Callie and me now. Callie more than me, so maybe I can get on her good side when Callie leaves for college. But do I want her there?

I can't believe his mom threw Nico under the bus like that. I glance over at him, and he's visibly upset. He's white-knuckling the steering wheel, and perspiration is dotted along his temple. His phone has been ringing since we left, and when he turned it off, I figured it wasn't a good thing. He didn't turn it off to give us attention, which he has done before. No, it was to ignore whoever was calling.

I swallow hard as I glance back at Callie. She's got her body in a ball, crying into her knees. I'm proud of her. She's so fiercely protective and loves with her whole little body. I just wish she had chosen a different way to handle this—or better yet, not say anything at all. No. That's not true. I would have handled this the same way she did if I had known. I absolutely love Nico and Callie's relationship, but she can't be talking to his mother like that.

Though the thing that bothers me the most is that Nico didn't tell me.

When we get to the shop, Nico pulls in but doesn't put the truck in park. He hasn't looked at me since his mom uttered the word. I clear my throat. "Put the truck in park, Nico. We haven't eaten, and I'm not having you go home hungry."

"I'm fine. I can go through a drive-thru," he says, and I'm staring a hole in the side of his face.

"Nico, just come in," Callie adds, but he doesn't move.

I reach out, cupping his wrist. Finally, he looks over at me, those beautiful, troubled brown eyes meeting mine. "Please."

He clenches his jaw, and then he nods before putting the truck in park and turning it off. We all get out and head inside. As I lock the door to the shop behind us, I say, "Callie, go set your phone and my laptop on the counter. Then go to your room."

She looks back at me with her brows raised. "Why?"

I look at her, dumbfounded. "Seriously? You can't speak to people like that. I don't care if you were right. You do not disrespect someone—"

"She disrespected him! It was not right. I don't care who the hell she is."

Either she or I will not make it to her eighteenth birthday. "Calliope. Do as I say and go to your room," I warn, and tears fall from her eyes.

"If you hadn't had the shock of learning what you did, then you would have defended him too. You—"

"Calliope, I swear to God, if you do not get up those stairs, I will take away gym and make you cut up onions for a month."

She scrunches up her face in complete horror. I wait for her to come back at me—we're a stubborn pair, she and I—but thankfully, she turns on her heels and heads up the stairs. I hear the door upstairs slam, more steps, and then her door shut. I set my purse on the table and exhale. When I look up at Nico, he's standing there awkwardly, probably wishing he were anywhere but here. I push off the table and pat his chest as I walk by. "Let me make you a sub."

"You don't have to," he says as I pass by. "You could just yell, get it done, and I'll leave."

I pause behind the counter. "Why would I yell?"

"Because I didn't tell you."

I hold his gaze. "I'm not going to say it doesn't bother me that you didn't tell me. It does. It feels like you didn't want to share that part of yourself with me, but it doesn't change how I feel about you, Nico. That label, as Callie so sweetly put it to your mom, doesn't change anything. It explains a lot," I say with a smile, "but it doesn't change a thing."

He swallows hard.

"What else are you hiding?"

His eyes meet mine. "Nothing, and it's not that I didn't want to tell you. I couldn't."

I start to make him the sub. I decide if I gawk at him, he won't feel comfortable and will not be open with me. "Why couldn't you?"

"I was terrified that you wouldn't want to be with me."

I want to pause; I want to run to him and wrap my arms around him so tightly. "That's not true. At all," I say, looking up as I set down the cheese. "If I had known, I could have helped the night of the gala."

He nods slowly, tucking his hands into the pockets of his slacks. His light-blue shirt has come untucked, and he looks a mess. A beautiful, stunning mess. "There is no helping me when I get like that. I just gotta ride it out."

I add some roast beef. "Okay, well, I would have liked to have known that. I was worried."

"I know. I'm sorry."

I add another layer of cheese. "When did you tell Callie? I assume she's known?"

"Yeah, since before we started dating."

Why am I jealous of my sister? "Why did you tell her and not me?"

"I don't know," he answers, and I know he means it. "I'd never told anyone before her."

I look up then. "Not even Chandler?"

He shakes his head. "No, I just told him a couple weeks ago. I was working up to you, but I'm scared."

"Nico, you have nothing to be scared of, and I'm sorry if I—"

"No, no," he says quickly, coming to the counter. "It wasn't you, our relationship, or anything—it is all me. It's my insecurities from living a life where I was the weird kid who got made fun of. Kids weren't nice to me because I couldn't control what I was feeling. For the longest time, I just couldn't. Now, as an adult, I've learned a lot, and I go to a lot of therapy. But sometimes, I can't get a grasp on all this emotion inside me. I felt awful for snapping at you before the gala. To the point that I had a panic attack when I got home, and all I could think was, *She's gonna leave me. Why would she want me?* I knew I had to tell you, I had to explain myself, but then you called that morning to check on me and invited me over for lunch, and I got scared again."

I gaze into his eyes, my whole body shaking, and I want to cry for him. But Nico isn't one to feel pity for.

"I mean, I have an out-of-this-world gorgeous woman who wants to be with me. Who enjoys me, and I don't want to lose that. I didn't want you to think you had no future with me because of my diagnosis. That I probably never will be able to handle big situations like that—"

"But if I knew, it would be easier for me to understand, and I can find tools to help."

He shakes his head, and when a tear rolls down that gorgeous face of his, it breaks me. I cover my mouth as he says, "I know, Aviva. You would be on the damn WebMD or whatever site you can find to be supportive. But then what happens when you realize our kids could come out like me?"

My heart stops, and I hop onto the counter, surprising him. I cup his face, looking deep into his eyes. I feel him swallow as tears start to gather in my eyes. "If our kids came out half as loving, kind, and funny as you, then I don't know how I would be able to stand it. I would be so overfilled with love. So complete that nothing could touch us. Do not, Nico—for real, listen to me—do not feel like your autism holds you back. If anything, it makes you who you are, and that's a damn great man." I lean my head into his, my body vibrating for him. "And if we, by chance, have these kids we're apparently thinking of..."

He wraps his arms around me, pulling me off the counter and close to him. I touch my face to his, our noses side by side as we stare into each other's eyes.

"You will be the example for them. So, you gotta be proud, and you gotta be the cocky, amazing man I am falling head over heels in love with, because our kids will be nothing less than a pain in the ass. I mean, look at me. Look at Callie. Are you sure?"

He laughs as he gathers me in closer, pressing his lips to mine. "I've never been so sure of anything in my life."

I close my eyes as the tears roll down my face. Our hearts pound together while we cling to each other. "What did you tell me that one time? I can't always think of the bad side of everything? That could apply here."

He shakes his head seriously. "I don't want to lose you."

"Nico, I'm terrified to lose you. You have nothing to worry about here."

His eyes search mine, and knowing that he usually doesn't look people in the eye pulls at my heartstrings. He kisses my nose as he whispers, "You have nothing to worry about."

Oh, heart. Oh, poor heart. "Nico, I want you to know that when I lost my mom, I seriously lost every beacon of happiness. All I had was Callie and Jaylin, but I swear, I faked most of it with them. It took you coming into my life to break open that part of me, and I can't thank you enough. Really. I can't."

He kisses my nose. "I mean, I am a joy and a delight."

We both grin. Of course, he would quote that asshole upstairs. "And while I love your relationship with Callie and I know it was hard for you to watch me yell at her earlier, you need to be on my side about this. She cannot talk to your mom like that."

He inhales heavily and then lets his breath out. "Callie was right, though. I'm pissed at my mom."

"I know, but Callie called your mom an old lady."

He grins. "Sorry. I'm on her side."

I let my head drop down against his jaw. "You two are going to be the death of me."

He kisses my forehead. "Don't worry. You took her phone away. I'll deal with my mom, and everything will be fine."

"She hates us," I say on a groan as I look up at him. "Callie more, but still, your mom knows I raised that opinionated, loud kid, and she's just like me—"

"I know—she's perfect," he says with a grin. "And like she said, who cares if my mom likes you guys or not? I like you, and I think how the three of us feel is all that matters."

I get lost in his eyes. "So, if Callie didn't like you, we'd have a problem?"

He scoffs. Back is my playful Nico, and everything inside me wants to celebrate. "Please. I'm awesome. That kid had no chance. Just like you didn't."

I laugh as I lean into him. I can't even disagree because he is completely right.

Now I know I had no chance whatsoever once Nico decided I would be his.

* * *

Callie is at school and Nico is at practice, so since I'm alone, I try to get ahead on the week. I have to cater for the IceCats four times in the coming week. As much as I love the money, the process stresses me out. I feel like I can't get it all done, but somehow, I do. Nico suggested I hire help, but I don't want to pay someone to do a job I can do. I guess I could hire some high school kids, but then I'd have to micromanage them, and I already do that for Callie. I don't want to do it for anyone else.

I turn on the mixer, and it struggles to mix the dough, but it gets the job done. I walk to the front to check my proofer and then my ovens. I hate having the ovens out here, but Mom said it makes the customers' mouths water. I believe they could smell them from the back because I'm sweating like crazy out here. I switch some things over and start a prepping area for the veggie trays I'll make. I had to Google how to make pretty trays since I didn't want to embarrass Nico. Apparently throwing everything on a tray isn't professional-looking. How was I supposed to know? This is my first catering job, but Jaylin made sure to let me know.

As I move through the shop, doing what I need to do, my thoughts, as always, float to Nico. He's been dodging calls from his mom, and I almost feel bad for her. I don't agree with the way she handled things, but she wasn't out to hurt him. She was confused, and to be honest, so am I. I'm unsure how I feel that he hid that part of himself. I showed him every scar and told him about my fucked-up life, but he never once told me he is autistic. It all makes perfect sense, and I'm surprised I didn't catch on before, but I don't know if I'm bothered because he didn't tell me or because he told Callie first.

I think this may be a jealousy thing.

I want to know everything about Nico. I want him to tell me all of it, but he confided in my sister about a huge part of his life and not me. Like I told him, it doesn't matter—he's still Nico to me—but I can't help but wish he had been honest with me from the jump. Nothing would have changed; I would still be in my feelings for him, but I did want to know.

When the door opens, I wipe off my hands as I say, "Welcome to Willz. Give me one second."

I turn just as Nico's mom reaches the counter. "Hello, Aviva."

My heart kicks up in speed as I put down the towel. "Hey, Myra. How are you?"

"Well, thank you." She looks around, a small smile on her lips. "This is a wonderful place."

"Thank you."

"Willz?"

"My mom's name was Willow, and she wanted it to be like the *Fresh Prince of Bel-Air,* so she added the z." I tuck my hands into my apron. "Can I get you something?"

She shakes her head. "No, I'm not hungry. I came to apologize."

I pause and then slowly cross my arms. "I don't feel that you owe me one. It's more to Nico than anything."

She nods. "I know, and I have apologized to him, but..." She pauses to clear her throat. She sets her large purse on the counter and folds her hands on top of it. "I need you to know how overprotective I am of him."

I hold her dark brown gaze. "I don't blame you. I'd be the same—well, I am with Callie."

She quirks her lips. "That girl is a firecracker."

I'm still embarrassed. "She is, and sometimes that's an issue."

She slowly shakes her head. "It's not. I thought I was the only one who would ever be able to defend or stand up for Nico, but she proved me wrong. If the way she acted is how you would handle things, I have nothing to worry about."

I clear my throat. I was terrified this lady would hate me. "You don't. I would be the same way."

She looks away and draws in a deep breath through her nose. "Nico, ah, my Nico is a blessing. I was with a horrid man, but Nico was the light. When he was diagnosed, I was scared that I couldn't love him right, and I suspect that's also why his father left. He was a coward."

He sure as hell was. Bastard. I look up just as she does, her gaze holding mine, and I see such pain in her eyes.

"I know I overstepped, and I hope you don't think I'm an awful person. For so long, he was unable to tell me what he felt. Then when he figured it out, he was made fun of. Kids were awful to him, calling him names that still hurt me to this day. When he asked to play hockey, I knew it was what he needed. I didn't know at the time he was using the gear to hide from the bullies, but it helped. It made him who he is today."

My heart aches for the boy Nico was. Then I remember the helmet in his kitchen. "Does he still do that?"

She nods. "There is a helmet he uses at home to recenter himself. It's hard for him to stop feeling fear when it comes."

My stomach twists for him as she goes on.

"He's always been loud, quirky, and with no filter whatsoever, but what I've noticed lately is that he's been slowing down. He never listened before, never paid attention. He always just jumped and did what he wanted without caring about anyone. He didn't have girlfriends because they didn't understand him, and he didn't slow down enough to think of what they were feeling. With Shelli, it was like that. He didn't pay attention to what she was doing and saying; he just felt. A lot. She was pushing him away the whole time, just wanting sex from him."

I clear my throat. I hate the jealousy that is eating at me. "Did he love her?"

She shakes her head. "No, he was infatuated with her. He wanted to love her, and I thought that when she chose the other man, it would ruin relationships for Nico. I was very wrong."

I find myself holding my breath as she exhales. With her eyes on me, she says, "Lately, I've noticed a huge difference. I thought it was the new therapist, but then I watched him with you and Callie, and I knew it was you two. He doesn't want to mess this up, and it thrills me." She reaches over, taking my hand in hers. "Thank you. Thank you for being kind to my son, for being patient and for loving him, because he loves you with his whole soul."

Everything stops. Do I love Nico? "He makes it easy."

She laughs. "Nothing about Nico is easy."

"That's the damn truth," I say with a grin. "But at the end of the day, he makes me happy."

"As do you for him. It's incredible to watch. I'm so happy for you two and Callie. He has taken to her completely."

I smile. "I love their relationship. Even with the ten-year gap, they act the same age."

She laughs. "They're both very lucky to have you."

My heart warms. "Thank you."

"I hope you don't hate me."

I shake my head. "Not at all. I think emotions were just high, and everyone was nervous. Things were said, and I don't think they were meant to be hurtful. I was surprised he didn't tell me either."

Her smile falls as her eyes stare into mine. "He's never told anyone. Every time he did when he was growing up, people would call him stupid or weird. I thought he would have told you with how much he says he loves you, but I think the pain of his childhood held him back. I'm sorry I couldn't protect him from that. I'm sorry it bled over into his adult life and he struggles."

My gut hurts as I hold on to the counter. How could anyone treat him like that? "Don't apologize. I completely understand. I'm a mother hen too. We have to protect our babies, and Nico and I are fine. We talked it over, and at the end of the day, his autism makes him who he is, and I love all of him."

Holy shit. What did I just say?

Her eyes light up. "I know, and I thank you for that."

"You don't need to. Again, Nico makes it easy. I really want you to fix things with Nico. He loves you too much."

She pats my hand. "I will. Thank you," she says softly. "This is a wonderful place, and you really are an amazing woman. I am very glad Nico has found you. He would do absolutely anything for you."

I grin. "Thank you."

"Can you tell Callie I am sorry for offending her yesterday?"

No. "I will."

"Thank you," she says, and then she grabs her purse. "I'm gonna go see Nico for lunch. We'd love for you to join."

I hold out my hands. "I gotta work."

She nods, though I notice she's disappointed. "Don't forget that you need to enjoy life. No point in working if you can't enjoy the benefits."

With that, she leaves, and as I watch her get into her car, her words turn over and over in my head. Before, I would work myself into the ground. I had to get ahead. I had to pay off my mom's bills and make Callie a good life. Now, I feel like I'm finally getting ahead, and I am accomplishing my goals. The benefits are like neon signs in my face, and I hate that it took someone helping me get out of debt to see that. I regret not enjoying the little things before, when now, I get excited just to see Callie do homework. Before, I worried I wouldn't be able to send her to college. Now, I see she can do it all and then some because someone took away the things that were distracting me and holding me back. I worried myself sick for nothing. I would have been fine. I could have been happy, but instead, I didn't allow myself. It infuriates me, but I'm also thankful.

And shit. Did I tell Nico's mom I loved him?

Shouldn't I have told him that first?

Well, I guess even without my impending doom of debt, I'm still a mess.

CHAPTER TWENTY-NINE

ico

"DID YOUR MOM GET HOME OKAY?"

"Yeah, she landed this afternoon," I say, turning onto my road. I'm running a bit late for the rehearsal crap Amelia is making me do. I can walk with Carter in my arms; it's not that hard. There is even an aisle for me to walk down. Shit, I stop pucks coming at me at over 100 miles per hour; I can walk with a kid and a dog. Sadie can lead us, really. Hell, maybe she'll calm me down.

Doubtful.

"She said to thank you and Callie again for dinner last night. She had fun."

"We did too, even though I think Callie is still a little bitchy."

"She is," I laugh, shaking my head. That girl can hold a grudge, but I don't blame her. I'm still resentful of the way my mom threw my shit out like that. Luckily, Aviva still likes me—or at least what we did last night seems to make me think so. "But it's fine. She'll get there."

She exhales loudly. “I don’t like it. Maybe I should ground her more.”

“Because that will make her love my mom,” I say dryly. “We’ll talk about it later. I’m pulling in at Chandler’s. Wait, where are you at?”

“I’m running so late. I had a dinner rush, and then I had to go sign some paperwork for a leotard at Callie’s gym. I’m getting ready now, so I’ll be over in about an hour. I won’t miss dinner. I’ll just miss you complaining about walking up an aisle.”

I grin as I get out of my truck. “You know me so well.”

“I do. See you in a bit.”

“Bye, baby.”

I hang up, tucking my phone into my pocket as I walk up the driveway. I thought my mom staying for two weeks would make things messy since she apparently loves throwing my shit out in the open, but really, it was fun. She got along with Aviva and kind of with Callie. It was nice to have my three girls together. I know I felt all kinds of things, and I think it only made me fall for Aviva even more. I’m ready for some time with just Callie and Aviva—and some really, really alone time with Aviva.

Gotta get through this rehearsal first.

Chandler’s place is packed with cars, from vendors to family. That need to run is deep in my gut, and I consider hightailing it out of this bitch, but I promised Chandler I would be here. I won’t let him down, not when he has always been there for me. So I take in a deep breath and let it out slowly as if I’m in net. When I feel like I can do this, I head up the stairs, open the door, and walk in. I see everyone on the back porch, but then Amelia comes out of a bedroom with Carter in her arms. “Hey, you’re late.”

I shrug. “Sorry. I got caught up at therapy. Apparently I’m growing up.”

She nods with an impressed look on her face. “Who would have thought it?”

“My thoughts exactly. Give me my man.”

“So, what makes you believe you’re growing up?”

I grin at Carter as I smush his cheeks. "I am picking up on social cues and trying to think before I act."

"Like impulse control? Something you've never had."

"Right? I'm getting there. Watch out, World. I might be an adult soon." She laughs as I cuddle Carter in my arms before leaning over to kiss Amelia on her cheek. "You look stunning."

Her face warms with color as she runs her hands down the flowy white dress she's wearing. It's a weird material, like a tent material, really, and it floats around her, showing the outline of her body as she moves. Her hair is braided, and her makeup is done how she used to wear it all the time until the kids came. "Thanks, Nico. I'm proud of you."

I grin at her. "You are? Do you like me yet?"

She scoffs, rolling her eyes. "Where's Aviva?"

"Running late. She's coming."

She nods. "Well, come on. I think everyone is waiting for us."

I kiss Carter's head. "Duh. We're the party."

She laughs as I follow her through the kitchen to the porch. Soon, I'm greeted by Chandler's mom and dad, and I try to ignore all of Amelia's family members who are here. Chandler's mom distracts me, gushing over me, while his dad talks about my game play. There are so many people in such a small space. Apparently Amelia's whole damn family is here, and that alone is like sixty people. I swear they're like a pack, all ready to tear you to pieces if you dishonor one of them... I need to stop watching *Game of Thrones*. Thankfully I don't see Shelli yet, and I'm hoping maybe she skipped. I really don't want to play nice with that fuc— I mean Brooks. Aiden Brooks. Nope, can't do it. He's a fuckbag. Nothing to do with Shelli; he's just a dick.

Chandler comes over, patting me on the back, and I give him a cheesy grin. "You're doing great," he whispers, and I stare into his eyes, cheesy grin still not moving.

"I want to die."

He laughs. "I know. I'm sorry. Come on, let's go down on the beach."

I follow him down the stairs and onto the beach. I don't notice

Chandler's dad is following until I see the legendary Shea Adler. I almost trip over myself, but I thankfully make it to the sand before turning around.

"Hey, Mr. Adler."

Shea looks at me like I'm junk. I don't think he cares for me. I know he knows I banged his daughter, and I think I might have called him an old man when I met him for the first time. What? I was nervous, and in my defense, I was freaking out, drunk, and trying to get Shelli back. Basically an emotional basket case. "Merryweather. Good game last night."

"Fucking right. Won't let you guys beat us anymore." Why do I sound like an idiot when I talk to this guy?

"Remember who has the Cup."

I guess those Nashville Assassins colors run deep, 'cause he narrows his eyes.

Chandler chuckles nervously as I gawk at him while Shea walks past us, talking to Chandler's dad. "That guy hates me."

Chandler nods. "Me too. It's okay. Apparently he accepted Aiden into the family, which I don't understand. I'm way better than that dude."

I make a face. "Duh. He's a fuckbag."

Chandler smirks as he shakes his head. "Be nice. Not really trying to stress out Amelia. She's actually calm, even though she's struggling with her dad not being here."

Amelia's dad passed a while back, and I imagine it's hard not having him here to walk her down the aisle. "I'll be nice, only for her."

"You're so kind," he says dryly. "Where is Aviva?"

"She's coming," I say, and I want to laugh at how Aviva is just a part of me. If I'm here, where is she? It's nice, and damn it, I miss her. I'm ready for a week off to spend the whole time with her. I figure she's gonna put me to work in the shop, and I won't mind. I'll be with her.

"Everything okay with your mom?"

"Good."

"Awesome," he says just as Shelli catches my eye. She comes down the stairs in a drapey teal dress that cuts down the front, showing not only the swells of her breasts but her belly button. She's lost weight. She's not as thick as I remember, but she's still very beautiful. Her hair is long, darker than it was. When her eyes land on me, I wait for the desire to swirl in my gut. It's one thing to hear her name and feel nothing, but seeing her potentially could be a different hockey game.

It's not.

All I can think is she has absolutely nothing on Aviva.

Shelli takes in a deep breath as she reaches the bottom of the stairs. "Hey there, Nico."

She goes for a hug, and I meet her for one. "Hey, Shell. How's life treating you?"

"Good, thanks. Working at the Assassins compound and planning our wedding."

I nod. "I heard. Congratulations."

"Thank you," she says, and she seems surprised. "I'm marrying Aiden."

"Yeah, I know."

She looks as if she is waiting for something, and I look at Chandler and then back to her. She looks annoyed as she says, "Okay then."

"Okay," I say as Chandler puts his hand on my shoulder. "So where is the fu—"

Chandler laughs as he cuts me off. That's probably for the best. I don't want to see the dude, and I sure as hell don't want to talk to him. "Let's go get this started."

So, we do. It's painful, stupid, and I hate every second of it, but then watching Amelia being walked down the aisle by her big brother, Ryan, kind of hits me in the gut. It's obvious how much the dude loves his sister. I don't have siblings, but I kind of think of Callie as the little sister I never had or wanted. Ryan holds Amelia so delicately, and it's just a rehearsal. I bet I'll be like that when Callie gets married. No one else is walking her but me. Aviva might fight me on that, but I can take her. A grin pulls at my lips, and it's crazy how my mind is working now. I never wanted any of this. But now, I can't wait for tomorrow. It's going to be beautiful. I'm ready to see my best friend live his dreams. I'm ready to live my own.

When we're done, everyone gathers along the beach for drinks and appetizers. Since it's entirely too many people in one spot, I stand in the water as it runs up on my ankles. It feels amazing, so I hold Carter in the water, and he kicks playfully. He's gonna be a water baby; I'll make sure of it. When the little guy lets out a shrill of happiness, I realize I want one of these little buggers. It would be fun.

Man, this wedding has me in my feels.

When I feel an arm slide around my waist and Aviva kisses my cheek, my heart explodes. I grin over at her, kissing her lips.

"Is Amelia going to kill you?"

I shrug as I stand up, cuddling the wet little fat baby into my chest. "Probably."

She shakes her head. "No one answered the door, so I just walked in."

"That's cool. You get everything done?"

"Yeah, and then I had to drop Callie off at Sammie's for some team-building thing? I don't know. I told her I had to pick her up at four tomorrow for the wedding."

I look her over in her hot little halter dress and grin. "Hey there, hottie."

She scoffs. "Hush, before I take you on this beach."

I hold up Carter. "You dirty woman. I have a baby."

She giggles, but before she can say anything, someone runs up on me. I move into Aviva as the girl steadies herself, looking up at me. She's a mini Shelli, but thicker with more auburn-colored hair. She's beautiful, with big blue eyes and thick lips. I feel like I know her, like I've met her. But one thing is for sure. The girl is drunk off her ass. She smells as if she swam in the bar.

"Are you Nico Merryweather?"

I hold Carter close to my chest. "I am."

"I'm Posey Adler," she says, jerking her thumb into her chest, but she does it so hard, she somehow hits herself in the chin. She doesn't even flinch. "And I know you don't know me and that you've fucked my sister, but I know that you like to fuck. So, can you fuck me?"

I'd like to say that I'm shocked, but it isn't the first time someone has asked me this. Aviva, though, she's shocked. "What the—"

I grab Aviva's hand. "It's okay."

"It is not," she says, her eyes wide. "Not only do you not know him, but he has a baby in his arms. That's ridiculous."

Posey points at her. "Shh, you. Stop cockblocking."

"Oh, I'm gonna cockblock. He's my fucking man!"

Aw, she makes me feel special.

Shelli comes out of nowhere and steps between Posey and me. "What in the world is your problem? Take your drunk ass to bed."

"Who's drunk?"

We all look back to where Shea Adler is glaring down at us. "No one, Daddy. I've got this," Shelli answers quickly.

He looks at Posey. "What's wrong with you?"

"I'm drunk, Daddy!" she yells, throwing up her hands, almost falling into the ocean. "You sent him away. You decided he wasn't good enough for the Assassins." She jerks her head back and cries out loudly. She loses her balance, though, and falls into the water. Shelli sighs dramatically but doesn't move to rescue her.

I point to her. "You gonna help her up?"

"Nope," she says simply. "Maybe the water will cool her off. She's been on a whole other level since she found out our billet boy was sent to Nebraska."

Shelli looks over at Aviva, and I watch as she sizes her up. With a very fake smile, Shelli says, "I don't think we've met. I'm Shelli Adler."

I wrap my arm around Aviva, pulling her in close. Shelli's eyes move between us as I say, "This is my girlfriend, Aviva Pearce."

She slowly nods, and I feel Aviva tense in my arms. "How wonderful. It's nice to meet you. I don't know where my fiancé Aiden ran off to. He plays with my brothers like he is still a teenager—" Her words fall off when Posey sputters water.

We all look down at her, and I say, "I don't think Amelia would be happy if she drowned."

Shelli sighs dramatically. "Let me get her inside before Amelia freaks out."

She gathers her sister, and I glance over to Aviva with an amused look on my face. "That was something."

She doesn't look the least bit happy, and that's just wonderful. "Yup."

"You okay?"

"Fine."

"Don't sound like it."

Aviva looks up at me. "That was pathetic."

I nod. "Yeah, but not the first time." By the way her face changes from pissed to even more pissed, I realize I should have left that part out.

"Does it happen often?"

"I mean, I'm a good-looking dude."

"Nico!"

"What? I don't give in. I'm with you."

She exhales harshly, crossing her arms. "And that's Shelli Adler? Jesus, her pictures online don't even come close to the reality of her. Did you see her rack?"

She shakes her head, and I scrunch up my face. "Are you serious right now?"

"Just let it go."

"No, you brought it up."

She goes to walk away, but I grab her by the wrist. "Whoa, killer, slow down. Talk to me."

"No," she says, pulling her wrist out of my hand. "I look like shit, and even the drunk girl was gorgeous. And then you tell me women do that to you all the time? How do you think that makes me feel?"

I wish Carter could talk. Surely he'd be on my side. "It should make you feel like a fucking goddess because I only want you." She won't look at me. "No one even comes close to you, Aviva. No one."

"Shelli's breasts are stunning, and to know you've had them in your mouth, hands, and then I have nothing there, it fucks with me."

This chick is insane. I grab her by her wrist and start for my house. I walk over to Amelia first, handing off her baby.

"You leaving?" she asks, and I nod.

"Yup. Gotta go talk sense into this woman of mine."

Before she or even Aviva can say anything to stop me, I'm already pulling Aviva down the beach. She tries to ask me what we're doing, but I don't have time for that. When I say something, she will listen and she will understand. We don't have to go far before we're at my house.

We enter through the back door, and as soon as we step inside, she asks, "What are we doing? It was rude to leave like that."

"I don't give a shit. They're happy I stayed as long as I did," I say, still pulling her through my house. I take her into my bathroom and turn her to the mirror. She looks back at me, confused, but I don't care. "You see this face," I say, pointing at her. "It's the first thing I think of when I wake up. To me, you're the most gorgeous woman I've ever seen." Slowly, her scrunched-up face loosens as I grab ahold of her ass. "This ass. Baby, for real, I dream of this ass. It's probably the best ass I've ever seen. Then this back? It gives me all these funny fantasies of subs because I know you don't go to the gym, so it has to be from slinging subs."

She sputters with laughter, and I untie the back of her dress. It's another halter top that I know she is comfortable in, but I wish she'd wear a tube top or even a low-cut something. I don't care. I want her to feel sexy. I pull down her dress, revealing her bare chest with two large scars. I move behind her and place my hands on her chest. "This body keeps me in knots, and to me, you look ten times hotter than Shelli does, even with her tits hanging out. I'd rather see this, the marks of your courageous fight, than anything Shelli—or any woman, for that matter—can offer me. I don't want it. I don't want them."

A tear rolls down her cheek. "But—"

"But nothing. Not only am I in love with the outside of this body, I'm in love with your soul, Aviva."

Her breath catches as her eyes meet mine. "You love me?"

"Oh hell, Aviva. You know I do. How could I not? Look at what I see. I treasure you. I get to love this gorgeous, hot, and wicked smart woman. How can you not see that?" She tries to turn in my arms, but I won't let her. "Look at yourself." She's reluctant, but she does.

Problem is, I can't make her see the truth of what I feel when I look at her. That overwhelming love.

"Aviva, do you not love yourself?"

She shrugs. "I do. I just don't like the way I look."

I shake my head. "That's unacceptable. You are perfect."

"Nico, my chest—"

"Is perfection," I say, staring at her. "What can change that for you? Do you want breasts?"

Her lips quiver as she nods. "I do."

"Then get them when Callie does. I'll take care of both of you, or I'll have my mom come in."

"Nico, the shop—"

"Can close for a fucking week, because I can't keep doing this!" I yell, making her jump. "You can't love me if you don't love yourself, and that pisses me the fuck off."

She blinks, tears rolling down her face. "But I do love you."

My heart stops. I wanted to hear those words and I want to believe them, but how can she when she can't even love herself? "You can't fully love me until you love yourself. I can't keep having this conversation with you. I can't keep defending my love for you. I love you with my whole heart, and I know you'd never hurt me because I know I'm fucking awesome, and who could you replace me with? No one." I point to the mirror, where tears are falling quicker down her beautiful face. "Now, love this woman before us and know I would never hurt her or try to replace her. How can I? I can't replace perfection."

With that, I walk out of the bathroom with tears burning my eyes because I don't know if she is capable of loving herself.

And that scares me to the core.

CHAPTER THIRTY

viva

I can't replace perfection.

You can't love me if you don't love yourself.

Nico's words roll over and over again in my head as I stare at myself in his mirror. Tears are flowing down my face as the scars on my chest taunt me.

If you want boobs, get them when Callie does.

I close my eyes as the tears leak out. He doesn't understand. Without pulling up my dress, I head out of the bathroom to find him on the bed, his phone in hand. He looks over at me. "Come to bed."

I glare. "You don't understand," I say loudly. "I have hated this body for nine years. You can't just demand I stop!"

He lays his phone down, putting his hands behind his head. "Yes, I can."

I'm flabbergasted. "No, you can't."

"I can, because I love it. There is absolutely nothing on you to hate,

Aviva. You have this notion in your head that you need boobs to complete you, and you don't."

"But that's my cross to bear, and I'll get there. But how dare you say I can't love you—"

"You can't," he says so calmly. "You'll always think I want better, and that's not fair to me or you. I really don't want anyone else, I promise. I happen to love you and only you."

My jaw is hanging open. "So what? You want to end this?"

He rolls his eyes, letting out a sigh. "What in the hell? How does I love you mean I want to end this?"

"Because why do you get to love me, but I don't get to love you?"

"I don't doubt you love me, Aviva. I mean, come on. I'm a catch—"

"Your cockiness knows no bounds."

He nods. "Yeah, so?"

I can't even argue with him. "Oh my God, you drive me crazy."

"I'm aware," he says simply. "But like I said, I can't keep doing this dance with you. Love yourself, know I'm not fucking around on you or that I want to. I love you. I love that body, and I don't need you to have boobs. I need you to smile."

I shake my head, crossing my arms over my chest as my lip quivers. I hate how I am feeling. So defeated, so worthless. "I don't know how to love myself."

Something changes in his eyes. Gone is the cockiness, replaced by concern. "It's easy, Aviva. Just know you are perfection, and the rest will fall into place."

"How, when I know I'm not? I'm missing a key piece, Nico."

"Funny, because your key piece to me is your soul."

My heart is going crazy in my chest, as are the butterflies in my gut.

"Now, come to bed so I can love on that body of yours and show you why you should love it too."

I just blink. "Why do you drive me crazy?"

"Because it's fun," he says, sitting up and pulling me to him. He kisses me in the middle of my chest and looks up at me. "I love you, Aviva."

I wrap my arms around his neck as he slides his hands down my dress before cupping my ass. I lean my head into his, pressing my nose right below his eye. "I do love you too, Nico."

"I know."

My face breaks into a grin, and my heart soars.

But I'm terrified he's right.

How can I love him when I don't love myself?

As the sun sets, Amelia slowly walks down the aisle on her brother's arm. He holds her like she is a flower, and tears threaten to fall from his eyes. He's wearing a pair of khaki pants and a teal button-down shirt. I was surprised by the minimal decorations for the wedding, but then I saw Amelia's dress. It's a showstopper. Made of only lace, it has tons of beads, crystals, and sparkles that have her gleaming in the setting sun. It's long, dragging on the beach as she walks, while the back is completely bare, showing off her incredible muscles. The lace in the front is cut in a way that shows a lot of skin but also keeps her covered. She isn't wearing a veil, and her hair is flowing down her shoulders. She looks stunning, and Ryan, he's an emotional mess.

I met him yesterday, and it's obvious that his sister and his wife are his life. After losing their dad to cancer, he said walking Amelia down the aisle would be very special to him. It's sweet. Almost as sweet as watching him with his wife; he can't keep his hands off her. Sofia is a gorgeous and stunning gymnast whom Callie has talked to and about nonstop. She owns a gym back in Nashville and offered for Callie to come train if we ever go there. She's apparently pretty badass and has convinced Callie that she needs to go to Bellevue for college. I was hoping she'd stay in state, but let's be honest, that girl is too talented to stay here.

I look up at where the preacher stands with Chandler, who's crying like a baby. Tears gush down that man's face, and it guts me. He looks so handsome in a white button-down and khaki pants. It's obvious he loves Amelia more than anything. Soon, my tears are flowing, and I know Nico is going to tease us all. He's standing there with a shit-eating grin while holding Carter, who is wearing a matching teal shirt and khaki pants. Even with how adorable Carter is, my gaze keeps falling on Nico. He looks so damn good, so damn happy, and I can't wait to cuddle with him later.

His words still haunt me, and I've sort of come to hate them. I don't want to believe that I can't love him without loving myself, because right now, I feel like I love him more than anything. Which may be the problem. He's right. After yesterday, watching Shelli's sister try to get him to sleep with her, and then seeing Shelli, who is basically a goddess in heels, I was riddled with jealousy. How could I measure up? I don't feel like I'm anything even comparable, yet he only looks at me.

He must know I'm thinking of him, because his eyes fall on me as his grin widens. Carter lays his head on Nico's chest, and my heart soars. Nico's going to be a great dad one day, and I pray I get to be the mom. I love that man. When his eyes shift to where Ryan is giving Amelia away, my heart stops.

"I trust you," Ryan says, grabbing Chandler's hand. "You're my best friend and the man who was made for my sister. Protect her, cherish her, and love her."

Chandler's a blubbering mess, but he nods. "Done deal, bro."

"And there is no return policy. She's yours."

Amelia laughs through her sob, and I notice her mom is bawling her eyes out. Amelia's family is all so beautiful. It's really unfair to have so many good-looking people in one family. Shouldn't someone have a boil or something?

"All mine," Chandler says, stealing my attention back. He takes her hand, and for the next twenty minutes, I'm swooning.

Callie leans into me, tears dripping down her cheeks, and I wrap my arms around her. "She's so beautiful."

"She is."

"I can't wait for you to get married," she whispers, and I kiss her head.

"Me either."

She is as surprised by my confession as I am. She curves her lips as she threads her fingers through mine. We watch as Amelia and Chandler stare into each other's eyes and the sun warms the scene.

"The couple has written their own vows, so Amelia, please declare your love for this man."

Amelia clears her throat and then presses her lips together as she stares up into Chandler's eyes. It's easy to see she is struggling and that the emotion is too much. She blinks away some tears and then brings their hands to their chests. She takes in a deep breath. "I found you young, but it didn't work out. I went another way, and you did too. I always think about how life would have been if we had tried to make things work, but I now know that we had to take our separate paths to find each other again." She sniffs, and soon, my tears are flowing faster. "I was bruised and broken when you found me. I felt as if I wasn't worthy of anyone's love, not even my own. I hated myself. I hated life. I hated everything. I was trying so hard to rebuild my life, but what I didn't realize at the time was I needed a partner to do it with."

Yup, pretty sure there isn't a dry eye on this beach.

"Chandler, not only did I fall head over heels in love with you, but I fell in love with myself. I love who I am because of you. You give the gift of your love and your support daily. Carter and Hannah don't even know how lucky they are to have you as a father yet, but I know how lucky I am to have you as my husband."

Chandler closes his eyes and drops his head to hers.

"I will love you until the day I die, Chandler Moon."

Oh, my heart. I watch as Chandler gathers her in his arms, holding her so close, but then my gaze falls on Nico. He is watching them with a dreamy look on his face, and he makes me feel what Amelia is speaking of. I want to love myself. I want to believe I'm the perfection he speaks of. I want to love my life the way Amelia does, and lately, I feel I have. So much is changing, and it's all because of that man right there.

As Chandler clears his throat, Callie cuddles deeper into me. "Do you remember the first time we kissed?" he asks Amelia.

Amelia grins. "I do. In a dark corner of the Bellevue Bullies' house."

"Behind my back," Ryan calls out, and I snort with laughter. Apparently Ryan had said that Chandler couldn't date Amelia. I'm guessing that memo was ignored, but I don't think Ryan can be upset. Their love is overwhelming.

Everyone laughs softly as Chandler nods. "It was so loud in there, but I heard everything you said. That moment is when I knew I loved you, and every moment since we met back up has felt like that moment. There is no one in the world I want to live life with but you. I want to pull the car over and dance with you to every song that reminds us of us. I want to raise our babies and show them what true love is. Because, Amelia, what we have is the real deal," he says, his voice breaking. "I will always be there for you, supporting you and loving you, so that you know your worth." He gathers her face in his hands, and his voice is so low as he says, "I love you, Amelia. Let's do this life together."

When they kiss, the beach erupts with cheers and applause, which wakes up both babies, and they start wailing. Chandler and Amelia part, laughing before grabbing their babies from Nico and Shelli. When they come back to each other, my heart aches with happiness. Chandler kisses Amelia, and I swear someone better have gotten that picture. But even with the gorgeousness that is their love, my attention drifts to Nico. He's grinning so widely as he claps, and he doesn't look too nervous. I can tell he doesn't want to be there, but he loves Chandler and Amelia. When his eyes meet mine, he winks, sending my gut into a fit.

I love you, he mouths, and my heart soars.

I love you too, I mouth back, and I've never meant four words as much as I do those now.

I wrap my arms around Callie and kiss her head. "Hey."

She looks up at me. "Yeah?"

"I love you."

She beams up at me, and soon, I feel that overwhelming love. "I love you too."

As I stare into my sister's eyes, I don't want this feeling to end.

When I notice Nico walking toward us, I stand up, and Callie does too. He comes right for us, wrapping his arms around us both. "Big crybabies."

"Shut up! It was beautiful. I bet you'll cry at your wedding," Callie teases, and Nico snorts.

"Probably," he agrees, and then he kisses my temple.

He looks down at me, and I love his smile. I want to do something I never thought I'd do. "I want to go."

He nods. "Me too, but I promised I'd stay for the party. Thankfully, no best man speech." He shudders. "I would freak."

I shake my head. "No, I want to go to Barcelona with you two."

Callie's eyes widen, and Nico grins. "No way."

"Yes. Can we still go this weekend?"

"The shop?" Callie asks, and I shrug.

"We'll close it for the weekend. I want to have fun."

"For real?" Nico asks, and I nod.

"For real."

He looks over at Callie, who is now jumping up and down, and then calls to Chandler, "Hey, Chandler."

Chandler looks over at us, grinning from ear to ear.

"Put us on the plane thingy, 'cause we're going!"

I'm terrified to leave my business for a weekend, but I want to live.

I want to live with Nico and Callie.

CHAPTER THIRTY-ONE

viva

On our drive home, Callie is still trying to pick out a profile picture for her Instagram. "I like the one with the stones on the one little road where Nico started playing the Ed song the first time."

I nod as I turn into the shop. I swear I would be okay if I never heard that song again. Between Callie and Nico, I think we listened to it a billion times. It was cute, though, watching her dance to it in the middle of the street. I took so many pictures and plan to blow up the one of Nico spinning her while they danced. The trip was worth closing the shop, and I'd do it again if given the chance. I could never have dreamed of the memories we made. It was so much fun.

While the trip was something we will do again, my first hockey game was pretty badass too. I had absolutely no clue what was happening, but the food was good, and Nico was super-hot. The IceCats lost, but we still had a blast.

"I think the one we took at the game tonight was awesome."

She shrugs, but apparently, it wasn't. For the last week, all I've heard about was how she wants to live in Barcelona and never leave. It was amazing. We only had two days, but in those two days, I have never been happier. The nerves I have that I'll fall behind are still there. But I've been able to save so much money from doing the IceCats catering, and I have to keep reminding myself of that. I did the books the day we came back, and I felt a little better. In true form, though, I stress.

"I think the one of Nico twirling both of us is my favorite."

I raise a brow. "You have one of both of us?"

She shows me the picture, and my smile grows. Nico is in the middle of us as he spins us. My red dress flows, as does Callie's blue one. He looks stunning in a pair of shorts and tee, and yup, that's the best picture ever. "How did you get that?"

"I had someone take it. And I did a boomerang."

I make a face. "I don't understand boomerangs, but send me that picture."

"Done," she says, and then she tucks her phone between her legs. "Is Nico coming over?"

"Yeah, but he'll probably be late."

She nods, threading her fingers together. "Why doesn't he just move in?"

I whip my head around to her. "What?"

"He's over all the time anyway, and he has crap at our house and we have crap at his. We might as well just merge our crap together."

I blink. "Callie, please, be real."

She glances over at me. "Aviva, we're a family. I think he should move in. Or us with him."

I take a deep breath, and while I would love to wake up every morning to Nico, that's insane. He'd probably laugh in my face. He likes his space, and I like mine. But I like it more when he is around. "Maybe in a year if we're still together."

She makes a face. "You know he isn't going anywhere, right?"

I swallow hard and my heart aches. She is already attached to Nico, loves him, and it makes me nervous. If something does happen, she'll be crushed.

As would I.

But she's right, he won't go anywhere. We're a cute little family. I don't answer her, though, as I turn into the parking lot of the shop. We head inside, and I lock the door and set the alarm. Nico is coming over, but I gave him a key to get in the other day and he knows the code, so I head upstairs to shower and clean up. I don't know how I feel about this jersey. It's entirely too big. Callie's swallows her whole, and mine hangs on me like a potato sack. I'm not a fan, but I did enjoy wearing Nico's number. By the look on his face, I know he loved it too.

Callie heads to bed since she has school tomorrow, while I get in the shower. Nico is leaving tomorrow, and then we leave Saturday for the conference. I'm excited to go because of how excited Nico is. Even Callie is pumped, but I think it's because of all the free stuff we'll get. She loves that sort of thing. As I wash my body, I can't stop my mind from wandering to what Callie said about Nico moving in. That would be crazy. Right? Yeah, he is here all the time, and we only go to his house on date nights, but he wouldn't want to live here. I'm insane. It's been like five minutes; we are nowhere near ready to discuss moving in or anything.

But then, why does it feel so right to want him to?

Once I'm washed, I get out and put on my robe. I wrap my hair up and find myself picking up my phone to call Jaylin. She answers right away.

"Whatup," she says on a yawn. "It's late. I need my beauty sleep."

"Callie said Nico should move in."

I'm met with silence for a moment. "How do you feel about that?"

"I don't know. It's only been a few months. Like three."

"Yeah, but he's there all the time, isn't he?"

"He is, but he has the freedom to leave and get away from me."

She snorts. "I doubt he needs that freedom. Have you asked him?"

"Not at all. I feel crazy thinking it."

"Ask him, then."

I wrinkle my face. "Would you move in with someone after three months?"

"If I loved them, I would."

"Hmm. This is weird."

"What?" she laughs. "Feelings?"

"Yeah, they're tricky."

Jaylin scoffs. "But they're so much fun."

When my door opens, Nico fills the doorway, looking tiredly sexy. His hair is brushed back and wet. His suit is fitted, but the first three buttons of his shirt are unbuttoned while his tie hangs loosely. "Nico just got here. Let me call you back."

"Ugh, I'm so jealous you're about to bang."

I hang up, shaking my head. "Hey you."

He grumbles, but still, he sends me a small smile. "Sorry I lost," he says, coming to the bed and crawling over me.

I wrap my arms and legs around him, kissing his lips. "It's okay. Amelia said that you guys got screwed and that power up shouldn't have happened."

He shakes his head. "Power play, baby," he corrects me before kissing my lips. "I really need to watch hockey with you."

"You do," I agree as he presses himself into me.

"Did you have fun?" he asks, chewing at my bottom lip.

"I did. I ate the popcorn pretzel tree thing. Not bad."

"Told you."

I grin against his lips. "It turned me on, watching you."

He groans against my mouth. "Oh yeah?"

"Yup," I say, rubbing myself against his slacks.

"Watching you there did something to me. I want you so bad."

"Do you?"

"So fucking bad," he murmurs against my mouth before kissing me once more.

I fall into the kiss, feeling it all over. His hands find their way into my robe, untying it and cupping my sex. I arch into his hand as his finger slides between my lips.

"Damn, you're so wet."

"I want you."

He growls against my mouth as he rakes his teeth over my lips, nipping at my jaw before sucking on my neck. I want to moan so loudly, cry his name, but Callie is in the next room. He makes his way down my chest, kissing and nipping, driving me wild.

"I'm freshly showered," I mutter, and he bites my stomach.

"Mmm, I love when you talk dirty to me."

I snort-giggle until his tongue glides along my stomach, licking at my belly button as he pushes my robe away, revealing my naked body. He kisses down my thigh to my knee before running his tongue back up my thigh and along the slit of my lips. I roll my eyes up into the back of my head as he continues the slow torture. I hold on to his shoulder when he moved the tip of his tongue along my lips. When he opens me, I arch up into his mouth, and he devours me. His tongue and fingers stroke me in all the right ways. When he slides his thumb into my pussy, I have to cover my mouth to keep from screaming. He presses his thumb into me harder, in and out as he flicks the tip of his tongue against my clit. I feel everything tightening, and soon, I break. I cry into my hand, gathering the blankets with my fingers as he sucks me into oblivion.

I don't feel him move or even undress. I'm lost. Completely gone. But then he is filling me to the hilt. One fluid motion, quick and hard. I grab ahold of his thighs as he pounds into me, holding me by my ankles with my legs up in the air. I look up to see he has no control on his face and he is taking what he wants. What he needs. And I am A-okay being on the receiving end. His body slaps into mine, and his cock feels so damn good in me. It's so thick, filling me in all the ways I never knew I needed until I met him. His eyes are hooded, gorgeous, and sexy, and soon, he slams into me, a moan bubbling in his chest as his fingers bite into my ankles. He jerks into me once, then again, and finally, his head drops back as he fills me.

When he falls onto me, I wrap my arms around his neck as my heart pounds with his. He kisses my neck, my jaw, and then my earlobe before bringing it into his mouth. I giggle softly and try to stop him, but I don't really want to. He smiles against my jaw before kissing it once more. "Hey."

"Yeah?"

"I didn't wear a condom."

I wait for the fear. Anything. But nothing comes. "I'm on birth control."

He pauses for a second and then mumbles, "Okay."

It's almost like he is disappointed, but surely he's not. "Did you not want me to be?"

"I figured you were, but it doesn't matter either way."

"No?"

"Nope. I like you a little bit."

I know what he is implying, and I'm surprised how much that pleases me. With a grin on my face, I ask, "Just a bit?"

"Just a wee bit," he teases, and then I turn my head to his.

His grin grows as I demand, "Kiss me."

"Don't have to ask me twice."

As we fall into the kiss, I'm aware I don't know what the hell the future holds, but I'm starting to realize my future starts and ends with him.

* * *

My alarm goes off at the butt-crack of dawn, and Nico groans.

"Why? It's early."

I chuckle tiredly as I cuddle into him. "Gotta get the bread in the oven."

"Screw the bread. People need to slow down on carbs anyway," he says, and I laugh as I kiss his jaw.

"But then how will I make money?"

He kisses me. "You don't need it. I'll take care of you."

I snort. "Because I'm all for that."

"Damn it, why you gotta be a strong woman? Be a gold digger. It's way easier."

I laugh loudly. "You're insane."

He holds me closer. "Don't leave this bed. I demand it."

"I've got to."

"Bullshit."

"Sleep. I'll come back up before I open the shop."

"Naked?"

"So naked," I say, kissing his cheek.

He's weird about morning breath, and I can't blame him. Mine is awful. I head to the bathroom and get washed up before heading downstairs. Callie should be down in an hour or so, but I'll get most of the work done. She's been busting ass in school since competition season is coming up fast. She wants to get ahead because she's an overachiever like that. As I get to work, a small smile plays on my face while the radio blasts the top hits. I'm dancing, singing, and having a great time. I know I have a hot man upstairs, and Callie is safe and healthy. I feel good. Really good.

When I hear someone on the stairs, I look up to see Nico coming down in just his athletic shorts.

"What are you doing?"

He sighs ruefully. "I can't have you down here working by yourself. I want to help."

Oh, this man explodes through the walls I try to keep up. "You don't have to. You worked late last night. In and out of bed."

He sends me a flashy grin. "Yeah, but by working now, the reward is being with you." My face breaks into a grin as he kisses my cheek. "What do you want me to do?"

"Can you start cutting meat?"

"Yup." He puts on an apron and then some gloves before getting to work. I have to admit, I love working with him.

"Callie said something funny yesterday."

He looks up from where he is cutting the roast beef. "I'm not surprised, but tell me anyway."

I smile. "She said you should move in."

I watch his body language and wait for the freak-out. His jaw gets tense and so does his back, but he's thinking it over. I thought he would just yell out hell no, but he's actually thinking. When he looks over at me, I give him a weak smile.

"What did you say?"

"I said it was kind of early."

I'm met with silence as he piles the meat onto a tray. He doesn't look at me or even comment, and I find that I'm just watching him. When he glances over at me, he shrugs. "I mean, I already kind of do live here."

"I know."

"But it has only been three months."

"I know," I say once more, sounding like a parrot. "But how does the idea make you feel?"

When I'm answered with a grin, my heart soars. "Good."

I smile back. "Me too."

He nods slowly. "Okay."

"Okay."

We hold each other's gaze. "So, am I moving in?"

"I don't know," I say, and he laughs. "How about we just keep doing us?"

He thinks that over for a minute. "Or we can start looking for a place to make ours."

My heart just about stops in my chest. "Really?"

"Yeah, a bigger place because I don't want to move again when we decide to have kids."

My eyes widen. "Wow. This conversation is real."

He nods. "Way too real." We grin at each other. "Maybe we should go back to just doing us? Together, though."

"Oh, totally together."

He nods, and I sigh deeply. "But after Christmas, start looking." I meet his gaze once more. This is really real. "If you want."

"I do."

"Okay."

"Okay."

When the sound of a guitar starts on the radio, Nico looks over at the speaker and turns it up before holding his hand to me. "Have you heard this song?"

I take his hand, and he pulls me in. "Yeah, it's one of my favorites."

I love anything James Arthur sings. But "Falling like the Stars" is a beautiful love song.

"It reminds me of us."

My heart tries to come out of my chest. "It does?"

"Yeah," he whispers against my lips. "And all I think is that I want to do what Chandler said, dance to all the songs that remind us of us."

I will not cry, but with so much emotion in his voice, I nod. "I'd love that."

So, slowly, we dance in the kitchen. As the music plays, I rest my head on his chest, not wanting to do anything else but this. Chandler was right; there is nothing better than dancing with the one you love at any time. Nico holds me close, kissing the top of my head until the music stops and my phone rings.

"What the hell?"

I move out of his arms. "I like my playlists on my phone!" He laughs as I grab my phone. When I see it's Jaylin, I make a face. It's really early. Why is she up? I answer the phone, "Hey. It's—"

"I know. Listen, I just got a fax from Dustin."

My stomach drops, and I clutch the phone.

"He is selling the shop building."

And there it is—the other shoe.

Everything stops, and my blurry gaze falls on Nico. I can't even speak. A sob is choking me, and then I'm crouching down.

Man, this isn't a shoe that's dropped.

It's a brick.

To my face.

CHAPTER THIRTY-TWO

viva

NICO COMES TO ME, cupping my elbow. "What's wrong?"

"Someone wants to buy the shop."

There is no reaction from him, and I'm sure he's as shocked as I am.

"Jaylin, my lease is still for another six months. I thought he said he would give us the first opportunity to buy."

Her voice is strained. "I know. I'm trying to figure this out. I wasn't going to call yet, but I knew I had to because we need to know if we are countering."

"Countering?"

"Yeah. I need to get the loan going as soon as I find out how much I need to outbid the other person by."

"Outbid? Jesus, what the hell? I don't understand. Why he is such a slimy turtle-dick asshole?"

"Turtle dick?"

"I'm angry, okay?"

"Yeah, he is a turtle dick," she agrees. I love her. "I don't know, Vee, but what do you want to do? Do you want me to fight this? Outbid the jackass who is trying to get the place—" She stops. "Let me call you back. That's him."

She hangs up, and I let my phone rest at my ear. "I don't understand. Why is he being a jackass? This is my shop."

Nico rubs my elbow. "I'm sure it's okay. Don't worry. It will work out. You won't lose this place."

"You don't know that. Dustin wants money and…fuck! What am I going to do?"

He grabs me, pulling me in close and holding my chin in his fingers. "Baby, I promise. Don't stress. This will all work out. Jaylin is a shark. She won't let anything happen to you." His eyes burn into mine. "And you say the word, and I'll give you the money."

I shake my head. "She's going to help me get a loan, and I'll pay it. I don't want to take your money," I say quickly, my mind racing. I don't know how this could have happened. Why would anyone want this place? It's mine! It's been in my family for fifteen years. Nothing else could ever go in here; the walls smell like subs.

"Take it. I don't want it. I want you to smile," he says, grabbing my face. "It's okay. This will work out."

I drop my face onto his chest and breathe in deeply. I don't understand the sense of calm that washes over me at being in his arms. Before, I would have freaked, had a panic attack, and probably made myself sick, but Nico keeps me calm. Which is insane since he is a bundle of nerves all the time. For some reason, though, he knows how to handle me, and I hope he knows I've got him covered. As he strokes his thumb along my jaw, I almost believe this will all work out.

Almost.

When my phone rings, I pull away and answer it without looking at the caller ID. "Hello?"

"Okay, so wow… This is so crazy," Jaylin says, her voice shaky.

"Crazy?"

"The place has been sold."

My stomach drops once more. "But how—"

"To you, Aviva."

I blink. Confused. "Huh?"

"She bought the place for you. She paid the money and wants your name on the deed, with Callie as a co-owner."

Nico is staring at me. "What?"

"It's been sold. To me."

Nico lights up. "Good! The loan is good?"

I shake my head. "No, someone bought it for me," I say slowly, unsure what the hell is happening.

"I got a name. Florence Tremblay. And the only reason I got that was because I called her lawyer. He's out of Buffalo, New York, and I demanded answers. He said he doesn't know much about her but that she wanted to make sure you were taken care of. He wouldn't give me her number or anything, but I'll get it, don't worry. I don't know who this chick is, but if she's buying shops for people, maybe she can buy me some stuff."

My stomach is in knots. "I don't understand."

"I don't either, but I'll find out."

The line goes dead, and I look up at Nico. "Some woman bought me the shop because she wants me to be taken care of."

He just blinks. "Do you know who she is?"

"No, and I don't know why she would do this," I say, and then I grab my computer from the office.

"What are you doing?" he calls out to me.

"I'm going to Google her."

"You have a name?"

"Yeah." But when I type it in, nothing comes up. I look up to see him on his phone. "Are you searching?"

He looks over at me. "Huh?"

"Are you searching too?"

He nods. "Uh-huh. Sure am."

I love him so much. "I'm not getting anything, but Jaylin will figure it out. She'll find her, and then we're gonna have a talk." He looks tense, and I'm bewildered. "What?"

"Nothing. I'm just a little confused. What will you talk to her about?"

"I'll demand that she let me pay her back!"

"Okay, that's a good plan. And if she says no?"

"Then I have no clue what the hell I'll do," I say slowly. "Why would she do this for me? She doesn't even know me."

He shrugs. "I don't know."

I'm beyond bewildered. I don't understand why anyone would do this. While the fact that I will never have to deal with Dustin again is appealing, I don't want someone buying the shop for me. I had an issue when Jaylin wanted to. But now a complete stranger? I don't think so. How can I accept something like that? I am still struggling with someone paying my mom's bills. I sent the amount I usually paid on the bill to the YMCA After Breast Cancer program instead. Even doing that doesn't make me feel right. I feel like a charity case.

As Nico wraps his arms around me, he kisses my lips. "Hey, it's all okay."

"I don't know, Nico. I feel pathetic."

"Why? You mean so much to someone that they want to help you and make your life and Callie's better."

The only person I know who would do that is him. I look up at him. "And you didn't do this?"

He shakes his head, his eyes burning into mine. "No, but I would if you'd let me." I swallow hard as he cups my face. "Listen, don't think about this right now. You guys are leaving for the conference tomorrow, and you're going to have a blast. Don't worry about it. Everything will work out."

As much as I want to believe him, I don't. I knew things were too good to be true. Yeah, it's awesome someone bought me a shop, and anyone else would be dropping to their knees thanking the good Lord above, but what happens when they come back, demanding things from me? I'll owe them, I'll have to do what they want, and that makes me apprehensive. I don't want to owe anyone, because if something happens to me, it all falls on Callie.

Like it did on me when I lost my mom.

* * *

I SIT between Callie and Jaylin in the packed ballroom. A stage is in the middle of the room with chairs surrounding it. The room is full of women of all types, shapes, and sizes. I have never been around so many women in my life. While I know Nico wanted to be here with us, he wouldn't be able to handle this. Too many people. Plus, come to find out, men aren't allowed in here anyway. I'm not sure why. Even Security is women. I guess Lacey is all about girl power, and I, for one, love it.

The conference has been amazing, and we've gotten so much information and, to Callie's delight, so many free samples. We've met so many women and heard so many stories of survival. It's amazing, and I am truly enjoying myself—when I stop thinking about everything that is happening outside the conference. Jaylin hasn't been able to find out anything about the person who bought the shop or what their motive is. I know there has to be one, and it makes me sick to my stomach to think about it. I just want to know. I want to talk to them, and I want to demand that they allow me to pay them back. I've gone back and forth on if I should be happy about this or not. I mean, it's awesome to be out from underneath Dustin, but this feels like a handout, and everyone knows I hate those. Jaylin doesn't believe it's bad, but she wants to know too so that I can figure this out.

"I am so excited to be here! Did you know Lacey had a mastectomy just before she turned eighteen?" Callie exclaims beside me.

Jaylin is on her phone, typing violently, as I glance over at Callie and nod. "I did. Her story is amazing."

"She lost her mom too, young like us."

"Yeah, Nico said that when we go to Nashville, we can have dinner with her. We were supposed to have dinner tonight, but she has to fly out. I think one of her kids is sick."

"Aww! That blows. But cool about Nashville. Can we go there like now? I have so many questions. Plus, it didn't say online what gene she had, but I wonder if it's the same one we have."

"I think they are all the same," Jaylin says. "Cancer gene, out to kill ya."

We both nod as the lights dim, and then out of nowhere, the crowd loses its mind. Yup, Nico wouldn't be able to handle this. I miss him. I notice that Jaylin is still on her phone, so I reach over, pushing it out of her hand. She glares back at me. But she does tuck it in between her legs as Lacey King takes the stage. This isn't the first time we've seen her this conference, but under the stage lights, she looks even better. I've seen some beautiful women, but Lacey is stunning. She has long, luscious blond hair and big lashes that I can see from our seats. She wears a black pencil skirt with a pink breast cancer shirt, and when she waves, people are screaming like she's a Jonas Brother or something.

Soon, I realize why.

I am on the edge of my seat as I listen to her talk. She takes over the room, demanding the attention of everyone in here. I'm in awe of her story, how after watching her mom die, she fought her own cancer and then decided on her mastectomy. She talks of her family, how it was hard to fight cancer without her mom, and how hard it was on her father and brother. In a lot of ways, it validates my reasoning for getting rid of my breasts. I didn't want to go through what my mom did alone—or put Callie though that.

When Lacey comes to the side of the stage near our seats, I find myself holding my breath. "I met the man of my dreams when I was almost nineteen years old. I fell hard for him. But sometimes, especially as kids, things don't work out. We were young, he was on the fast track to the NHL, and I was trying to find me again. Yes, we did break up, and he went his way and I went mine. But the good news is we found each other again, and now we are happily married with the most amazing kids in the world."

The crowd claps loudly, and so do I, watching her in awe.

"There are a lot of moments in my life where my husband has completely blown me away and made me feel like the most perfect woman on this earth, but the moment that still touches me to this day was when we were kids." A small little grin sits on her face as she presses her hand to her stomach, the mic at her lips. "As we know with mastectomies, they leave nasty scars, and I hadn't gotten my implants yet because my dad wouldn't allow me to since I was so young. So, the thought of being intimate with a guy was terrifying. I remember telling Karson about it, and he was confused at first, but when he saw my scars, he treasured them. He didn't care that they were there, that I didn't have breasts or anything. He didn't love my breasts. He loved *me,* and to this day, I will never question his love because of that moment."

I'm holding my breath, and soon, I find myself pressing my hands into my chest.

Nico. Nico does that.

"Who here has had a mastectomy? Stand up for me."

Most of the room stands up, including Jaylin. Callie smacks me, but I hesitate until Jaylin pulls me up beside her. My heart is in my throat, and I feel my skin tingling as Lacey places her mic in the stand.

"Thank you. Now, do you hate your body? Do you resent your scars?"

I notice a lot of women are nodding. Not Jaylin, but most everyone else. I turn back to the stage and zone in on Lacey.

"I know. It's hard to love something that society says isn't beautiful." She moves her hands out in front of her. "As you can see, this room is completely full of women. There are no men here, and I want you to do something with me."

My jaw drops when she takes off her shirt, throwing it to the ground. She has implants, but even with the beautiful tattoos on her chest, I can see her jagged scars beneath them. "I want you to remove your shirt with me. Then throw that bra to the floor."

I'm in shock as people start following her instructions. Surely there has to be someone offended here, but no one says anything. People are cheering, clapping loudly as more and more women remove their shirts and bras. When I look at Jaylin, she's topless, standing proudly.

Tears burn in my eyes at her beauty, her strength.

I want that.

"Aviva. Do it," Callie urges.

I want to.

What in the world am I doing?

"I love this body," Lacey says, tears in her eyes. "And I'm proud of it. Say it with me."

I don't say it at first. I don't utter a word; I just listen to the many women around me who are saying it. When Callie threads her fingers through mine, I look over at her, and she's saying the words. My heart cracks in my chest, and I ask myself, *How can I hate this body when Callie's is going to mirror mine soon?* I can't have her doing what I am. I am alive. I am loved, and damn it, I am happy.

So, at the top of my lungs as I pull off my shirt, I yell the words until tears stream down my face and I believe them.

I love this body, and I am proud of it.

* * *

"NICO, IT WAS ABSOLUTELY PHENOMENAL."

I'm basically bouncing, and I can hear the excitement in his voice when he replies.

"Baby, that's awesome."

"She is so uplifting. We all took our shirts off—"

"You were topless? Hot."

"Nico, focus!" I laugh as I stand inside the café, waiting for Jaylin and Callie to get a snack. "We're topless, all these women with their scars, and we're all pledging to love our bodies. It was amazing. Perfect, even. I have never experienced something like that, and then I'm yelling so loudly that I know Lacey heard me. She pointed right to me and even yelled 'Yes!' Because I have to believe it, Nico. I can't let Callie grow up hating herself. It's pointless, especially when she is so loved."

He sighs softly. "That's right, Aviva. Man, you don't know how happy I am to hear you say that. I am pumped you had a good time."

"Great time! I bought her book and her journal, and I'm really going to work on this. I don't want to hate myself. I want to love myself."

"Good, because I love you, Aviva. I love you so much, and I'm so proud of you."

My heart hurts from how swollen it is with love. I'm so inspired. I let out a long sigh. "I love you more, Nico. You really have changed so much for me."

I wait for the cocky comeback. But instead, he says, "Right back atcha, baby. My therapist said I was a grown-up the other day."

"Aw, you're a real man, Pinocchio!"

He laughs. "I love you, baby. Listen, I hate to let you go, but I have to hit the ice. Be careful going home, and I'll see you tomorrow."

"I can't wait."

"Me either."

We say goodbye, and as I hang up the phone, I see Jaylin walking toward me with Callie. A weird look is on her face as she holds her phone in her hand. I raise my brows as she stops in front of me.

"That was my informant."

Like a rock, I fall from my happiness cloud of rainbows. "Oh?"

"I know who Florence Tremblay is."

I bring in my brows. "Who?"

"Florence Myra Tremblay kept her maiden name when she married Marco Merryweather," she says.

I scrunch up my face, but then it clicks.

My heart stops, and everything goes cold as she says, "She won't speak to me. Told me to talk to Nico."

I knew that shoe was going to fall—I felt it in my soul—but I never expected it would be because Nico lied to me.

CHAPTER THIRTY-THREE

ico

WHEN I GET off the plane, I turn on my phone, and it starts vibrating and beeping like crazy. Sixteen voice mails and thirty-three texts. I raise my brows as I click on the texts. It only takes one of them to know I'm in deep shit.

Callie: Aviva knows, and she is on a rampage. Take cover.

Jaylin: Dude, really? She's going to kill you dead.

Mom: The lawyer found out, called me, and I told her to contact you. I told you that you should have been honest from the beginning.

I exhale heavily as I hit my mom's name. I probably should call Aviva first, but I'm not stupid. I need to know what is going on. Once I'm in the truck, I start it as she answers.

"Oh, Nicolas, she's pissed."

"What happened?"

"She called and demanded I let her pay me back."

"What did you say?"

"I told her it was all you."

"Really, Mom?" I ask, dropping my head to the steering wheel. "I thought we decided that it was you with my money."

She scoffs. "She was pissed, and I'm sorry, but she's scary. Plus, I think you need to own up to this. I didn't know she would be so upset. Usually women love when men do things for them."

"Eh, that's normal women who see it as an act of love. I'm with a strong-willed woman no one has ever done anything for."

I take a deep breath and rack my brain for how I'm going to handle this. She's going to yell, but I can handle yelling. Since I decided to do this and everything has been taken care of, she has been so much happier. She isn't worried about making ends meet, and she's living. I mean, she closed the shop to go to Barcelona because she wanted to. I knew then I was doing the right thing. She just has to realize that. She has to realize I did it because I am unequivocally in love with her.

"Well, I suggest you get ready. She did not seem happy, and Callie, that sweet thing, was in the background trying to defend you, but Aviva wasn't having it."

Callie. That's my partner in crime.

"It's okay. I can handle Aviva."

I hang up and put my phone on the seat. I don't know if I want to go to her house or mine. Maybe she's sleeping and isn't thinking about what I did. She probably isn't that mad. Probably happy it was me and not some stranger.

Who am I kidding? She's gonna skin me alive.

I reach for my phone and dial Chandler's number. "Hey, you okay?"

"Well… Eh, listen, a little backstory. I paid Callie's gym fees for the next two years, I paid off Aviva's mom's medical bills, and then I bought her the shop. How do I keep her from killing me?"

I'm met with silence. "So, do you need the plane to leave the country? Or should I just start planning the funeral? Am I on the life insurance policy?"

"Chandler, be real. Surely she can't be that mad."

He scoffs. "If she is anything like how Amelia has described, I think she is that mad and you are that dead."

"But I did it because I love her."

He lets out a long breath. "Dude, I know, but she isn't going to see it that way. She's gonna see it as pity because that's all she knows."

"Whatever. That's bullshit. She loves me," I say, and I'm almost to the house when I see Aviva's car. "Well, shit."

"What?"

"She's here."

"Well, nice knowing you. I'll tell Carter and Hannah stories of you—"

I hang up and park behind her car. If I block her in, she can't leave. I get out and lock up the truck after grabbing my bag. I don't want to be yelled at, but I'm ready for it. I know what I did was for the best, and she'll realize that once I explain myself. She'll be okay. We'll be fine. I'm not worried at all.

When I reach for the door, I pause. What if it's not going to be fine? What if she freaks out on me and does something drastic? I mean, I knew better. I did, but I didn't care. From the moment I met her, all I wanted was to make her happy. I wanted to make her smile because she needed to. No one as beautiful as she is should be so sad all the time. Not when I have the means to help her. It makes sense to me. Surely it will to her?

Okay, now I'm worried.

I push the door open, and she's there, on the couch. Her eyes are wild, and her lips are pressed together firmly as she stands slowly.

"Oh, hey."

"Don't *oh, hey* me," she snaps, and I nod as I shut the door.

"Okay," I say. "What's up?"

She glares. "What's up? Are you serious, Nico? How could you?"

"What?" I know I shouldn't be acting like this, but maybe if I play dumb for a moment, she'll calm down.

Wishful thinking.

"Nico, stop!" she yells, her eyes burning with rage. "You lied."

I hold up my palms, shrugging. "Eh, not technically."

"No, it's very technical."

"I didn't do it. My mom did."

"With your money! I don't even know what you were thinking. I didn't even think you could lie!"

I give her a look. "I'm autistic, Aviva. I can lie just fine."

She glares. "What the hell, Nico?"

"What? I didn't lie about anything else. Just that."

"That doesn't make this better. How could you do this when you know I don't take charity? I don't want to owe you anything!"

"You don't," I say simply. "It's yours, no strings attached. I don't want anything but for you and Callie to be happy."

"I don't need your money to be happy! I just need you."

"Well, I come with the money. And the thing is, Aviva, you were drowning. I have all this money. I wanted to make sure you were taken care of no matter what happens between us. You've been struggling for a while. It's time for some good to come your way."

She looks as if I slapped her. "How dare you? I am not a charity case."

I make a face. "Never said you were."

"By doing this, you have."

I glare. "That's bullshit."

"You knew I wouldn't be okay with this. You knew I didn't want your help or anyone else's, yet you did it anyway! That's why you hid it. How could you? I feel so betrayed."

I shake my head. "It's not even like that. I did it because I love you—"

"If you loved me, then you wouldn't have done it!"

"Not true!" I yell back, my eyes burning into hers as my breathing kicks up. "We're talking about moving in together, kids, marriage. I mean, fuck, Aviva, what happens when we get married? All your debt comes with you, and then what? Am I supposed to let you struggle while I'm rolling in dough? Let your asshole of a landlord treat you like shit and see the stress eat you alive? My job is to love and support you, and I feel I do that really well."

Her eyes widen. "We aren't married, Nico!"

"Not yet, but you better believe we will be, because I'm not going anywhere. I want you, I want to marry you, and I want to make you happy. Believe me, I would have told you, but I wanted to wait until maybe we were on our deathbeds."

I said that to make her laugh, but she doesn't. Her eyes are aflame with anger, and soon, tears start to gather. "You lied to me."

I let my shoulders fall as I sigh loudly. "Yeah. And I'm sorry if that upsets you, but my intentions were good."

"I feel like a pathetic charity case who can't pay my own bills, so my boyfriend has to bail me out. I didn't need a hero, I didn't need your money. I just wanted you."

"Aviva, I feel like you're blowing this out of proportion—"

"I don't want to see you anymore."

My mouth gapes open. "Well, now you're really blowing this out of proportion. Are you fucking serious?"

Tears fall quickly as she takes in a shaky breath. "I can't be with someone who lies to me and goes behind my back—"

"You act like I'm cheating on you!" I roar, and she stands there, stone-faced. "I paid off some shit to help you get ahead, and you want to break up with me because of that? That's fucking stupid, and you know it. Take all of my money, Aviva. I want you to have it because you are the most important person in my life. I love you. Take it," I say, throwing my wallet to her.

She catches it, her eyes practically on fire. "I don't fucking want it. What part of that don't you understand?" She throws the wallet back, and I let it hit the ground. She slowly shakes her head as she wipes away her tears. "You lied about this, about your autism—"

"I never lied about my autism. I just didn't tell you!"

"You hid it from me, just like you did this."

"For fuck's sake, Aviva, I withheld information because I didn't want to upset you. Be real here. I did nothing wrong! Maybe a little shady, but not wrong."

"No, I am being real. It's not my fault you don't understand boundaries—"

"Whoa, wow," I gasp, my chest tightening. "Thought my autism didn't matter."

She presses her lips together. "I didn't mean it that way."

"Well, you fucking said it."

She looks away. "You know what, I'm gonna walk away."

"The fuck you are. You're staying here."

"No."

"Yes. We need to fix this."

She shakes her head. "We can't. Not tonight. I don't know if we ever can."

I take a step toward her, and she backs up. "Get your stubborn head out of your ass and realize that I did this with good intentions. I did this because when we get married, we can start a life with no worries in the world. I don't fucking need the money, Aviva, I need you."

"Funny... That's all I wanted from you. You—nothing else. I would have figured it out."

"Why? When I can take all your burdens away and we can be happy?" She moves past me, and I try to grab her. "I don't want you to leave. I want to talk about this."

"For what? So we can yell and scream at each other while going round and round? You don't think you're wrong, and I know you are, so there is nothing else to say."

She pulls out of my grip and heads for the door. She needs to go. To cool off.

"I have you blocked in."

She shrugs before taking my keys from the bowl next to the door. "I'll move it and leave them on the front steps."

The door slams behind her, and I don't know what just happened. All these emotions are swirling deep inside me, and soon, I realize they are making me sick. Her words turn over and over again in my head, and I almost don't believe them. I look at my helmet that is lying there, waiting for me to hide, but I don't reach for it. I don't want to hide. I want her to listen to me. I go to the door, pulling it open as she gets out of my truck that she's parked in the yard.

"So, you're breaking up with me?"

She shrugs as she throws my keys to me. "I don't know, Nico. I need time to cool off."

"Because I paid all your debts? Way to treat me when I do that for you."

She stops mid-step. "And that, right there, is why I didn't want you to do this. You don't realize because you don't think things through, Nico. But you've basically made me feel trapped. As if I could never leave you. And that's why I'm leaving."

I rush down the stairs, running to her and stopping her before she closes the door. I hold the door in my hand as she looks up at me with tearful eyes, but I shake my head. "Hear me out." I crouch down and take her hand in mine. She wants to fight me on it, but I hope she doesn't. "I hear you, and to be honest, I didn't mean to say that. I don't want this to be held over your head, which is why I asked my mom to do it with my money. I know that you didn't want anyone to do it, and I get it. I do. You are a strong woman who can do this all yourself, but I am a man who wants my woman to be happy. I want to care for you. I want to make things easier for you because I love how you wake up with a smile on your face. I love how you just seem lighter—"

"Let me stop you there," she says, squeezing my hand. "All that wasn't because of the debt being gone. It was because of you."

I press my lips together, and soon, tears are in my eyes. "I don't want to lose you over this. Aviva, I did it because I love you."

She looks away, inhaling shakily. "I don't want to lose you, but I don't know how to forgive you for this. Especially when you feel no remorse whatsoever—"

"I'm sorry I upset you, but I'm not sorry I paid those bills," I say, and she brings in her brows. "I swear to you, Aviva, I did it because I know I'm going to marry you, and I would have paid them then. So, what's the problem with doing it now?"

She removes her hand from mine. "Because at least that way, I wouldn't have been made out to be a charity case." She starts the car and looks over at me. "I would move if I were you."

I do as she says because there is no talking to her. I step out of the way. "Please call me tomorrow."

She shrugs. "I don't know."

Then she shuts the door and drives off.

As I watch her drive away, everything is shaking. I don't want to believe this is over; she's just mad. But even so, I feel like she's taken my heart with her.

And hell, she might as well keep it, because it's hers.

CHAPTER THIRTY-FOUR

viva

I CLUTCH my pillow and rub my face into it, hoping to get rid of the tears. When I'm not working, I'm in bed, and it's really getting pathetic. It's been three days since I've seen or talked to Nico, and I want to say things are better, but they're not. I'm still spitting mad at what Nico did, and I still can't believe he did it. He knew I would be upset. But, as angry as I am, I can believe he would do this. He doesn't think, he just does, and he does it with his whole heart. When I drove away, it killed me to do so, especially with the tears in his eyes. I know I said I couldn't be with him because of this, but that was the anger talking.

I'm just so mad.

I've worked so hard for what I needed and wanted for Callie. Never taken from anyone. But then Nico comes along and does what Nico does. Whatever the hell he wants. And I encouraged it. Loved it. He made me feel good, made me feel loved, and while I know he did it with purity in his heart, I don't want him just to save me when he feels

I'm drowning. I wanted him to discuss it with me, tell me his plans. I would have told him no, and if he did it anyway, I would have known it was him. Instead, I've stressed for months that someone is out there helping me and giving me things when I don't deserve them. Instead, it was being done by the man I love. And while I still don't feel I deserve it all, Nico does. His love knows no bounds, and I wish instead of angry, I felt appreciative. He loved me enough to make things easier for me. But the problem is, I don't understand how.

When my door opens, I look up as Callie comes in.

And then Jaylin.

"Great, the cavalry."

Jaylin laughs as she crawls into the bed and under the covers. Callie climbs onto the covers beside me, moving my hair out of my face. "Are you okay?"

"Fine, just pissed."

"I know," she says, and she smiles. "He won last night."

I nod. "Good to know I don't affect his hockey playing."

"I still think you do," Callie says, and I roll my eyes. "He looked sad through the whole game."

"He's an adult. He's fine."

She gives me a hard look. "Aviva, are you truly surprised?"

I scrunch up my face. "What?"

"Come on. It's Nico. Surely you had to have thought he was the one doing this. I did."

"I did too," Jaylin says from the other side of me.

I go up onto my elbows to look at them both. "And no one thought to say anything?"

Jaylin shrugs, cuddling in my blankets. "I figured, who cared as long as you were happy?"

I glare. "But it bothered me that someone was doing it."

"But you were happy," Callie says, and I look back over at her. "You were finally doing things for yourself. Smiling more and living. I mean, you dropped everything to go to Barcelona. Aviva, you'd never have done that before."

"And I know you want to be a strong woman, hear me roar, but the thing is, you are," Jaylin stresses. "You fought to stay afloat for so long. And yes, it sucks he lied, but he did it for a good reason."

"Because he loves you," Callie adds, and our eyes meet. "He loves you so much, Aviva. I know he shouldn't have lied, but I don't think you can really break up with him for it."

Jaylin nods. "It's a little silly to do that when you feel what you feel for him."

I shake my head. "How can I be with someone who lies to me?"

Jaylin lets her head drop back, and Callie lets out a long breath. "Here we go."

"What?"

"Self-Sabotage Sally in full force."

I make a face. "He sabotaged us by lying and paying for something that wasn't his place to pay for. He bought me this shop—"

"Because he knew how much Dustin upset you," Callie stresses. "And if, for some reason, Dad comes back, the place is ours."

"He made sure you and Callie were taken care of, no matter what. When he dropped the deed off yesterday, he told me that, no matter what happens, he wants you to know that everything is yours. He doesn't want a penny back. And if this is it, keep his heart—it belongs only to you."

I groan loudly. "Man, what a line."

Callie grins, and Jaylin says, "Nico knew how upset it made Callie that you were worried about her gym fees and knew how much she wanted it all to go away. They're best buds, and the thing is, Aviva, he always thinks of Callie too. With your mom's bills, you were suffocating, and his reaction was to take it away because he didn't want that for you. I don't know… I wouldn't be mad at him. I'd be grateful that someone loves me enough to want to take care of me."

"I don't want anyone to take care of me—"

"Why? Would you expect Callie to say that?"

I make a face, turning to look at her. "You better not."

"I don't, because I know you do it out of love," she says slowly. "The same with Nico. He loves us, Aviva."

I close my eyes before dropping my head to the pillow.

Jaylin moves her hand over my back. "I know you want to hold on to that pride like a cat trying to keep from falling into water. But maybe this time, you should think of what you're pushing away. Do you really want to leave a guy because he made sure you and Callie were taken care of? You stayed with Mike, who treated you like dog shit, and now you have a guy who worships the ground you walk on, and you want to leave that?"

"He lied," I stress, and Callie nods.

"Yeah. And he's sorry. He really is."

I make a face. "He's sorry he got caught."

Jaylin shakes her head. "No, he's sorry he upset you."

"But not sorry for paying off all those things."

They both shake their heads. "Yeah, no. He's not sorry for that."

"At all," Callie adds. "He wants the best for us, and he said that if that means we go on without him, he'll figure it out."

I furrow my brow. "How do you know that?"

"He's downstairs," Callie says slowly. "Waiting for you."

I roll my eyes, dropping my face once more onto my pillow. I haven't seen him in three days, and I do miss him greatly. I want to stay mad, but Jaylin's right. Do I want to throw away a man who would do anything for me just because he did what he always does? Lives life with no holds barred and no remorse? I love that about him; I encourage that because it inspires me to live the same. He says what he feels, and he loves so damn hard. I just wish he hadn't done this behind my back. I push off the bed, and Callie and Jaylin jump up quickly.

"What are you going to do?"

"Don't break his heart."

"He makes you so happy. He doesn't think things through, but he means well."

"You know him better than anyone. He didn't do this to hurt you."

I shut the door on them before they can leave my room. I let out a sigh and then head downstairs. When I hit the stairs, I hear the song playing that reminds him of me. It's ending, but then it restarts. I make a face as I come down and into the shop.

Nico's behind the counter, waiting for me.

He looks tortured, and I know I mirror him. I swallow hard as I cross my arms. "What are you doing here?"

"You haven't called."

"I know."

"I've called."

"I know. I watched the phone ring."

He narrows his eyes. "I don't want to fight, Aviva. I miss you. Bad."

I bite my lip. "I miss you too, Nico, but—"

"No, hear me out," he says quickly, holding his palms out to me, and I perk my brow. "Welcome to Nico's I'm Sorry shop."

He waves his hands over the three subs in front of him, and I can't help it. I laugh.

"The what?"

"Sub Shop of Sorrys. It's a working title. Play nice."

I raise a brow at the stupidity of it as he goes on. "We have a Number 0, The One Nico Really Likes—where I do whatever you want, whenever you want, however you want." I scoff, and he winks. "It's the dirty sub of sexiness. Lots of salami."

I snort as I shake my head. "Of course you'd start with that sub."

"Hey, can't blame me for all the naughty time I like with you." He winks once more. "I feel banging this out will be good for both of us. I'll even let you choke me a bit. Safe word: subs."

I laugh out, shaking my head. "I'm supposed to be mad at you."

He nods before he points to the second sandwich. "I know. That's why we have the Number 00, the I Don't Want a Life without You. Yeah, I played decent last night, but I came home sad because I didn't have you. I'm growing, Aviva, but I want to grow with you."

"Well, that's a heart-clencher."

"Yeah, I needed you to know that, so I threw it in there. It's your favorite too, tuna."

I grin as he moves on. "Then finally, the Number 000, the Nico and

Aviva special. It's three zeros for me, you, and Callie. It's where we have a great life and ignore my stupidity. Do everything that makes us happy and forget the stupid things I've done. But we appreciate them because I would only do them for you and my mom because you mean that much to me."

"That option has appeal."

"I thought so. It's my favorite sub," he says, and then he leans on the counter, his eyes burning into mine. "I fucked up. I know this. I shouldn't have lied and done everything behind your back. I'm sorry for the lie and doing it in secret. But, again, I'm not sorry for doing it. And let me explain why."

I feel like we're just going round and round, but then, his eyes don't allow me to argue.

"I watched my mom struggle and work hard to make ends meet. She's just like you. She didn't want help. She did it her way and I came out great, but it was hard to watch. I always said when I got older, I would make life easier for her, and I did. I saw how happy it made her, how all the stress left her body in an instant. And all I could think when I saw you struggling was that I had to do it for you." He swallows hard, his eyes pleading. "It didn't matter if you would have broken up with me the next day. I was going to pay everything off and make things easier for you. But the more and more I was with you, with Callie, the more and more I knew I was doing it for our future."

I press my lips together, watching him, and my heart feels as if it is beating out of my chest.

"I can have a million women throw themselves at my feet, and I'd still only want you. I want to be there to tell you every morning how beautiful you are. I want to kiss you every chance I get. I want to dance in the streets of Barcelona with you again and again while we listen to that damn song that drives me bananas. I don't care because we'd be together. I want to go to every single meet of Callie's. I want to watch her grow. I want to be there with you to cheer her on. And damn it, Aviva, I want to have kids with you."

Emotion takes over, and I can't keep the walls up much longer. He has a way of knocking them down with no warning at all. My lips start to quiver as he holds my gaze.

"I promise I won't lie ever again about anything, even if I think I know best. I've known for a while that I can't just jump into things like that, but I didn't care. Now I care because I refuse to do anything to lose you. I never meant to make you feel like a charity case, and I never saw you as one—"

"I know that, Nico. I do," I say as my voice breaks. "I know you only did it out of love, but you can't blame me for my pride being a bit stung."

He nods. "I know, Aviva, and I'm sorry for dinging it. The last thing I want is to hurt your pride or anything on you."

I nod slowly. I believe him totally. "I know."

"I can't lose you. I *won't* lose you, Aviva. Never in my life has anyone understood me or been so patient with me. I'm usually terrified to be myself, but you accept me for who I am."

"Because I love you."

He points to me. "Exactly. Just as I love you. We do really crazy things when we love people."

I cock my head. "What crazy thing have I done?"

"Loved an autistic guy," he says with a shrug.

I shake my head, scrunching up my face. "Nico, really. Using that as a line?"

He grins. "It's not a line."

I hold his gaze. "Then, Nico, that's not crazy. That's natural for me."

His eyes get misty as he exhales. "See? I would legit buy a billion sub shops just to hear you say that. Just to know I'm enough for you."

I shrug. "I'd say it without the endless sub shops."

He nods. "Which is why it was so easy for me to give you everything you deserve." He reaches out, taking my hand and pressing his thumb into my palm. "The best part of me is you," he says, and my heart takes flight. "And I need that part. So, tell me what to do. Beg? I can beg."

I laugh softly because I know he would beg. He doesn't care what people would think as long as he made this better. "You wouldn't beg."

He scoffs. "For you, I would, and I'm not ashamed of that." He steps closer to me, and I don't move. His cologne hits me in the face, making me dizzy, but still, my eyes stay on him. "Do you want me on my knees?"

"No, Nico, you don't have to beg."

"I don't?"

"No, but you do have to promise never to do that again."

"Never. I won't buy you any more shops."

"And I want you to let me pay you so you can make a profit from the shop."

He looks intrigued. "In blow jobs?"

"Nico—"

He holds up his palms. "Fine, free subs and endless kisses."

I quirk my lips. "Or the rent I'm paying."

He shakes his head before snaking his arm around me. "Or we take that money and send it to that YMCA thing you like supporting. And I get my subs and kisses."

He brings me in close, and I let him, my chest resting against him. "Only if I get my triple zero sub."

He curves his lips slowly, his eyes darkening as he slides his nose along mine. "Since I made it only for you, it's yours. Along with my heart, my soul, my life."

"Wow, the lines are real tonight."

He nods. "I watched a lot of romantic comedies when you weren't speaking to me. I wanted to pull out all the stops."

"Without me? Rude."

"You eat all the candy."

"And you love it."

He nods. "I love you."

Without another thought, Nico cups my face and drops his mouth to mine. I lean into the kiss. I should have known I couldn't stay mad at this man for long. His heart is too pure, and it's all mine. I'm sure he'll do more things in the future with zero impulse control, and the crazy thing is, I'll still love him.

When he pulls back, he kisses my nose as I whisper, "I love you more."

With a smirk that is unstoppable, he nods his head. "I know. I am pretty amazing."

Yeah. Yeah, he is.

EPILOGUE

ico

"I DON'T KNOW how I feel about buying a house when we're also buying two sets of boobs."

I glance over at Aviva with a dry look. "I feel like if you guys get boobs, I get a house. I'm tired of sharing a bathroom with crazy-pants back there."

Callie scoffs. "Hey, you aren't easy to share with either. You shave entirely too much, and your hair is everywhere."

I roll my eyes and notice that Aviva is looking at the houses I sent her as she starts to speak. "I don't know. With you about to start the top plays—"

"Top plays?"

She glances over at me. "The championship thingy."

"The Cup finals?"

"Yeah, that," she says offhandedly, and Callie lets out an annoyed sigh.

"Can you pay attention, or do you like that Nico corrects you?"

I look over to notice Aviva does love it. "You brat!"

She snorts and shrugs. "I like the attention."

I grin. "Attention whore."

"Only for you," she says with a wink. "But yes, the play-offs. You're leaving a lot, and I don't want to move us by myself."

"I'll pay to move us," I remind her, and then I clear my throat. "Plus, I really want to live next door to Chandler and Amelia. And the house is going to go fast."

"Oh my God, your bromance with him is borderline worrisome," Callie teases, and I flip her the bird, to which she laughs. "But hey, I can babysit and make some cash."

"Yeah, I need you to pay off those boobs," Aviva says, and I make a face.

"I have a joke."

"And I'm so proud of you for not telling it since I know it's inappropriate," she says as she looks at the house that is by Chandler and Amelia's. "It is a really nice house. Five bedrooms and four baths. You'd have your own bathroom, Callie."

"Is it far away from you two?"

"Forget it. She's sleeping in the closet like that Potter kid."

"You're not funny!" Callie exclaims, but I happen to think I'm hilarious. "But it is a nice house," she says, looking over Aviva's shoulder.

"It is. Maybe we should take this one?"

"I think we should."

To say I'm excited is an understatement. The season is going great for the IceCats, and we're the number-one seed in the Eastern Conference. Callie had a great season and placed top three at all her meets. The shop is doing awesome, and we've donated a lot of money to the YMCA's ABC program for breast cancer survivors. Aviva has also been going to meetings with Callie and Jaylin. The best part, though, is we're still astonishingly in love with each other, which is why we need a bigger place. I don't like her small place, and she hates mine. We need more space, and when we find it, I'm asking this girl to marry me. She'll say yes, and when we go to Barcelona after the finals, we'll take my Cup and get married.

Aviva has no clue about any of this, but it's going to happen.

I can feel it in my bones.

Just gotta get through Boobageddon.

When we reach the hospital for Aviva's and Callie's pre-op appointments, my stomach aches a bit. Makes me nervous to know both my girls will go in for surgery. Callie's will be longer and more extensive, but I'll worry the same for both of them. Thankfully my mom is coming to town to help since I start the finals in two weeks. The doctor isn't too worried about their recovery time, but I'm freaking the hell out.

I park the truck and get out as Aviva does the same. Callie hops out of the back and looks at me. "You nervous?"

I nod. "Freaking the shit out."

She taps my chest. "Because of germs or us?"

"Shit, I hadn't even thought of the germs!"

"Great, Callie. Great," Aviva calls, coming over to hold my hand. I bring them our hands up and kiss the back of hers. "It's going to be fine. This is so routine. They just slap the boobs in, and we're done."

"But Callie's makes me real nervous."

She waves me off, though I see the fear in her eyes. "She's going to be fine. I was. Don't worry."

I make a face. "Are you sure you two can't just skip the boobs?"

"Nope," they both say, and I groan loudly.

These two are going to kill me. Aviva likes to say Callie and I gang up on her, but I really think it's the other way around. They know that I'll crumble and do whatever they want. I want to make them happy, and I like how they make me feel. The last couple months, I've really grown as a man. I actually did my first interview for the IceCats a week ago. Yes, it wasn't live—and yes, I had a panic attack—but I answered two questions. So, I think my therapy is working. I'm not sure, but in a way, I don't care as long as I feel good. I feel good not doing interviews and just playing great hockey. No one else feels that way, though, but Aviva doesn't push me. She's just supportive enough to make me feel I can do anything, and I know she'd be there if I fell.

Which makes me love her even more.

Nerves are eating me alive as we head inside, but Aviva is cool as a cucumber. Even Callie is. They're excited and happy, and while I'm not, I can now add scared shitless of germs on to the list of today's fears. I hate hospitals. We head to where they are doing their pre-ops, and I wait as they talk to the nurse. Over here, I don't have to hear anything, procedure-wise, and maybe I won't be where people have touched anything. I don't lean on the wall; I just stand in a spot I don't think anyone has touched while I wait for them.

Aviva finally comes over to me and crosses her arms as she stands beside me. "We have to go give blood. Do you want to come with?" I make a face, and she smiles. "Please come hold my hand? I'm nervous."

Damn it. I nod. "Okay, but don't expect me to talk."

She laughs as I take her hand, and we head into the room with Callie. Once back there, they go over the procedure, and then the nurse looks at both of them. "We'll need you both to take pregnancy tests to make sure you're not pregnant."

Aviva looks over at Callie, and she gives her a look. "I'm a virgin, but you need to test her with the way those two go at it."

The nurse's eyes widen as Aviva turns bright red. "I'm gonna punch you in the boob."

"Now? Or the new ones?"

Aviva grabs the specimen cup as Callie does the same. "It'll be a surprise."

They both head into the bathrooms as the nurse looks at me.

"Sisters," I say with a shrug. "But in Callie's defense, Aviva and I do bang a lot, which is okay. We're in love and getting a house. I'm really nervous about the boobs—like, I don't think she needs them, but she wants to feel like a woman and all that, but have you seen her ass? I mean, it's a great ass. She doesn't need anything else, but I really want her to be happy. Ya know what I mean?"

The nurse draws in her brows. "Yes, I'm sure it will be fine."

I nod. "Yeah. I hope so."

Finally, the girls come out, and of course, they're still bickering. "You don't tell a nurse that!"

"She's heard worse," Callie throws back.

"Have a seat, ladies, and I'll get your blood." They both sit down, and Callie goes first as another nurse comes in. "Can you test the samples?"

She nods as our nurse drains Callie. I look away before I puke. I don't know how they are so calm. Aviva laughs beside me, and when I look at her, she grins. "You're the color of a sheet."

"I'd pass out if I weren't scared of the germs on the floor."

She snorts, and then she's next. When the nurse comes back out, she clears her throat. "Did you take Calliope's blood?"

The nurse nods, and the other nurse looks stricken. "Well, that's pointless. She can't have the surgery."

I furrow my brow as Callie's jaw drops. "Why not?"

"You're pregnant."

Everything stops. I'm going to kill whoever did this to her. Aviva's eyes widen, and I look at Callie as she cries out, "I am not. I haven't even had sex!"

"What are you thinking? These tests don't lie!" I yell, but Callie is shaking her head.

"Nico, don't look at me like that. I swear, I haven't. It has to be a mistake. Aviva, it's a mistake! Tell us it's a mistake! I seriously am not having sex. Yes, Landon may have touched me—"

"For the love of God, shut up," Aviva mutters, and when I look at her, she's gawking at the nurse, her eyes wider than saucers. She clears her throat and says, "I know it is."

Callie and I look at Aviva, and I ask, "What?"

"It's a mistake," she says, and then she points to the cup the nurse is holding. "I peed in that pink cup."

Callie lets out a long breath. "Oh, thank God. I'm blue. That's not pregnant, right?"

"Right."

But then she whips her head to Aviva right as things click in my head. Aviva meets my gaze just as I ask, "You're pregnant?"

We both look at the nurse, and she nods. "I just realized that it does say A. Pearce. I don't know how I mixed them up. I'm sorry."

"So, I'm pregnant?" Aviva asks, and Callie still looks as if she's seen a ghost.

"And I'm not."

The nurse nods. "A. Pearce is pregnant. C. Pearce needs to drink more water."

I'm having a hard time breathing as Aviva meets my gaze once more. I'm just staring at her. I'm taking in the most beautiful woman on this planet who continually gives me all my hopes and dreams. I stand up, walking over to her before taking her face in my hands. "It's mine, right?"

She narrows her eyes to slits before she smacks me and yells, "You're always playing!"

But I stop her from hitting me, pulling her into my arms. She comes into me, laughing as our lips meet in a joyous embrace. I wrap my arms tightly around her as she does the same, and when we part, it's only to look into each other's eyes. I hear Callie crying, and I almost feel like I could.

"I love you, Aviva," I say, kissing her nose as my heart explodes in my chest.

Her eyes brighten as a smirk comes over her sweet lips. "You're damn right, you do. I'm the best thing that's ever happened to you."

"That's my girl," I say, my heart skipping a beat. I'm not saying she started loving herself overnight, but she's trying, and I'm so damn proud. I gather her tighter in my arms, and before I kiss her, I whisper, "Yeah, you are."

And as our lips meet, there is no fear. There is only excitement because my future has this woman in it.

Along with Callie.

And whatever bundle of joy we bring into the world.

The END

ABOUT TONI ALEO

My name is Toni Aleo, and I'm a #PredHead, #sherrio, #potterhead, and part of the #familybusiness!

I am also a wife to my amazing husband, mother of a gamer and a gymnast, and also a fur momma to Gaston el Papillion & Winnie Pooh.

While my beautiful and amazing Shea Weber has been traded from my Predators, I'm still a huge fan. But when I'm not cheering for him, I'm hollering for the whole Nashville Predators since I'll never give my heart to one player again.

When I'm not in the gym getting swole, I'm usually writing, trying to make my dreams a reality, or being a taxi for my kids.

I'm obsessed with Harry Potter, Supernatural, Disney, and anything that sparkles! I'm pretty sure I was Belle in a past life, and if I could be on any show, it would be Supernatural so I could hunt with Sam and Dean.

Also, I did mention I love hockey, right?

Also make sure to join the mailing list for up to date news from Toni Aleo:

JOIN NOW!

www.tonialeo.com
toni@tonialeo.com